Ian K Pul

I was with Dad, walki
childhood home, one Sur
been to 'The Swan' for a couple of drinks. Mum was
preparing Sunday lunch. His retirement was
approaching and I asked him if he had any plans. Out
of the blue he told me he was thinking of writing a
book. Absolutely not what I was expecting him to say,
however I thought that it was an excellent idea and I
told him so. Wow, that would be something!

Dad passed away a few years back, approaching the
grand old age of ninety-two. Mum had died some years
earlier. His life had never really been the same after
her passing. He didn't write that book in the end.

About a year after Dad's passing, an idea for a story
started growing in my head. I had never written a novel
before. I'd never had the seed that blossoms into a
complex narrative develop in my thoughts. Nothing
even close to that really.

Pretty soon I had the whole story: beginning, middle
and ending. When I began writing it down, transferring
my subconscious script into written word was
relatively straightforward. It was like transcribing a
remembered verse or song. All the detail was already
there for me. I had help from good people getting some
of the words and punctuation right, but the story more
or less stayed the same.

I've thought about that particular conversation with
Dad a lot since I started all this.

I like to think Mum and Dad would have enjoyed my
book.

I think it would have made them laugh.

Ticket to Eden

by

Ian Pulham

A CIP catalogue record for this title is available from the British Library.
ISBN 978-1-8381526-4-2

Paperback published by Eventispress in 2022

Printed & Bound
by Biddles, King's Lynn

Everything changed, many thousands of years ago, when it dawned on homo sapiens that they had reached the top of their world's food chain, and they revelled in their newfound majesty. Like the heavyweight boxing champion of the world, they were smart, cunning and certainly more vicious than the competition. They were the lords of all they surveyed. But they were not benevolent lords. They treated the co-inhabitants of their world appallingly. They disrespected their home with destructive abandon, and they very noisily bickered among themselves.

But they did have a good run.

The fact is though, nothing lasts forever.

My story begins a long way down the line, at the point where our metaphorical boxing hero enters the ring for that last big fight.

Part 1

'Tell me about the monsters Jack.'

1

Dawn was breaking when we came across Branco's vehicle lying on its side, battered and broken. There was dried blood all over the cab's smashed windscreen. Vultures and eagles were feasting on the contents within. What was left of Branco now amounted to little more than a birds' banquet.

It was two days after the initial drop-off from the six trailers, one of which had never left the site. Tony and I had instructed our drivers to position our armoured personnel carriers facing the body of this trailer that hadn't managed to escape.

My radio crackled into life. 'Nothing happening here Jack. Hit it with a flame thrower, do you think?'

Tony clearly didn't want to hang around here any longer than was necessary. Touch of Italian impatience coming to the fore.

It was fully daylight outside now. The sun didn't waste any time in Oman. I looked to my right at the dusty track that led to our ultimate destination, Ras Madrakah. It was only half a mile away, but the morning haze blocked any potential signs of habitation. Aside from Branco's truck there was little to see in this parched landscape. Rocks, some hardy brush, little else. The early temperature outside would be in the twenties and rising. Why people would want to set up a cult in this godforsaken place beggared belief. People, ey?

'Knock yourself out.' I smiled as I replied to Tony. We were in a grim place. You had to extract some humour where you could.

Almost immediately he launched his flame thrower at the fuel tanks. As we hoped, there was enough fuel inside for them to blow and the subsequent blaze soon engulfed the entire vehicle. What was left of Branco received a cremation which was better for him than when we arrived.

With his vehicle now burning into an anonymous wreck in an anonymous landscape, it was time to move on.

We contacted our base to report the incident with the lorry. Other than that, we only felt the need to speak to them when anything of significance happened. They were tracking us and therefore could let us know how long until we came upon the remains of the settlement. We were not speeding along. Our approach was cautious. My driver, Omar, was Royal Army of Oman, as was Tony's. For them this was a shitty clear-up operation. They hadn't seen the drone footage of the attack. Their pre-op briefing hadn't included that.

All the time Omar's steely gaze was fixed on the view directly in front of him. No glancing to the side. No looking at me sitting beside him. All his focus was geared towards getting the job done and getting out. And I was sitting beside him, occasionally wondering how I'd ended up in this place. A recurring theme in my life. The briefing Tony and I had sat through prior to the mission had, among other delights, suggested the creatures were no longer active in the area. Well, they didn't seem to be.

We were close to Ras Madrakah now and there was a lot of activity. It was a blurred black mass at first sight. Tony, who was in front of me initially, radioed across to let me know he was instructing his driver to bring his vehicle to a standstill until we established what was actually in front of us. After a moment, the view became clearer. The word was out. There were thousands and thousands of Oman's indigenous bird population gathered for the feast of feasts. We're talking about an area not much more than a square kilometre that made up the settlement space for 'The Family.' A hundred yards to the right was the sea. This area, that had up until a few days ago been a tented village that was home to upwards of one thousand souls, was now a carpet of torn cloth, twisted metal poles and bits of people. You would now struggle to identify the remains of anyone.

The initial attack had left their bodies decapitated, burnt and smashed, and then the birds would have begun tearing up what remained.

I looked across at Omar. His gaze remained fixed on the sight in front of him. No visible emotion. He hadn't come across anything like this before surely, I thought. I was struggling to take it all in. I obviously couldn't display any sign of weakness, or my authority would have been shot. I could feel my heart pounding as I tried to distance myself from the detail and focus on the task.

'I'm thinking hit it with the flame throwers again, Tony. You begin on the left perimeter and we'll start on the right. Back and forth until we meet in the middle?' Seemed to me a plan. Tony came back almost immediately.

'Yes Jack. Like the combine harvester machines in the fields.' There was a little chuckle after he said it.

That was a shock. Tony was clearly tougher than I had him down for. We had met for the first time the previous day and the only real conversation between us happened in the couple of minutes we had before our mission briefing. He had told me he was born and lived in Turin and was a passionate Juventus supporter. I'd then made a joke suggesting there would be little tribal rivalry between the two of us, me being a follower of West Ham making European clashes a rarity. He'd had a little chuckle at that. He was the same age as me, twenty-five, and had been working for the same people in Turin for four years, around the same amount of time I had been working for my people in London. He was a good-looking guy too, classic La Dolce Vita style. I imagined he would have been a riot on a night out. And we were probably both selected for the same reasons, being privy to stuff in our worlds of smoke and mirrors. I knew little more as regards Tony's domestic situation, but I knew it wouldn't generate too many waves if I didn't return from this.

We instructed our drivers to position our vehicles as discussed, ignited the flame throwers and began our grisly treks up and down the former encampment. No autumnal greens and goldens here, harking back to Tony's quaint image. We were in amongst the reds and blacks of blood, fire and scorch. It engulfed our windscreens, the view constantly raising and falling back as we ran over body remains. The sky was black with smoke and cinders. And the birds followed behind us as they would have followed the combines, though our birds were gathering barbecued flesh as opposed to stray seeds. The whole operation took us an hour. We parked up and took a breather from it all. I didn't want to look back at our handiwork. I fixed my gaze in the direction of the sea, wishing I'd listened in school.

Omar sat staring out in front of him, as he had from the start. In our vehicles, silence. Outside the birds were still active. No signs of anything else.

But we still had the hotel to deal with, situated as it was around a hundred yards on from the campsite. This had been the head bad boys hang-out, with 'Charlie', the spiritual leader, lording it up over his subjects. Gran's stuff had told me all I needed to know about the original Charlie and his Family. Guess if you're of a mind to start your own death cult, these were appropriate unhinged role models for these people. And credit to them, they'd made nuisances of themselves enough to warrant the desire of powerful men to rid the world of their presence, albeit by means utterly beyond anyone else's comprehension or understanding. At this point in time no one except a 'privileged' few were aware of what had been let off the leash here.

Other than the birds there was no activity around the hotel. It was not a massive building. There wouldn't have been any call for one. It had two floors and it would have consisted of twenty rooms tops. All the windows were broken. All the glass in the building was smashed including what appeared to be the entrance to a reception. Many birds gathered at the front, pecking away at the remains. And there were a lot of remains. There were signs here that victims had been picked up and launched with great strength at the hotel walls. We could see the cracks in the brickwork and the bodies beneath that would have smashed or exploded on impact. It wasn't just people. There were the remains of cattle and goats among the dead. It was like these were the victims of a cruel game of sorts. Of course, Tony and I had seen the rough drone footage of the entire attack, and yes, this phase of the attack had possibly been a bit of evil R & R.

'We're going to have a look round the back.' Tony was back in serious mode now.

'OK. We'll hold our position here and keep an eye out for any activity.'

Once again Omar and I were sitting in silence, both staring out of the windscreen. I knew what I was on the lookout for. At that stage Omar didn't, but he would have seen enough to make him extra vigilant. This was the first occasion during this exercise when we had been faced with a hiding place that could provide the element of surprise as a weapon. There was palpable tension in the air now. This hotel was a whole new potential danger.

Still no sign of hostile activity. Silence!

When the radio suddenly crackled into life with the sound of Tony's voice it was as if someone had smashed a sledgehammer into our windscreen. I sensed Omar's body jolt into a raised rigid pose, as did mine along with the couple of missed heartbeats. Bloody hell Tony! He had good reason to radio us though. He had found something and suggested we join him at the rear of the hotel.

Omar drove our vehicle around the side to where Tony's was positioned. The rear of the building was open planned. There would have been no need to construct perimeter walls in the initial design of the place due to the remote nature of its situation. There was merely a hedge not even a few feet tall, and within this was a simple garden area with a swimming pool. Between the swimming pool and the actual building was a patio area designed for alfresco eating and drinking. What had caught Tony's eye was that the patio, rather than being occupied by tables and chairs, was now taken up with the fallen frames of two of the creatures. They occupied the entire patio area, their colour a drab light grey. The juxtaposition reminded me of one of those more bizarre record sleeves from a bygone era. A pyramid sitting in someone's living room, or a bunch of large glass orbs lined up in a desert maybe.

Nothing was moving where we were, and the only noise was our engines. No birds were remotely interested in the creatures, making the only marks on their bodies bullet holes from which oozed a yellowy gunk. We sat in silence staring at this odd scene for some time. Out of the corner of my eye I could see Omar also looking straight ahead still. I confess that was a relief. He would have been well within his rights to give me the gaze and inquire as to what the hell I had gotten him into. And I wouldn't have blamed him if he had. This was outside anyone's training brief. At least I had been allowed to see the damn things in action. Yes, the drone footage had been patchy, but you could make out the creatures towering over their intended victims before they struck. You could see their oversized individual single eyes focusing on targets, selecting one or two of their six legs to behave more like tentacles as they gathered up cult members. I had seen people decapitated with one bite of their cruel beaks, the remains spat straight back out. I saw them spit some powerful corrosive goo that burnt through flesh like a powerful acid. And I saw them toss victims high into the sky and watch them smash onto the ground before they trampled over them in search of the next victim. The drones also picked up their ungodly screams which would have scared the shit out of you before even you'd seen what they were capable of. They also showed what looked like them communicating with each other through shifting colours across their metallic like skins. The godforsaken souls in their path never stood a chance.

And after that film show we'd still agreed to proceed with the mission. Why? Simple, the bonus payments. Not sure about Tony but if I survived, I'd receive enough cash to buy a house. Guess our bosses were hedging their bets on paying out.

If Omar and Tony's driver had, to a certain extent, been kept in the dark as to the perpetrators of our mop-up operation, I now opted to keep to myself the disturbing fact that these two dead creatures left fifty-eight from the original drop off unaccounted for. I hoped Tony had adopted a similar policy of secrecy with his driver. These guys knew we were in a 'situation'. That was enough. And so far, there was still no sign of anything hostile moving towards us.

We weren't finished here though. All the glass at the back of the hotel was shattered as well and the large frame of the patio window had taken a battering. Bits of masonry hung or lay on the ground by the creatures' bodies. There was no sign of any people. My guess was this had been the entry point for the creatures. There had been a standoff, yes, they had lost two of their own, but once inside the building it would have been a massacre. Without doubt it would not be a pretty picture inside now. Fortunately for us, it appeared a lifeless one.

I radioed Tony suggesting we torch the creatures and he quickly agreed, so we moved our vehicles inside the grounds. We were separated from the creatures by the swimming pool, which was a regular hotel pool, not large by any means. We aimed the flame throwers at the creatures and let rip. Whatever their odd skin was formed out of it sure was combustible. They went up like a bonfire.

So far, we hadn't left our vehicles at all during the mission. Our brief was we should avoid doing so unless events necessitated a need to. Was this one of those occasions? Should we take a look inside the hotel? Part of me was curious to do so, to see how the ruling elite of the Family ended their days. Maybe there were more of these fallen creatures inside? If there had been anything, or anyone still alive in there they would surely have been alerted by the blaze out back. I looked across at Omar. He was in no way a coward, but his posture told me he had no intention of going anywhere.

The creatures, still engulfed by flames, continued to burn. We looked around as far as we could within the confines of our vehicle. Mercifully no further rogue activity to report.

Our pause for thought was interrupted after a minute or two, by an ear-piercing crack of thunder that, although I tried to hide it, did cause me to wince in pain. Simultaneously, there was a bright light and the hotel briefly expanded and then fell on top of itself, creating a massive dust cloud that slowly dissipated into the cloudless sky above. If Tony had been having the same thoughts I had been having, he had evidently also decided against leaving his vehicle. Along with the flame throwers our vehicles were each equipped with two rocket launchers, for 'extreme' situations. He didn't bother to radio us for confirmation, he just went ahead and launched one and have done with it. Good lad!

We reversed our vehicles back out of the garden area of the ex-hotel and positioned ourselves in such a way as to have visibility of the scorched beach area, the flattened building and the sea. All was still apart from a few birds still scavenging for charred scraps. No sign of any other activity. Tony contacted our mission leaders with an update. He also confirmed there was no sign of any of the creatures in the immediate vicinity. We were ordered to remain where we were and await instructions.

No one said much. Omar did tell me he had a wife and two boys aged five and seven, who he lived with in a small town south of Oman. I explained to him that I was single, worked in Whitehall and lived in a town called Dunstable around thirty miles north of London. That was about all we discussed. It was the first time we had engaged in any idle conversation during our whole time together. He may have been one of the toughest men I had ever encountered, but when Tony radioed to let us know our command had given us the green light to vacate the area, the sense of relief inside our vehicle was palpable.

There was no hanging around. As soon as was possible our drivers had the vehicles at top speed moving along the dusty track away from Ras Madrakah. I sat and reflected on what we had witnessed during those terrible few hours. I guess we were lucky. We were still alive!

And I considered that within not much more than a few months, weeks maybe, the combination of the local wildlife and the intense heat of the sun would re-design the landscape we were leaving back to how it had been before the Family had arrived. Nature was good at that. The hotel would be gone, obviously. As would any other signs of recent human occupation. As I stared out at a part of the world I would never visit again, I hoped that my mind and soul would be equally efficient at erasing the detail of what had happened in that awful place.

2

How on earth did I get that gig from hell, you may wonder? The only way I can answer that properly is to start from the beginning. My beginning to be exact.

Up to the age of twelve I would describe my life as uneventful and, compared to many, fortunate. In hindsight, Mum and Dad were wonderful parents. We lived in a nice area of Dunstable. Every now and then we went on day trips down to London. School was OK. I had friends. They were happy days.

When I was a child, we used to visit Gran at regular intervals. She lived in a large two-storey house in Richmond Park Road in Charminster, a suburb of Bournemouth. She was in her sixties by this time. It was a higgledy-piggledy household, full of plants and paintings and books and music. Always music playing. I loved going to visit Gran when I was a kid and I know Mum and Dad did too. We would sit in her large, slightly unkempt garden. I would be rushing about finding 'dens' to hang out in while the grown-ups drank wine and talked and laughed. And as this is a happy memory the sun was always shining.

Our holidays with her continued to be an annual event. As I grew older, I would spend my time rummaging through her books and paintings and records. And there my fascination with the period-in-time Gran grew up in began.

Now comes the sad part. I had now turned twelve years of age, and that was when Gran developed early-onset dementia. In no time at all it became impossible for her to function on her own. She was seventy-two years old. She had to be cared for and that meant her upping sticks and moving into a special care home. There were a lot of these care homes in the UK. You had to be cautious though. The standards did vary. And they were not cheap. Clearly, we wanted Gran to be in the best of care, and we also wanted her to be closer to us than Bournemouth was. Eventually we settled on a place just over ten miles outside Dunstable.

It was peaceful. It came very well recommended, and because of this it cost a fortune. The only way Mum and Dad could pay for this was through selling her lovely house in Richmond Park Road. There was no joy in making that decision. I was only twelve at the time, but I was inconsolable when Mum and Dad told me. That was how it was. That was how our democratically elected government decided how things should be done. I suppose to some that seemed a fair way to carry on. The profit generated on your home subsequently funding your later years. Yes, that had merit I suppose. For Mum, Dad and me it was heart-breaking. My childhood was never the same again.

We would visit Gran. The carers there all appeared wonderful. We would wait in a private meeting place, and one of them would bring her to us in her wheelchair and leave us, realistically for as long as we wanted. We generally stayed not much more than an hour or so. Mum would brush her lifeless white hair. She would give her a drink from a bottle. One of those bottles children drink from with a spout type of affair. It was all horrible. We talked to her, but we had no clues as to whether she was understanding anything. Her head remained upright, but her eyes did not appear to register anything. Her skin now looked grey and leathery. There was no shine to her anymore. The best we could do was to make things as comfortable for her as we could. Effectively the move away from her home had done for her, and yes there were pangs of guilt in our house. It was now in the hands of greater powers as to what would happen next. After just over a year in the home, Mum received a call one evening telling her that her mother had passed on to the next life. She was seventy-three. Mum cried all night. I cried. Dad was wonderful looking after us. He would have been dying inside too. I guess I had been lucky. Up to this point in my life I had been mentored by exceptional people. At my insistence, when Mum and Dad had sold Gran's house, they had salvaged all her good stuff. By that I mean the books, the magazines, the artwork and the records. And a lot of photographs. Now I could immerse myself in all this full time, not just during holidays. It was a fantastic education. I was studying all the subjects you study at school when you're thirteen. Some of what they told me stuck, but everything I read and listened to in Gran's archives became embedded in my memory, never to be forgotten. I would most certainly have known less about the history of the Family and the notorious Charlie of the late sixties, were it not from reading Gran's magazine articles from the time. I became aware of the music that was supposed to have inspired these horrific actions. Gran's books would tell me about the art that inspired the music. And so on. At school I would be trying to understand quadratic equations. Gran's books told me what a 'Foon' was and the effects from being injected with scopolamine. This was proper learning. Not the bloody Schleswig-Holstein question.

We were still recovering from Gran's passing when, two years later, Dad had a massive heart attack. The day after, he was gone too. It was just Mum and me now. All the joy we had in our lives only a few years previously had dissolved, like an aspirin in water. But no number of pills could take away this pain.

I don't blame Mum. It was a tough time for both of us. She had to make decisions, and they weren't always going to be great. The one I'm going to talk about next was a shocker though.

3

I had just turned sixteen when John Thims walked into my life. Well, meandered would probably be more accurate. I was entering the last two years of school life. Mum wanted me to stay on and get a good educational foundation. My previous mediocre exam results had just about allowed me to do that, and besides, what else was I going to do? But I just was not academic. Some stuff stuck but not much. However, the phrase 'one may smile, and smile, and be a villain' did.

Mum had got to know this guy on a dating site. She told me she had no inclination after Dad's passing, but after about eighteen months she had started dabbling with the internet. For me it felt an odd thing to do, such was my love for Dad, but who was I to deny her carrying on with her life? And at first this John Thims seemed OK. He was older than Mum, a good ten years in fact. He had a shock of grey hair, and I suppose you would say a pleasant manner about him. Mum's friends seemed to like him, and within two months they were married. He was always vague about his work. It was to do with the military. It involved the government, or civil service maybe, and he was based in Whitehall. He was high up the ladder. He was a decision maker.

It all started well enough. Unfortunately, sixteen months later, by the time I had scraped through my final school exams and turned eighteen, Mum couldn't get far enough away from him.

It had soon become clear that John Thims was all about himself. His half-baked parenting was in effect one long handover.

'Ask your mother.' 'That's more the kind of thing your mother would like to see/do.'

It didn't really bother me. I spent my time out of school either studying – toil, immersing myself in Gran's legacy – wonderful, or visiting friends' houses getting wasted – rite of passage. It was Mum who had to bear the brunt. She'd married the pratt, hadn't she?

'I don't know', was his stock response to anything. I soon found swapping the word 'know' with 'care' came closer to the truth. The only time he became remotely animated about anything was when a new car was due to be delivered, or some fancy holiday was on the horizon. Over time his dedication to this self-serving existence wore Mum down. It was incredibly sad to see.

The good news, I suppose, was I managed to convert my mediocre exam results at sixteen into mediocre exam results at eighteen. Encouraged by Mum, I somehow managed to find a university that would have me. This meant I would now be leaving home, which allowed Mum to tell me the following. She was going to divorce John Thims, sell the house and start a new life in Australia. Wow! That was a blow. The John Thims bit I fully understood, but Australia? She gave me a day to take that in before she expanded on the detail. It so happened that she had befriended an Australian chap, Craig, on social media. They had shared their past stories, and in time he suggested they met. Unknown to me, and presumably John Thims, they had met while he was in England for a short break. They got on famously and she decided to take a leap of faith. It was when she told me he was a cricketer that I responded in shock. Investment banker I could have coped with. Hedge fund manager, anything but an Australian cricketer. That hurt.

I left home at the beginning of September. John Thims had left to live in London initially, totally bemused by the whole affair. Mum had sold the house and was arranging for her stuff to be sent to her new home just outside Sydney. We tried to make our goodbye as painless as we could. There were tears of course. Obviously, we could keep in touch. That was not hard to do then. I had everything I needed in my car when Mum handed me this little external hard drive. She must have spent months covertly transferring all of

Gran's stuff onto it. Music, books, newspaper cuttings, magazines, everything. I welled up.

'Aw Mum, that's really nice. You've given me a mix tape like that film we watched.' I was in awe of her but couldn't resist making fun of her.

'You really can be a cock when you put your mind to it, can't you Jack?' she quite justifiably replied.

She knew I was messing, so she was not hurt.

'Oh, I did put some of my bits on there too,' she continued.

I looked at her with comedy dread.

'You will like Radiohead one day,' she said, and to all intents and purposes that was it. I drove away and she stood at the edge of the fence surrounding our garden waving and crying at the same time.

Did I mention before that I was not particularly academic? I managed to bluff university for the first year, however, by the end of the second the game was up, and I left with my tail firmly between my legs. Naturally, without a clue as to where to go or what to do. At this point something strange happened. I was sitting in a pub in Holborn a few weeks after leaving uni, when I spotted John Thims. It goes without saying I tried to avoid his gaze initially. He was literally the last person I wanted to meet, but he saw me and came over. I was on my own so it would have been unnecessarily rude to wave him away. I told him of my aborted attempt at academia. He smiled.

'It was always what your mother wanted. I knew it wasn't for you.'

He bought me a drink. I figured if he were going to character assassinate me, the least he could do was pay for the privilege.

'What are your plans now?' was his next rather obvious question.

I told him I was staying with a friend back in Dunstable and as for work, or career, or whatever you wanted to call it, I didn't have a clue. At this point John Thims did something that at the time seemed totally out of character.

'I may have something,' he said.

As I had never seen him do anything selfless in all the days I had known him, I was suspicious. I was also unemployed and drifting. I kept listening.

'It would be involved in military intelligence,' he continued.

I said to him that I didn't think I was in any way military minded, and with my recent experience of thwarted self-improvement still fresh, couldn't see much evidence of any great intelligence on my part either. He smiled.

'That won't hold you back,' he said. 'Just turn up each day, and sign everything they put in front of you.'

And that was it. He gave me a department and a name to report to, the following Monday at nine in the morning. And then he drank up and left. No interview. No need to bring documents for a CRB check. No need for a CV. Just be there at nine.

That was the last time I ever saw John Thims.

4

The work was ridiculous. My work-station was a desk and a desktop, alongside thirty colleagues with the same set up. Our superior sat in his office, separated from us by a temporary wall, probably chipboard or something cheap, and a door. This being an office set in buildings in Whitehall, the age of the buildings made this set up seem even more tatty. It's fair to say that I didn't really understand what was expected from me, realistically, for the first year I was there. The best way I can think of describing what I was required to do, is to compare it to an experience my buddy from schooldays, Ian, had when he was starting out in a career in journalism. He told me once he got a couple of days freelance with a Sunday tabloid rag. They put him in an office with a typewriter and told him he was doing the letters page for that Sunday's edition. After an hour they came back to him and asked how he was getting on, so he told them that they hadn't given him anything to type yet.

'You make them up. No one ever sends us any letters worth printing,' was their reply.

So that Sunday's letters page was the best collection of twisted perversion nineteen year-old Ian could dredge from his adolescent psyche. This was what we were asked to do. Invent ridiculous stories, macabre set-ups, really let our imaginations run free. And if our stuff appeared good enough, it would be edited and placed into context by our manager, before it was submitted to specialist subversive operators to use against the state they reckoned it would be most effective against.

Once I properly understood what this was all about, I became particularly good at it. Clearly, I was a born and gifted liar. So much so, after a couple of years I started getting promotions and becoming more involved in tailoring stories to specific targets. Russia was a constant focus of our elaborate nonsense. They did it to us, didn't they? The only regimes we were told to leave alone were America, India and China. Apparently, we were keen to be friends with them.

All this worked well for me. The pay was excellent, allowing me to rent a decent flat in Dunstable. I could drive into work inside an hour or get the train in if I fancied it. I was in my early twenties and I was doing fine.

More importantly, I had rekindled my friendship with Tom who I had grown up with. We had gone to the same schools, but as the years passed, we no longer shared the same classrooms. Tom was very, very clever. He was easily the cleverest person I ever knew. In fact, he was probably one of the cleverest people on the planet at that time. He was exceptionally good at all the core subjects, and he excelled at the sciences. With all his intellect, Tom had remained a good egg. We stayed friends during our mid 'teens, meeting up to watch movies or just to chat. He took an interest in Gran's memorabilia, which he could have ignored as unnecessary interference in his busy, busy brain. I think he saw something in my passion for her stuff that mirrored his feeling for science.

One thing, though, he was hopeless when it came to small talk with women. This was a frustration for them as they desperately wanted to engage with him. By the age of eighteen he had become a gangly six-footer with blond hair: slight wave, unfortunately cut formally, with a general demeanour that resembled a *Thunderbirds* puppet. No flowing movements, more a combination of jerks and awkward twitches. Quite amusing at times, I am ashamed to confess. I guess he appealed to women insofar as they saw him as an enigma and were attracted to his apparent innocence. And he had intense blue eyes. He would look you in the eye when you were talking, appearing to listen to what you were saying rather than waiting for you to stop talking so he could start, like so many did. Those eyes encouraged you to bare your soul. All the time he was listening attentively, you were witness to his mind absorbing all you were saying to gain an understanding. It was flattering to be listened to so intently. It would only take a few tweaks to his attire, and some work on hair styling, and he would have been a cool dude. But at this stage in his life, he just didn't have any appropriate lines for the opposite sex. When it was his turn to speak, he just froze. Women possibly terrified him. At eighteen, or any age really, I was no ladies' man. I could converse though, and I knew an amusing anecdote or two. We all have our talents, don't we?

After Tom graduated from university with the highest grades ever, he also returned to Dunstable, and like me by this stage, rented himself a flat. He got himself a job at the Science Museum in South Kensington. As part of the deal, they allowed him to do his post graduate course at the UCL in Bloomsbury, mainly on a Friday. Thus, we could car share couldn't we, which paid for a few pub nights for me, but more importantly fuelled our continuing friendship. Pleasant chat on the way in, and a lot of laughs on the way home. Friday was always train day though, so we could have a drink in town after work and uni. The venue of choice was in the main the Black Friar by the Blackfriars Bridge train station. Easy. Tom would drink shandies. I would drink industrial strength cider. Tom would invariably oversee waking me up when the train rolled into Luton, giving me time to pull myself together before we got off. He was a good friend.

I would say this was the happiest time since I was twelve. Work, or should I say the lying, was going well. By the time I had been doing that crazy job for four years I was earning good money. I even had my own bogus social media account, which was an indicator that you were on the rise. I had never been attracted to social media outside work. It seemed to me to be a massively wasted opportunity. I had no desire to be part of that sinister underworld. Tom, being the top man that he was, completely agreed with me. As far as that was concerned, it seemed to be us two Luddites against the world.

Workwise, though, it was fantastic! Sometimes it felt like the whole concept had been designed with what we did for a living in mind. It worked particularly well when you were targeting a specific individual. You could do anything. Set up fake dates for example aiming to humiliate. It didn't matter if today's victim was male or female. Simply let them down, and repeat, and so on. Arrange to meet in locations that would be considered undesirable by their leaders. We could fix it so while they were waiting for their imaginary date, persons who would be classed as 'undesirables' by that regime, would be at the same location. Once they were compromised, you could capture it all through rogue CCTV. It wasn't difficult to set up. You could character assassinate through hearsay. My God, the only limits were your imagination, and how much of the dark side of your make up you were prepared to tap into. I reconciled my professional use of it with the fact that I rejected it outside of work. If our victims were mugged off by what we did, well destroyed is probably a better word, then more fool them for engaging in the stupid thing in the first place.

Having said all that, I did use it to connect with Mum. As she was the only contact I had, and, as she had moved to bloody Australia, in my head it was justified. We didn't talk loads, but enough to keep up with each other's lives. Life seemed to be good for her, which was nice to hear. I did miss her, but she deserved a break, so good on her. She in turn was saddened to hear of my educational ineptitude, but pleased I had got, from the limited amount I told her, what seemed to be a good job. And she was pleasantly surprised that I had got the start through John Thims. She reminded me that he was without doubt the most self-serving son of a bitch on the planet, and I should be on my guard. No hard feelings there then Mum. She did have a point though.

Tom and I continued with our little routine with the commuting. I was probably boozing a bit too much, but you can do anything when you're young, can't you? It was all good. Well, up to the point when I got the call to see if I was interested in a 'special project'. Life was never really the same after that.

5

Workwise Ras Madrakah made me. I was hot. Would this be through my ability? Probably not. I had come back, which I think surprised most of the people directly involved. I was now privy to a lot of stuff. I had had to sign a shed load of documents before I went on that little jolly. I had seen things out there that made me 'privileged', or 'a risk', depending on which way the wind blew. Whatever, I got assigned to advanced lying. Yet more money and now I was in the Premier League. I was lying to us: the people of the UK. Our section's brief was simple. Do anything to keep people indoors. The rationale behind this was also simple. If people were at home, they weren't out in the streets making mischief, and we could control them. It worked during the pandemics. People were at home with their families, so they became a single cell separate from all the other similar single cells. True, there was still social media, where nefarious groups could hatch sinister plans. We could disrupt them though, through our bogus accounts, and naturally could monitor what was always going on. People's personal data? We had access to all that, and algorithms, to save us wading through all the dross. You could fold up your television and watch it anywhere you wanted, ideally at home. Off to the loo? Take the TV. Watch TV. That is all we wanted people to do really. Whatever the networks claimed, in the main TV was a dumb-down. If everyone watched TV, they probably in time watched the same things, so they would talk about them at work. If someone didn't watch a particular programme, they would feel left out, so they would have to watch 'catch up'. We manipulated their 'likes' anyway. In time enough people would be watching what we wanted them to watch. Through this we could start to influence conversation. Control the people. Control what they were thinking and talking about as much as possible. Police on the streets? Don't need them. We used gang wars and violence and plagues as a tool. All that suggested mayhem, served a purpose for us. Stay indoors. Death of the High Street? Don't care. Shop online. Watch TV. Always. Play games. Watch TV.

Oh, and try to discourage books. People learnt stuff when they read books.

Did I feel any sense of guilt regarding my work? I'll tell you. I used to watch cop shows from the previous century. I was filled with envy at the way they carried on during their 'down-time.' I saw little of those freedoms and reckless abandon in the world during my late twenties. As far as I was concerned all I was doing at work was icing a particularly bland and boring cake.

Over time, people did indeed become fearful and insular. Music to our ears. Many European countries were already looking inwards as a result of the gradual break-up of the Union. And we could discourage travel to all these lovely places, through the wonderful gift of concern over the environmental impact caused by travel. Or disease maybe. Naturally, we, or should I say the worldwide ruling elite, didn't give a toss about the environmental impact of anything. Why would they? The apocalypse was not going to happen on their watch, and that was all that mattered to them. If you worked in a warehouse and you handed over a fork-lift truck with a flat battery to the next shift, you would be disciplined, if the warehouse was run properly. These rules did not apply to global leaders. This 'warehouse' was not run properly. They could hand over any old bag of shite to the next regime, spending the rest of their lives in a world of overpaid speaking engagements whilst writing dull autobiographies. Happy days indeed. Dictatorships kind of operated the same way. Only difference was at the end of any dictator's run, it generally involved being thrown to the wolves as opposed to luxurious living, although not always, if they were smart.

Naturally, they all came out with all the right soundbites, and even had global conferences to make it seem like they were trying to make it all better. Good for them. Truth was, frankly my dear, they didn't give a damn.

By the time he was twenty-six Tom had graduated from the UCL, naturally with near perfect grades, and was now a fully-fledged particle physicist. Still employed by the Science Museum, though now on a vastly greater salary. With this he could now afford to buy his own house, which along with our rejection of social media set us both apart from a large contingent of our age group. Tom never asked me how I was suddenly able to become a homeowner. I told him I had been promoted a few times, but I never really discussed details of work. In truth, all the things I had signed meant I couldn't anyway, and as for the team I was in; one was a Spurs season ticket holder, the other chap was obsessed with Craft Beers and his bang on-trend allotment, and the well-spoken and well-educated lady loved to be telling us of how she was a closet nymphomaniac. Why would I want to talk about them?

6

I had bought a terraced house in the road backing on to the Priory Church. Tom's was on the way out of town at the base of the Downs. Tom had also been developing a hobby. Three years previously he had rented a little bit of land just down the road from Northall, a small village two or three miles out of town. It was nestled in between a small gathering of industrial units and farmland. And with both sets of landlords' permissions he had set up several beehives, which he would tend after work and at weekends. I had been invited down there, a lot at the start-up, and on numerous occasions after. And we would dress up so we looked like characters in the movie *The Andromeda Strain*. I would watch Tom working the hives, extracting some honey, naturally. Never so much as to cause a revolt. He would watch them for hours. He wanted to understand everything. He had tiny cameras inside the hives so he could watch their 'dances' and their devotion to their queen. To be honest I was happy when it was time to leave. I had nothing against bees, but there did seem to be an awful lot of them, and I never really one hundred percent trusted that oddball protective gear. Sadly, Tom lost a few colonies over the years, and he would then have to start from scratch, setting up a new one in the vacant hive. It was a cause of constant frustration to Tom, quite understandably. He was forever reading journals and statements of beekeepers who had similar misfortune, all trying to understand why. He would discuss it with me. I always had to be careful what I said. I didn't want to appear shallow or disinterested.

'Would it not be a combination of factors? Farming methods, climate, other competitive creatures. Even the surrounding flora and fauna?'

He would pause, look up at you and smile and then carry on trying to figure it out. As far as I was concerned that was the least Tom's dedication to the cause deserved. It was when one of these discussions that I have described was closing, one early autumn evening in September at Tom's new house, that I received the call from Martina.

She was in London for a couple of days and would like to meet me. She was Tony's sister. I said I would ring back in the morning and confirm a meeting place. I didn't tell Tom who the call was from. I didn't even know Tony had a sister. Our informal chats had been brief, and he had never mentioned her. And I could not remember giving Tony my number, but it would seem I had, probably with one of those soppy 'ring me next time West Ham play Juventus' throwaways.

I duly rang her the following morning and asked if she was OK to meet that afternoon around four. I suggested a pub not far from Leicester Square tube. One of those ornate places: lots of glass, high ceilings. It was apparently a favourite with the celebrated actors and thespians of the early 1960s. They would use it to wax lyrical and cavort, before or after performing at one of the many famous theatres a stone's throw away. That's what Gran's magazines told me anyway. It seemed a suitably classy rendezvous to meet a young Italian lady. I figured choosing a restaurant would make me look too much of an upstart, maybe trying my luck. I had no idea who the clientele of the pub would be at four in the afternoon. Just had to hope there wouldn't be any dickheads. Martina agreed to the time and location.

I bunked off work early. That wasn't a problem, and the underground was kind to me, enabling me to arrive at the Salisbury fifteen minutes early. I ordered a pint of Guinness. The patrons looked non-threatening, around twenty in total and, mainly in their fifties or older. Men and women sitting together: men drinking alone, women drinking alone. Pretty cosmopolitan. A good mix. So far so good, I was happy with my choice of location.

The lady who walked into the Salisbury around ten past four was quite clearly Martina. She stood around five feet six. Shoulder length black hair parted in the middle. Olive skin, high cheekbones and piercing brown eyes. She was wearing a black blouse with matching knee length skirt and immaculate black heels. She was undeniably Tony's sister. Her elegance was matched only by her beauty. I guessed she was a couple of years older than Tony, by the mature way she carried herself. It just gave away a few more years' life experience and added to her aura. It was one of those entrances where, if there had been a piano player he would have stopped playing. Everyone in the bar gazed at her, men and women. I caught her eye as I got up out of my seat.

'Hi Martina,' I said.

She came over. 'Hi Jack.' And we did the two-cheek kissing thing. She sat opposite to me, arranging herself, while I ordered her a glass of her preferred choice of red wine.

'I wasn't aware Tony had a sister,' I began.

I was tempted to use the adjective 'beautiful', but something had suggested to me that phrases such as that would not be appropriate to this conversation.

'Tony always said you had a kind face, Jack,' she replied.

The use of 'always said' set my inner alarm bells ringing but I needed to pursue this, and I could not see a way of not asking, 'How is Tony?'

'Tony is dead,' was the reply.

She was dressed in black, wasn't she?

'He threw himself out of his hospital's top window two months ago.'

She clearly had had two months to deal with this; I had one minute. I had to consider not upsetting her or realistically making a fool of myself, while being careful not to say too much.

'Hospital window?' I stammered out.

She took a sip of her wine and told me the story. I knew Tony lived and worked in Turin. She also lived in Turin in an apartment. She became engaged around the same time Tony had been sent on that little away day with me. I hadn't spotted the ring up to then. Anyway, the plan was for her to be married last year, yet more and more of her time had been spent looking after Tony. He had been fine for the first six months or so after returning, but after some time she noticed he had started drinking. He was also becoming sullen of expression. She had asked repeatedly what the matter was, initially receiving no response. This soon developed into increasingly angry responses. She began to be properly concerned. And she started to receive phone-calls from the police. Tony was at the station. He had been fighting. He had been sprawled over a car bonnet unconscious from alcohol. And so on. She would drive to the station and drag him into her car after he was released, and then drive him back to his apartment, the other side of Turin to where she lived. She would put him to bed. He would just be rambling nonsense. 'Nice Mummy. Put silly Tony to bed. Tony been bad.' That kind of thing. And of course, she couldn't leave him. He was her baby brother. She would make herself as comfortable as she could on a chair to get some rest herself.

This continued for a while, then it went quiet. She wouldn't hear from Tony for a month. He wouldn't answer his phone when she rang. He was nowhere to be seen when she visited his apartment. Then he would ring out of the blue and they would meet, and all would seem fine. Maybe all that nonsense had just been a blip, and things were gradually returning to normal. She had even put off her wedding, through the need to get her brother back on track somehow. Her life had been put on hold. Up to that point her fiancé had been the model of understanding. Nevertheless, it was appearing more and more as if this pattern with Tony could continue indefinitely, and he had begun to suggest to Martina that maybe it was time to focus more on their own plans. Not at all unreasonable. Tony seemed to have calmed down. So once more they named a date, the following October, now only a few weeks away.

The first time Martina had seen Tony this year had been during March, and he had seemed OK. He had gained some weight, sure, and his general demeanour was still of concern. Clearly, he was still drinking, yet he was lucid enough to apologise for all the distress he had caused her and was totally supportive of her wedding plans. She left him in the same mood she had been leaving him every time during the previous year. A mixture of relief that maybe he was finally ridding himself of these demons that had inexplicably invaded his psyche, and an overriding sense of foreboding. The latter reared its head the following month. She received the first phone call for over a year from the police one Saturday evening. Could she come to the station ASAP? He was asking for her but was in no state to use the phone himself. When she arrived, she was shown to his cell where she identified him. He had no ID of his own on him. He was completely out of it but did recognise her, slurred her name and fell back onto his mattress. The police explained they had been called to a bar where he was causing a disturbance. They did not elaborate. Drunk and disorderly behaviour was not unusual in Turin on a Saturday. Their concern was the twenty grams of cocaine they had found on him. This was a new development for Martina. Tony, to the best of her knowledge, had never dabbled in drugs of any sort. He was just not that type of kid.

Kid!

Martina found the next part of the story strange, though considering that Tony's work set up was probably not dissimilar to mine, it made sense to me. Tony remained in police custody during May. Possession of cocaine was serious, particularly the amount he had on him, and the Turin authorities were unforgiving as regards Class A drugs. Martina naturally visited him when she was allowed, and he was full of apologies and regret. This was the only time etc., etc. The turn up was in June. He was suddenly transferred to a hospital on the outskirts of the city that specialised in mental health care. Tony was diagnosed with severe post-traumatic stress disorder. He was placed under twenty-four-hour supervision. Martina could visit once a week. In no time Tony was supposedly back to the same man she had been seeing a few months previously.

Yes, it had all been a silly misunderstanding. He had made a terrible mistake, but he'd been poorly, and with the right care he was sure he would be back on his feet in no time. The only difference this time was she knew Tony was now clearly lying. His shine had gone, and if she did not know better, he appeared to have a death wish. The doctors reeled off what they needed to say. Complete rest. Drugs to deal with his condition. Straight out of a textbook.

June passed into July with no alteration. Tony didn't seem any better or worse, but the light was gone from his eyes. When she received the phone call giving her the sad news of his demise, she was almost relieved. That was what she had come to London to tell me. That was why we were sitting where we were, in this grand old building in the heart of London's theatre land. She had been led here through my number appearing in Tony's phone. Maybe he had mentioned his West Ham buddy in England once in passing, and she had sought me out as a result. She then hit me with the request she had come all the way from Turin to ask of me.

'Tell me about the monsters, Jack.'

Evidently Tony had talked in his sleep during Martina's stopovers at his apartment. And having listened intently to her story, my initial expression of guilt gave me away. Well, I wasn't a bloody machine, was I? I probably hadn't spent more than a day in his company, but in that time we had seen and done more than some do in a lifetime. The crack about the combine harvester machines. He'd launched the rocket at that godforsaken hotel in Ras Madrakah, while I was dilly dallying about the price of fish. That was enough, without the horrors that had drawn us to that awful place. Of course, my body language gave the game away to Martina, but I couldn't tell her what she wanted to know. I couldn't tell her because I quite simply wasn't allowed to tell her.

And if I had, what good would it have done? Would it have eased her pain? Would it in some way allow Tony salvation in the afterlife? No. I would just have to sit the other side of the pub table to her, and be the horrible bastard I was handsomely paid to be. She was a smart woman. She had sensed by this point that I wasn't about to give anything away. I clearly did know something about what caused her beloved younger brother to disintegrate over the previous two years though.

'What does it mean?' she asked.

When she had been telling me Tony's story her expression had been business like but intense. She wanted to impart to me the facts as she saw them as accurately as possible. When she had sussed I knew the cause of Tony's pain, initially she became sad and there was a tear in her eye. Now she was angry.

'What does it mean?' she asked again, a decibel louder this time.

The customers in the Salisbury were sensing something was stirring here, and we were starting to generate interest. She then said some words in Italian very quickly still staring angrily at me. Her English was near perfect. My Italian was non-existent, and I had said nothing for ages now anyway.

'Maybe you are the monster, eh Jack? Why don't you say something? Has the cat got your fucking tongue?'

We had the whole pub's attention now including the bar staff.

'I can't say anything that will help you Martina,' I replied as truthfully as I could.

'Don't say my name. Don't you say my fucking name. My beautiful Tony is dead. Why aren't you dead? Why do you still live? Why aren't you haunted? I hate you, you dumb bastard.'

At that point, the tears arrived, and I sat where I was, waiting for the remainder of her wine to be thrown over me, or for one of the punters to step in and do a Sir Galahad turn.

Thankfully, she was done. I was a dead end. A dead loss more like! She got up, mouthed a bit more Italian as she headed for the door and that was her gone. I looked around the pub. Everyone was staring at me; at the bastard that had somehow reduced that vision of beauty to a foul-mouthed tearful wreck. Now was not the time to finish my Guinness. I got up from my seat and walked purposefully to the door, leaving the building before anything more could develop. I now proceeded to get as far away from the Salisbury as I could, and at all costs avoid running into Martina again. I must have walked around for an hour trying to process what had just happened. It was incomprehensible. How had all that unfolded? How was I the villain? That woman genuinely hated me. Why? Tony? After another half hour I began the journey back to Dunstable. I would be one unlucky swine if I bumped into Martina en route now. And once I was sitting on the train, I gazed aghast out of the window, as the metropolis surrendered to the greenbelt, still trying to understand what had happened back there. Bizarrely, I almost felt some comfort in the fact that Martina had been wrong about one thing. She had wondered why I wasn't haunted. Why I hadn't been affected?

If Tony had been a shooting-star, I was the slow burner. It is simply that people respond to horrific ordeals in different ways. I had my demons too.

7

Let us get this straight from the start. We are not talking large numbers here, three or four max. However, during the last couple of years all my romantic encounters had one thing in common. When it came to sex, I always insisted on using a condom. Always. Even if they told me they were using some form of birth control it didn't matter. I still insisted on using one. And always the same reason. I was not ready for the responsibility, which in fairness was partially true. I don't believe from the age of twenty-four to twenty-six I was. Some men are; I was not. Looking back, I wasn't maturely developed enough to cope with bringing up a child, to work in tandem with a partner/wife. To sacrifice my own needs for another. Although this aspect of my make-up denied me the joys of early fatherhood, it undoubtedly helped me deal with the horrors of Ras Madrakah, insofar as I didn't have the mental skills at that time to really take in all that had happened. Tony clearly did and that's what killed him. I still had that dumb shrug of the shoulders and move on attitude that made for ideal cannon fodder. But responsibility? I don't think so.

The ladies in question responded in different ways. One thought I was being chivalrous, one thought it was an insult to her. Like I was worried she had a STD or something. And so on. The bottom line is nothing came of any of these relationships, and I was probably drinking a tad too much to be taken seriously, even if they could overcome my little quirk.

As I said, that was part of the reason I did what I did. The rest, I'm sure, was a hangover from the horror. I had started to experience a recurring dream. Not every week, maybe not even monthly sometimes, but enough to allow me to recognise it and fear it. And when I had this dream, I didn't wake up bolt upright, eyes transfixed and sweating. It wasn't like that at all. It would be a dream among other dreams often during the same night. But this one started to resonate and seriously affect me.

It always started the same. I was living in marital bliss. I couldn't describe my wife's appearance. Her physical form was not the purpose of the dream. All that I was required to accept was that I was happily married, we lived in an ideal home and we had just become parents. In the dream I was always walking upstairs to see our new-born baby whom I loved very much. The baby was always crying. I would gather it out of its cot and try to soothe it in my arms. But it continued to cry. I know calling the baby 'it' is awful, but whether it was a boy or girl was immaterial to the dream. It carried on crying in my arms, and then it moved on to screaming. Its mouth now grossly exaggerated compared with the size of its tiny head, and its screams got so loud and ungodly. I was on fire now, not physically, but inside I was burning up with rage at this damn screaming abomination. So, I would grab its tiny torso in my right hand, and facing the wall of the bedroom with my back to the door, I would reach my arm back far behind my head, enabling me to catapult it forward, as forcefully as I could. When I let go ... It always finished there. Always the same set up. Always the same ending.

Now, thanks to the meeting with Martina I had the guilt germinating inside me too. The beautiful Tony was dead, the horror we had seen surely uppermost in his demise. Yet I survived, and Martina had called me a monster. Me, a monster? It began to fester inside me, so that over the next four years, up to my thirtieth birthday, I gradually unravelled. Tom and I still shared a car into London: sometimes his, sometimes mine. More his over time, as he had concerns over my ability to drive some mornings. There weren't any dry nights when I returned home from work anymore. Tom didn't visit my house much now either. It was a tip. It sometimes scared even me when I came in, then I would binge the place, but drinkers do not keep tidy households. I carried on. After a couple of years, I was getting the train in most days. I was getting sick to the back teeth with Tom and his bloody career, his bloody bees, and his wholesome goody guy aura. He had been my best friend in the world, and I was doing my best to push him away. For his part he knew something had happened to me. He tried at times to politely ask what he could do to help. I may have been falling apart but I wasn't stupid. I still had enough loyalty to people who did not deserve it, to know I couldn't tell him what was behind my decline. He didn't deserve the burden of knowing anyway. I still possessed enough decency in me to know Tom was a good man and I loved him for that. It was best we spent less time in each other's company for the time being. As it goes, I still managed to function at work. I turned up every day. I continued to sign everything they put in front of me. I had now acquired an edge, which in a lot of ways made me even more effective in what I did there. I had no scruples in my attempts to control now. If our aims were met by the UK population existing in ignorant solitude, so be it. Good! The years continued to pass by.

It was probably hitting my thirtieth birthday that in some way pushed me over the edge. A few days after the actual day I went over to Tom's place on his invitation. I hadn't seen him for months, and he wanted to have a belated birthday celebration for me. He had invited some colleagues he knew from work, who he thought I may possibly get on with. Some new blood was his thinking, male and female. Nice gesture, massive mistake. I was smashed when I turned up, late, and treated each new guest I was introduced to with disdain. I behaved horribly. I knew I was behaving horribly, and I knew it was an awful thing to do. Tom was still trying to repair whatever was wrong with me. Thing was I was in character by that point and there was no going back. When they asked how work was, I bluntly told them to mind their own business. When they discussed their own careers I sniggered nastily, dismissively, and passed snide cracks. Remember Tom had assembled all these people on my behalf, no doubt explaining to them over the time he had known them what great friends we were. I shudder now to think of it. And my pièce de résistance, to cap the whole evening off, was to announce to everyone, his friends, his colleagues, everyone, that as far as I was concerned Tom was an interfering, charmless, boring tool. And with that I left, naturally tripping over one of his stupid garden gnomes on my way to the gate.

I felt appalled by my behaviour when I staggered indoors. The next day I tried to contact him, but he was understandably having none of it. Subsequently, I adopted a strange strategy to somehow make amends for my boorish behaviour. Call it a form of self-harming perhaps. I decided to completely sabotage myself at work, which I achieved in only a matter of months. I missed deadlines, ruined projects that had sometimes years of work by others invested in them. I misdirected important emails. I misplaced important documents. I was spectacularly awful. And all this time, I continued to turn up to work on time and leave on time. By all outward appearances, I was the consummate professional. My team didn't really spot what I was doing, but they were not the brightest anyway. The senior management did though. You need to understand here that we were in the odd situation, whereby our work was technically military intelligence, but we reported to civil servants. People high up the chain would have been aware of Tony's demise. I'd like to think they would have been ignorant of my meeting with Martina, but the Tony thing would have put them on alert. Even with four years passed, I would have still been watched in case I developed any symptoms similar in behaviour to Tony's. It appeared now that I was. I was ordered to have a medical, physical and mental. Amazingly, I passed. I was fine, don't ask me to explain how. I must have had some constitution back in the day. That gave them a problem. I was the original man who knew too much. Ironically, what I did know had been so well covered up over the passing of years that many of my overseers didn't know specifically what I knew. A few did but not many. Fortunately, the UK had not gone down the route of killing off its employees in my line of work, who had gone slightly off the rails, and medically I was A-OK. They couldn't keep me in my present role though. I had become a disaster at that. I was given a couple of days' leave while they came up with a plan. When I returned to work all was revealed. I had been with the organisation ten years now blah blah blah! I had loads of valuable experience blah blah blah! Now was time for a fresh start to keep my creative juices flowing. They kindly offered me a nice fat pay rise and transferred me to the ultimate bullshit job ... Training!

As with my previous role it took a while to get to grips with this one, yet after the fog cleared it all fell into place like it always did. And once I understood that we didn't actually do any proper training as such, I was happy to join in and enjoy the ride. If something of any use to anyone needed to be taught such as elementary code breaking, diplomatic procedure; anything like that; we got proper experts in to train our people. On the other hand, the new-fangled drinks machine on the fourth level? We were all over that. And after we had been properly signed off to give guidance to our people, we would get them into our training rooms, show them some film, make them read the appropriate guff, and then get them to sign to say they had managed to stay awake for the last hour and were fully compliant with whatever it was they signing for. So, if the next day they went to get their morning latte with chocolate chip coating and fresh cream, and the machine decided to spray scalding hot water in their eyes instead, it was OK because they had signed the corresponding document. That was filed with the rest of our arse-covering documents in their personal records. Job done.

And as I had managed to pass the induction process to this department, which involved remaining emotionless whilst being introduced to Charlotte, the department head, who announced herself to me with the absurd line, 'Hi. I'm Charlotte and I'm passionate about training,' I was in.

With my career now effectively on hold forever, I had achieved that little short-term aim. It had been three months. Now it was time to make it up with Tom. I tidied up my house, properly this time. Paradoxically my drinking had been put on the back burner while I had been working on screwing up my career. I had needed focus to do that, plus I was still ashamed of my behaviour round Tom's. Sometimes you need something like that to set you back on the right path. Tom and me both adored cricket so I invited him round to mine to watch a one-dayer between the West Indies and England in Antigua. I would make us a bite to eat. And I would not drink. I figured the sport as a background would help soothe any bad blood. Understandably, he declined at first. We hadn't spoken since that fateful evening, but I persisted and as I knew he would, he eventually cracked. And naturally we had a marvellous afternoon.

My plan worked as well. Any awkward silences were averted by a dubious umpire call or a sumptuous cover drive. I even produced a half decent curry. We did not really discuss anything specific. That bloody evening was certainly off limits on my part, and we didn't speak of work except in superficial terms. Still, Tom was a clever man. I have no doubt he could detect I had attempted some form of quasi-spiritual self-cleansing exercise, and now maybe considered myself worthy of seeking forgiveness. He wouldn't have realised that this had been assisted by Charlotte and her unquenchable professional passion, but hey ho. Tom left my place around ten. He thanked me for the afternoon and evening. I sensed he was relieved I hadn't drunk anything other than water. And he said he would ring me the next week, and maybe he could return the compliment. That meant the absolute world to me. After he left, I did pour myself a large whisky. It was my first of the day so what the hell. For the first time in a long time, I felt good about myself. Also, I looked forward to going back to Tom's, so I could redeem myself, I guess. I realised things would probably never be as they once were between us. I had inflicted wounds that, (now at least partially healed), would leave scars. The scars remain forever. All you can hope is the passing of time allows you to notice them less. It would be good to visit Tom again. Maybe I could take Sarah with me.

8

It had been a few days after my appalling behaviour at Tom's little party, when I bumped into Sarah. We had both been waiting to be served in a bar in Dunstable that was notoriously a challenging place to get a drink. When the lady behind the counter did eventually make her way to our section, both of us launched into one of those 'This lady was before me' 'No I'm sure it was him first,' comedy routines, and then continued discussing what a pig it was getting any attention in the place while waiting for our drinks to arrive. And as luck would have it, we both returned to the same position at the bar at the same time for a refill. We smiled at each other and, once we got some attention, I steamed in and offered to buy her drink, which she duly accepted. We found a nearby table, and in a nutshell that was that.

I discovered she was a micro-biologist working for a research team based in the grounds of King's College Cambridge. I was naturally as vague as I could get away with about my work. She liked music and the arts and was particularly interested when I mentioned Gran's archives. She wasn't beautiful in the conventional sense, but she had a style of her own which I found extremely attractive. Her hair was almost punky, a short blonde spikey top blending into a shade of light brown around her ears. She had piercing brown eyes and soft pale skin. I was smitten!

We finished our drinks, and she said that she would have to re-join her friends whom she had abandoned for me. We exchanged numbers and made a commitment to meet again, which we did a few days later, and then again, a few days after that. She really seemed taken with me. I have to say I thought she was great. We talked about books, movies and music. She didn't dismiss cricket as dull nonsense, and she could be very funny when it took her fancy. She even dealt with my peculiar foibles as regards sex when that time came, in a caring and affectionate manner. Bloody hell! This was fabulous. Maybe I was recovering from being the biggest dick on the planet at last. By the time I had managed to accomplish the reconciliation with Tom, we had been seeing each other for three months. That was long term in my experience believe me.

She was more than happy for us to visit Tom the Saturday after he had come to mine. I had told her about Tom naturally, but I had omitted the grim parts up to then. After all, we were only three months into our relationship, and I could see no point in highlighting my dark side at that stage. After Tom rang in the week and confirmed the offer, I explained to Sarah that Tom and I had drifted off into our own worlds for a time, and this was part of the process of rekindling a lifelong friendship. That would do for the time being. She was a smart lady. Sure, she would figure out the full story over time. And Tom was politely intrigued that I was bringing someone, mainly because I had never done so before. Like I said, three months was serious in my world. When Saturday came, I got a cab from mine to Sarah's flat around eight in the evening. Her place was on the way to Tom's, virtually two minutes away, so our journey together was brief. She had her hand in mine for the journey. I think she sensed this was important to me, even though she was not to know she was the first lady I had taken to Tom's house. Or that the last time I had been there, I had put on an award-winning exhibition of obnoxious behaviour a Las Vegas stag party would be proud of.

Tom greeted us at the door with a big smile and beckoned us in. It was all a bit awkward, which Sarah found highly amusing. Men can be such twats. Before I could do the introductions, she opened with a cracker:

'Hi Tom. I'm Sarah. I understand we spend a lot of our working time sweating the small stuff.'

That was Tom sold. He smiled and replied, 'Well that makes us among the luckiest people alive Sarah, as we are privileged to see all the beauty that so many people miss out on.'

'So true. That is a wonderful description of what we do,' she said.

They both smiled, and all the awkwardness disappeared. She then looked at me and squeezed my arm as we walked into Tom's living room. At that moment I was probably at my happiest since I was twelve.

Tom's house was a little bigger than mine, but the layout was much the same. The living room had a dining table by the window looking out onto the garden. Adjacent to that was his sofa that wrapped around that corner of the room. In front of that was a coffee table and on the opposite wall the television was mounted. There were some plants dotted around the place and some prints on the walls. It was tidier than mine, however, he had left some books and papers and a laptop on the dining table which he apologised for as he cleared them away. Yes, it was all very pleasant and totally lacking in a woman's touch, a sight no doubt not lost on Sarah.

The evening was a joy. Tom even rustled up a half decent Spaghetti Bolognese. Careers were discussed up to a point. Not much you could say about mine, although I did mention I had recently engineered an internal transfer for myself that I was pleased with. Sort of true. Sarah was particularly interested in Tom's bees, and stated that she would like to visit the hives sometime in the New Year maybe, when they became active again. She turned to me looking for back up, which I was more than happy to provide. Wow, she was talking about next year already. And bless her she mentioned Gran's archives and my obsession with them. Tom laughed and said he had been living with them for years. The Doors, Martin Luther King, Roy Lichtenstein, *Uncle Tom Cobley and all*. Sarah said she liked talking to me about all that stuff, as it was the only occasion I showed any passion for anything other than the England Cricket Team or West Ham United Football Club. We laughed at my expense. Sarah could have added that my eyes also lit up when I was talking about Tom, but that would have embarrassed me, and she was too good a person to do that. We left all smiles, just after midnight and took the cab back to my place, with my arm round her and her head on my shoulder. We were in a special moment ourselves, and I had never seen Tom behave that naturally with a woman before. All his usual awkwardness left him after a few words with Sarah and never returned. Once again, I seemed to be in the company of exceptional people.

I thought it best to get in early that I'd always gone to Tom's Mum and Dad's for Christmas Day, effectively since Mum emigrated. It took the pressure off Sarah. Her parents lived down in Cornwall and it was probably too early in our relationship for her to be presenting me to them. The distance that they lived would have made us both turning up look like something more than it was at that stage. Sarah spent Christmas and the New Year in Cornwall, returning in the first week of January. It was great to see her again. We still seemed to be on the same track. She said she had told her folks about me and they had seemed to approve of what they had heard. And of course, we met up with Tom. Sarah gave him a belated Christmas present, a cookery book of all things. He looked at me as he opened it. Yes Tom, I had mentioned to Sarah his past kitchen disasters at some point.

Spring arrived, prompting Sarah to be allowed her visit to the bees with Tom and myself. The Andromeda Strain now had its female lead. We continued to gather round Tom's or mine most weekends and sit and chat until the early hours. These were the good times.

One evening after dinner at Tom's place we were discussing the world we now lived in, with flying cabs in the cities and driverless cars and all the other nonsense. Wondering where it would all end, that kind of thing. After a while on this subject Tom made the statement:

'As far as I can see the greatest advances that men, and women, will make over the next twenty years will be––'

'In medicine,' Sarah finished.

And with that they both caught each other's gaze and held the moment for what seemed an eternity. Something passed between them in those mysterious few seconds. They were emotionally naked in each other's gaze. A connection was made, leaving me sitting alone at the dining table in Tom's front room watching it all unfold. It was horrifying! You don't always need a twelve-volt battery to create electricity.

And at that same point I knew I was in trouble.

9

I had brought my car that evening. When Sarah and I called it a night around midnight I was stone cold sober. We said our farewells in the same manner we always did. No different to any other evening when we had performed the same routine. The only difference was I was now in a terrible world where I was looking out for any slight anomalies, anything differing from the norm. We got in my car and I drove the short distance back to her place. She was going to a Sunday market out of town with a friend in the morning. They would be leaving early. This had been arranged weeks ago and at that time I had opted for the Sunday morning lie in, so there was nothing sinister there. I kissed her goodnight, told her I hoped she would have a blast at the market, and drove away. Exactly as I would have done any other evening. When I arrived back at my place, I poured myself a large whisky and decided to finish the evening with some tunes. What's Gran got for me?

My eyes were drawn towards songs concerning love and loss, like a lemming is drawn to the edge of a cliff. Bloody Joni M. No music tonight then. I finished the whisky in silence and went to bed. I eventually drifted off to sleep after an age, running the Sarah and Tom thing around in my head. I was either imagining the whole thing, or they were falling in love. It changed minute by minute and hour by hour. The one thing I was now sure of was that I was thirty years of age and an emotional retard. I slept eventually and was woken late the next morning by the alert from my phone receiving a picture message. It was of Sarah and her pal Jane smiling and clutching their spoils from the morning's exploits. Sarah was showing me a couple of tops she had bought, and she was wearing a kind of 'Casey Jones' cap. They both looked like they were having a great time, and she put a couple of kisses on the bottom. No words. It was approaching ten in the morning and as I was still waking up

I could summon up nothing more profound than a 'They look nice. Glad you're having fun,' response back to her.

'They're rags Jack. No matter, it's a right old laugh. Jane sends a kiss. x x x.'

I got out of bed and walked to the kitchen. As I made the morning ritual coffee, I looked at the photo again. She was at the market with her pal Jane as she said she would be. She had contacted me as she would have in any similar situation. There was no subterfuge. I needed to get a grip.

The following months passed without incident. Well, that's true, but there was a difference now. We spent a lot more time by ourselves. Drinks, trips to the movies, that kind of thing. Normality. No meeting up with Tom though. Not through a falling out or anything like that. I would phone or text regularly. It was the summer now so there was a lot to discuss, being as the cricket season was in full throes. There was no mention of meeting up though. Sarah didn't broach the subject. She was pro-active with her plans for us every weekend now, and it was just her and me every time. I went along with this. I was suspicious that the dynamic may have altered somewhat, yet I enjoyed being with Sarah. That's a bloody lie. I loved being with her, and she seemed to feel the same about being with me. It was an almost ideal summer. Ideal apart from the stone in my shoe that made itself known from time to time. It wasn't like the couple who enjoy the summer knowing that when it ends he must go off and fight and probably be killed in a war somewhere. Not that dramatic. It was more like an unsettling prod that would manifest itself at any time, and then vanish in the laughter and sex. I guess as my thirty first birthday approached that August Sarah and I were having what people call 'that perfect summer.'

I had a small garden, and one particularly hot Saturday Sarah thought it would be nice to have a barbecue that afternoon. Just the two of us. We could cook the food and get slightly drunk while we were doing that. The insinuation was, after we had eaten, we could then go to bed and get intense. Couldn't fault the plan, so that morning we drove to the supermarket to stock up on the standard barbecue fare. That was when we met Tom for the first time in two months. I spotted him first, and his initial joy at seeing me for the first time in ages soon turned to something akin to panic when he spotted Sarah. He blurted out something, rambling to me, and then turned to Sarah and looked away, and then back and then away again. He didn't know where to look. He turned to me and tried again to say something, but by now he was so self-conscious the words did not come. He had betrayed me in an awful way, and he was struggling to hide his horror and self-loathing. But even with all this his gaze again returned to Sarah, with all the intensity and longing and loathing and wanting. He stared at her for a few more seconds, and then mumbled his farewells and headed off to the aisles of plenty at breakneck speed. To me he looked like a clown. And as for my Sarah, who was normally the model of self-assuredness and friendliness and exuberance? There had been the same looking at him and looking away dance with the eyes. She was shaking. She didn't want to look at Tom. He was the last person in the world she wanted to see, but she couldn't take her eyes off him. And her eyes. There was sadness. There was longing, and I am afraid to say there most certainly was love. After a time, she looked at me with such sadness that I struggled to hold her gaze. Then she gathered herself and spoke.

'I'm going now. Um ... I'll call you.'

And with that she turned and walked out of the supermarket. I stood for a time in the same spot. I didn't want to run into either of them again. We had only just started shopping so my trolley only had a few items in it. Fifteen minutes ago, or less, they would have grown into the makings of a feast, to begin a wonderful Saturday in August. How that had all changed now.

As always happens in these damn places, I was soon in someone's way. I guess they had no idea that my world had just broken. I wasn't of a mind to give anything away in my manner, even though the temptation to whack this pest of a woman in the head with the heaviest vegetable I could find was overwhelming. Realistically, I had been standing there long enough now. Out of badness I left my trolley in the way of everything, and left the building. It was just after midday. I headed to a pub where I was confident of not meeting anyone I knew, with the aim of getting wasted.

10

Dunstable people are never shy in venting their frustrations as to the town's limitations. In fairness the place is no different to a lot of mid-sized towns in Southern England. It has its good parts, and it has its not so good parts. Nevertheless, most people are united in their appreciation of the jewel, Dunstable Downs. Not a mile from the centre of town, they rise almost eight hundred feet and then drop down to the Gliding Club, providing panoramic views of the farms and villages below. Further out west the view takes in Ivinghoe and Ivinghoe Beacon and beyond to the Vale of Aylesbury. It is a magnificent vision, these villages with their farms and churches and surrounding fields, feeing more like a fantasy land complete with elves and goblins. Maybe a dragon hiding in the woods. There's no blot on that landscape. No warehouses or multi story car parks or any such abominations. The gliders which take off and land in the field that constitutes the Gliding Club's airstrip manage to add to the air of tranquillity that pervades the place. Silently skimming the air during flight like albatrosses returning from an epic journey. The local wildlife gives them a cursory glance, little more.

It had also served me well over the years as a refuge in times of stress. And it had never let me down. I had always left in a better place than that when I arrived. Sarah rang the next day, the Sunday, because she said she would. It must have been horrible for her building up the words and courage to do so. It was around one in the afternoon and the conversation was brief. We had to talk. Some resolution had to be achieved though how God only knew. I asked if we could meet outside her place and then walk up to the Downs via the section known as the Five Knolls. Her flat was literally a couple of minutes from the open park area that rose to the Knolls, so it was a natural suggestion as somewhere to spend time on a sunny cloudless day in late summer. It was also quite a steep climb initially, so my hope was that we would yomp up to the top then sit and have it out. I wasn't in the mood for walking and talking. She agreed and I said she would see me at two.

It was about a twenty-minute walk to Sarah's. I wasn't going to risk driving after the previous day's excesses, and I duly timed it to arrive outside her place at the allotted time. She was already outside. We exchanged pleasantries, all formal, no kiss, and headed along the rest of West Street to the park. I set a pace and Sarah understood my strategy straight away. We continued as the park rose to the climb that takes you to a gate near the summit, signifying the beginning of the Downs proper. We then marched over the Five Knolls, and then onto the area I had in mind. This was my favourite spot, probably anywhere.

I would say there were in the region of seven or eight people in the immediate vicinity. A couple sunbathing where the hill starts to fall towards the Gliding Club. It was just after two thirty and the temperature was hitting the thirties. There was a young couple with a small terrier. An Asian family and that was about it. The hordes congregated close to the visitor centre just under a mile away across the top of the Downs. There you could see all the kites and ball games and picnics visible from where we were. People were less inclined to venture to the area where we were, and that suited me fine. Sarah knew this was my special place, so she allowed me some time to take it all in. It had been a hottish summer and the fields below were now green with a copper-coloured tint. There were a few cars travelling between the villages but not a great deal of activity. No farm vehicles in sight. There were red kites amongst the birdlife overhead and I counted three gliders in mid-flight. All was as it would be on any summer Sunday up there.

Sarah now began to talk. She was composed, but there was a hint of desperation in her tone that I had never heard coming from her before. We should go away somewhere, just the two of us. Maybe move out of the area. She couldn't bear losing me. She brought in the 'love' word. This was the first time either of us had used it in conversation. She put her arms around me and nestled her head on my shoulder. There were tears in her eyes.

I wasn't gazing into her eyes though, by this stage. Something else had caught my attention. For some reason it had got noticeably darker during the previous couple of minutes, which at two forty-five on a cloudless day should not have been happening. I looked up and noticed the sun indeed didn't seem as bright as before. It seemed to be diminishing, not in its diameter but in its mass. On second glance I saw that it was not diminishing, it was dissolving! There had been birds about a few minutes ago, and I hadn't witnessed any dramatic uprising of the flock. There were no birds in the sky now. Or gliders for that matter. It continued to get darker, though curiously the temperature stayed constant. I looked around. Sarah had gone. In fact, everyone had gone, even the masses that had been playing and having fun by the visitor centre were gone. And the steady stream of vehicles constantly coming and going along the road behind me that separated the Downs from the Golf Club? All gone. Absolutely nothing moved. It was extremely eerie, and my heart jumped when I looked back up at the sun. The light was like dusk now, and the reason for that was the sun was now nothing more than a collection of fading blotches with darkness clearly visible through its mass. I had that awful thumping in my ears that you get when your heart is racing. Other than that, it was silence, and it was getting darker.

When I first heard the screams, it was easy to pinpoint exactly where they were coming from. It was the dozen or so houses on the left-hand side of the road that headed down to Tottenhoe, a half a mile below me to the right of my vantage point. The screams were coming from there. Not human screams though, not yet anyway. The light wasn't great, but I could make out the creatures. Their long diabolical legs or whatever the hell they were. The torso with the metallic look constantly shifting in colour, and at the head of the torso the cruel eyes and the monstrous wide-open beaks emitting the screams. They began their attack on the occupants of the houses. The occupants didn't stand a chance. I saw some being gathered in the creatures' beaks, and then the body parts outside fall away as the jaws clamped shut. I saw flesh burning from the creatures' spit, and I saw inhabitants gathered up by the creatures' tentacles then hurled at their homes. I heard their screams and then the sounds of their bodies smashing and breaking against the brickwork. Yes, I saw the bodies exploding in a mess of blood and bone like some conceptual artist throwing paint at his canvas. It was horrendous, and all I could do was sit and watch. I counted upwards of thirty of these creatures. They made short work of the houses and descended to the bottom of the hill. Thankfully, there was no cricket match happening on the pitch on the other side of the road. Realistically, all that meant was that when they reached the bottom of the hill they turned left onto Church Road, attacking the first set of houses on the corner, then moving onto the pub on the other side of the road. I could hear glasses smashing from within, and then saw patrons being dragged outside and given the same treatment as the inhabitants of the houses on the way down. People screaming, but the creatures' ungodly screams were louder. Scream, screech, whatever you wanted to call it. The sound felt like it was freezing the blood in my veins.

And on they marched. Onto the farms and livestock. They liked livestock, didn't they? I saw cows hurled into the air only to fall and explode as they hit the ground with a dull thud. I saw farmers and their families scattering only to be grabbed and given the same treatment. The church appeared to be empty, thankfully, so on they marched. They passed Doolittle Lane. Doolittle Lane indeed. No *Chien Andalou*? No *slicing up eyeballs*? No, not this time. I couldn't make out the detail here, as trees obscured my view, but I heard the cows mooing, and then the screams. Same outcome. And on they headed to Edlesborough. Well, most did. One group of five I think I could make out had branched off from the group and were now moving back through Well Head, in my direction. They moved with such speed. I remembered that from the flakey drone footage. These few didn't bother with the local inhabitants on the way. Their interest lay elsewhere. Within minutes they had crossed the main road and were all over the Gliding Club. Did they see the parked-up gliders as large resting birds? They made for them anyway, smashing the cockpits of three or four with their tentacles before they discovered they'd been duped. This deception most certainly saved the pilots who were now in their cars and driving away as quickly as they could. My problem was that two of the creatures had lost interest in the gliders and had instead decided to climb the side of the Downs that reached its summit just where I was sitting. Now I could see the tops of their heads emerging from the climb, around ten yards from where I was sitting. I remained motionless, until they stood directly in front of me, staring down with menace, their screams now deafening. Their colour changing from dark purples to dark blues with snatches of violet and bright green. A smell of blood and rotting flesh. They were on top of me and I could do nothing. I felt one of the tentacles reaching out and scraping against my leg.

'Jack! Jack! Where are you, my love?'

I moved my leg, but another tentacle grabbed it and began to pull me towards it. So how was it to be? Bitten in half? Spat upon, so I could watch my flesh burn away revealing my inner organs, as my life drifted away? Or maybe just hurled high into the fake night sky, and it all ending as my body splattered from the resulting impact with the ground? That would probably have been my preferred option. As it turned out it was none of these. The pounding in my ears grew louder and then everything turned purple, followed by a blinding light that immediately caused me to squint.

'Jack! Jack! What's wrong? Jack!' Sarah was shaking me.

Many years later, she told me how she had felt panic and slight hysteria at this point.

Naturally, I couldn't see my own expression, but I reckon it must have been dramatic. Eyes staring maniacally, mouth open, drool probably. I think Sarah was waiting for me to have a seizure, heart attack, stroke, or something ghastly. I continued to stare at her, probably for a minute, just holding our position. Perfectly still. And then it all came out. Ras Madrakah, the creatures, the mop up, Tony, Tony's sister, the nightmares ... everything. That was the Official Secrets Act smashed to smithereens then. When I had finished, I grabbed Sarah in a bear hug and sobbed. She was so cool. The few people in our vicinity must have been alarmed by my behaviour, and were looking towards us, showing polite concern. Sarah smiled at them reassuringly, keeping hold of me all the time until I was ready to move. When that time came, I released my hold slightly so I could look her in the eye. I said, 'I'm OK,' and moved to get up as did she. Once again, the sun was above us, and birds and gliders circled the landscape in their graceful aerial ballet. We retraced our steps back to her place in silence. I looked at my watch. It wasn't even four o'clock. We entered her flat in silence. Apart from my 'I'm OK' after the outburst, no words had been exchanged between us. Sarah took off her boots once we had got inside. I took off my shoes and we went into her bedroom. At that point we left everything outside. Our baggage, our history, our inhibitions, my little precautions. All left outside and our clothes left on the floor. We launched into each other and did not let up until after the sun had set. As we lay exhausted and covered in sweat, my arm cradling her head, I turned to her.

'I won't stand in your way Sarah. All I ask is we all remain close. You and Tom are the only people I have.'

'That pretty much makes me the shittiest person in the world, doesn't it?' she said.

Deep breath. 'It's just what happens,' I said. 'I don't know why God, or whoever, has designed it so it pans out this way,

60

but he has, so we need to deal with it, and that's what I'm trying to do.' I paused and then finished with, 'It ain't easy though, hon.'

She looked at me, and this time she started sobbing. And she said something very un-Sarah like.

'It's not fair, Jack.'

You don't say!

Part 2

Five years later

1

Charlotte never called me, about anything. Tasks were presented through e-mails. All correspondence came through her immediate underlings. I think I was to her a metaphorical bad smell. The reasons I came to report to her in the first place had been unclear. I was regarded with suspicion, and the safest strategy for her was to keep me at distance. I had no complaints. I was being ridiculously overpaid for the work I was doing, and I could come and go as I pleased. Hence, her phone call on that otherwise pleasant April Monday morning came as a shock. Next shock, she asked if I could come to her office straight away.

Her office was within an office, so to speak. You entered and walked into an open planned workspace, with officers hammering away on their keyboards. Charlotte's realm was separated from the rest by plasterboard walls located in the back-left corner of this uninspiring set up. Some looked up from their workstations. One said 'Hi.' It was not a jolly environment. I knocked on Charlotte's door and bowled straight in, as was my way. She looked up, startled by my bravado.

'Good morning ,Jack. Thank you for coming straight away. Please take a seat.' She motioned me towards the leather seat the other side of her desk.

'I must apologise. I so rarely see you or speak with you directly. We're all so busy and unfortunately the personal touch so often goes by the wayside.'

Get to the point Charlotte, I was thinking. Am I getting the bullet ... unlikely, but who knows? Had Sarah somehow spilled the beans with regards my confession on the Downs? No, never. Am I getting moved to some new hideaway for employees who could be a potential risk? I was looking directly at her sitting opposite me. I would have said she was in her late thirties. She was wearing the professional uniform, pastel blouse, knee length skirt. I imagined she would have been up for a good time in her youth, and possibly good fun to be around.

'Jack, forgive me for being the one to have to tell you, and if you have already heard I am so sorry. It is my sad duty to inform you that John Thims passed away in his sleep last night. You understand that his senior role within this organisation means we get to hear about events such as this very soon after they occur. May I offer my condolences and any realistic support you may need at this difficult time for yourself. Should you require time away to gather your thoughts and make any preparations, please feel free to do so. Let me know now, and I will make it happen.'

I remained sitting and staring directly at her while saying nothing. She would have interpreted this as shock I would imagine. I was staring at her trying to work out what the hell she was talking about. After a moment or two it came together. Ah yes, John Bloody Thims. I hadn't thought about him in years. Why would I? Charlotte would have been briefed as to my relationship with him, stepfather and all that, but it would have just been the bland details. She wouldn't have known of the mutual contempt, and why would she? But he had been a big deal I believe. He spoke regularly with cabinet ministers, among others, during his reign. Charlotte would not have wanted to screw up any protocol as regards me being told in case I used the connection against her. On top of that, as far as she was concerned, I came from a dark place anyhow. I could have told her the truth, that I didn't care. While not wanting to speak ill of the dead, he had never meant anything to me. Aside from this silly job. Other than that, he had been a negative influence in my life. But she didn't need to know any of that, so I just maintained my gaze, and thanked her politely for telling me.

'Yes, I think it may be for the best if I took some time out,' I said. She replied saying I could take as much time as I needed.

I got up from my chair, as she did hers. I shook her hand and thanked her again. I then walked out of her office, and headed towards the building's main entrance and exit. By the time I was outside, I had booked ten days' all-inclusive in Spain. Thank you very much John Thims.

2

Maybe if the Downs hadn't happened, and I had fought the Tom thing, Sarah and I could have stayed as a couple. It might have worked out OK. But maybe it wouldn't have. Couples do sometimes split after a time, don't they, sometimes acrimoniously. If that had happened, would she have saved my arse all those years later? I would say unlikely. And what would have happened with the cancer episode? As regards this story, Sarah and me splitting as an item at that time in our lives was for the best. The benefit of hindsight is a wonderful thing.

That doesn't mean it wasn't awful at the time. I think it is one of my finest achievements, that I behaved gallantly during the Sarah/Tom switchover. This is not to say I wasn't dying inside. I most certainly was. The girl you love suddenly goes off with your lifetime best buddy. That sucks in any language. Two things saved me. Firstly, confession most certainly is good for the soul. My confession to Sarah on the Downs, after the vision, proved the spiritual lightening of a heavy load. I honestly believed I had regained some sanity through emptying my guilt onto her that afternoon. Also, my feelings towards her had shifted. I still loved her I guess, although not the same as before. Maybe more spiritually than possessively. Secondly, and this is weird, I am convinced that I believed deep in my soul that Sarah and Tom were the right thing at that time, as was I remaining close to them. I had moments of self-pity sure, but that belief kept me on the path. As a result, I became a far better person I'm sure. If anything, it was Sarah and Tom who were racked with guilt. Though to be fair, not so much shame as to prevent Sarah becoming pregnant with almost embarrassing haste. In May of the following year she gave birth to twins, David and Michael. I was made their godfather. Nice touch.

I wandered over to see them all the evening after my chat with Charlotte. The twins were running riot as ever, and

Tom was attempting to take control without much success. They both expressed their condolences, not going overboard, as they knew the score. We chatted for some time, and after an hour or so Tom took the boys up to bed, stating he would be turning in early himself, as he had an early start in the morning. He gave Sarah a peck on the cheek, me a hug, and off he went leaving Sarah and me sitting at their dining table chatting. She rose and got me another bottle of cider from the fridge. Yes, I had had a few already through their generosity. Whatever the truth, Charlotte's news had been a shock of sorts, and when that happens friends rally round, don't they? It was around nine in the evening and up to this point the conversation had been fairly run of the mill. Sarah went quiet for a time and then asked me a real humdinger of a question.

'Do you think your stepfather had anything to do with that Ras Madrakah business?'

I didn't answer straight away, I just gave her the 'I'm thinking … quiet' look. It had certainly never occurred to me, but as I worked her question over in my brain, slightly hampered by the three bottles of 'Cornish Rattler' I had already swilled, it became clear that it was more than a possibility. He had been one of the top boys. He would have had the authority. If it were so, I then wondered how he would have actioned such a barbaric operation. At that moment, the only piece of advice he ever gave me came to mind.

'Just turn up and sign everything they put in front of you.'

That thought led to a vision of him sitting at his fancy desk arranging his 'to do' papers, and then grabbing a pen:

Acceptance of budget costs

for upgraded codebreaking IT   sign

Deployment of a further eleven surveillance satellites   sign

Tab for New York conference   sign

| Authorization to release sixty unearthly monsters on rogue armed cult | sign |
| Table government to make all Russian broadcasters in the UK illegal | sign |

My God. It sounded like a joke by Woody Allen. I let out a long sigh.

'It's possible,' I said.

It is fair to say anything was possible with that man.

'And then your involvement?' she said.

Once again it was possible.

'I'm sorry Jack. That was a horrible question to ask.'

But she was within her rights to ask. I had involved her in the whole ghastly tale that afternoon. I had made her privy to information pertaining to a diabolical operation that she should not have had any knowledge of. I was one hundred per cent sure she had never told anyone of it, including Tom. I had made it her burden as well as mine, so yes, she was well within her rights to ask me. We sat in silence for a while. If Sarah was thinking the same as me, she would have been wondering what other awful secrets John Thims took to the grave.

'Have you spoken to your mum?' she said, I imagine trying to wind the whole sorry subject down.

'This afternoon,' I said. 'She didn't attempt to feign any sorrow. She asked if I was affected by the news, which I wasn't. She's enjoying a nice life down there. Begged me to visit. Sobbed a bit with missing me. Told me she loved me. Usual stuff. She's a good person and I love her too, but she's a long way away and that is just how it is.'

We then talked for an hour about lighter stuff. Tom, the twins, her job, England's openers for the forthcoming test. I then finished my Rattler, gave her a little kiss and bid her good night. She told me to have a nice holiday, and I left and walked home with my head full of thoughts of the recently departed John Bloody Thims.

3

The funeral was the day after I returned from Spain. It was being held in a little church just outside Hertford, which was where he had lived for the last six years or so. I gave myself an hour to get there, which was about right. That allowed me the simplicity of being able to park up and walk straight in when I arrived, and sit at the back out of the way, thus avoiding any awkward standing about prior to being invited into the church. There were two senior knobs I vaguely recognised from work sitting seven or eight rows in front of me. At the front on the left side was a serious looking dame, with heavily lacquered, angry white hair, sitting next to two guys in their late twenties. I guessed they would be sons from a previous partner, and she was John Thims's recent widow. They all at some point looked around briefly before the service began, giving me an opportunity to size them up. They were not pretty people. If they were curious as to the numbers there, the total including them was six, and then the vicar. No organist. All the music was taped. So not many, and not much feeling of love in the building either. The vicar performed the whole service. No one stood up to read a eulogy or anything like that. The whole service was a by the numbers job. We are gathered here today. Stand up. Sing hymn. Sit down. Bit about the deceased. Amusing story (optional … not taken up, due to nothing remotely amusing to recount). Few lines from the Bible. Moment to reflect. Stand up. Sing hymn. Lord's Prayer. And then off out of the church to the sounds of '*Where Do You Go To My Lovely*', which I always thought was one godawful song. '*Ha, ha, ha.*' I didn't hang around, spoke to no one, and was back in Dunstable and at the bar of the Victoria inside an hour. Job done!

4

It was two years after the funeral when I noticed Tom was really struggling. I had kept up the visits to Sarah, Tom and the boys every month in the meantime, without any drama. I seemed to have a knack for getting the boys' gifts spot on, which was a surprise to me. The toy cars, toy trains, shirts, caps etc. were loved. It didn't seem to be lip-service. Sarah said they told her constantly that their godfather's stuff was great. And I was not trying to 'out flash' anyone either. That would have been inexcusable. I didn't spend ridiculous amounts of money, just seemed to get it right. Which was genuinely nice, and for me surprising. Added to this, for me, life was not bad either as I marched towards my forties. Work was steady and undemanding. I had Gran's legacy that Mum had put together for me. It gave me the right books to read. It gave me art to print off and frame, so I could make my house even more bohemian. I had the music, so the neighbours could have the treat of a bit of 'Purple Haze' on a bright Sunday morning. I had pubs to go to. I even had some friends in the pubs, and I occasionally got a bit of action, which was most welcome. I was OK. And Sarah was always fine and bouncy and funny. As I said the boys were always great when I visited. But it became apparent to me that Tom was becoming more and more withdrawn. We no longer travelled to and from work together. Ever. Tom said his people preferred him in early so he could work when fewer colleagues were there to interrupt him. I wondered if that was true. It also gave him the excuse to go off to bed early when I visited, thus leaving me with Sarah and the boys until it was their time. I voiced my suspicions to Sarah, and at first, she scoffed and told me I was imagining it all. She told me he was a good and caring husband, even though we both knew they never married. It was just an expression. In fairness after they first got together, when would they have got married, what with Sarah getting pregnant almost immediately, and most certainly not wanting a shotgun wedding? The twins dominated proceedings after that. As I said it was just an expression. And Tom was a wonderful father, which I didn't doubt for a minute. I was not imagining it though. I had known Tom too long, and Sarah could be a hard-nosed so and so when it took her fancy.

'Sometimes I think he's more bothered about his bloody bees,' she remarked, sounding more like a 1970s sitcom wife.

In time she admitted that I may have something. Tom was racked with guilt. And yes, it's weird that it should be so. That over seven years after Sarah and me became Sarah and Tom, he should now still feel a villain. But then Tom was not like normal men. He was a beautiful man, but he was fragile. Perhaps for the first time in a long time, he'd time to reflect on what had passed before. I knew Sarah was still crazy about him, but her 'it's done, get over it' attitude didn't always help matters. And as we were probably the worst two people on the planet to discuss this with him, what could be done? Well, as sometimes happens, events conspired to take the whole business out of our hands, and effectively put the matter to bed.

A few weeks later Sarah rang me one Saturday morning. Could I meet Tom and her in town for a coffee?

'Sure,' I said, 'The place we like. An hour?'

'Fine,' and she hung up.

This was unusual. We would normally go in this coffee place when we accidentally bumped into each other in town. Never arranged, so I was intrigued. But then Sarah could be a box of tricks, so best get presentable and see what it was all about. It was a sunny June morning. A lot of people were out and about as I arrived at our place, exactly an hour later. The building itself was a retail unit, so no design awards there, still the interior worked OK. Serving area to the right as you walked in, with tables and chairs arranged in the middle and along the exterior wall on the left. Some art on the walls. Sarah and Tom were there already, sitting beside each other, backs to the wall in the far corner. The boys weren't with them. I was to sit facing them, and my coffee was on the table all ready for me. OK, this was the serious set up. I sat down and started to extend pleasantries. Sarah cut me short. Tom was silent and looking at me with an incredibly sad glint in his eye. I took a deep breath and prepared myself, as clearly something horrible was coming my way. Sarah continued:

'Look Jack, it's like this. I thought it was time I should get myself checked out, so I did about four weeks ago. The results have come back. I've got cervical cancer and it's advanced.'

I started to well up. This was the reason I had my back to the rest of the clientele. How could someone as beautiful as Sarah have something as horrible as this in her body? I started to cry properly, and soon received a sharp kick to the shins.

I looked straight at her, 'Sorry. How long have you known?'

'Three days.'

I looked at Tom. His expression had not changed. I let out a sigh.

'Do the boys know?' I said.

'Not yet. And if I get my way, they aren't going to hear about it. We're going to fight this thing. Tom and I are going to find a way to beat it. Between us we are the best qualified and have the best skill set. We've been going over this for the last day and a half, after we calmed down.'

'We've got a plan. This is a cue to make the world a better place, Jack.'

'I admire your resolve,' I said, 'and yes, if anyone can beat it, you two are the ones I'd put my money on.'

Tom's expression had now changed. He was looking at me and smiling. 'We've only told you Jack. You're the only one we want to tell. You've got something special in the way you're put together, and right now Sarah and I need that.'

'You've got me Tom. You've got no worries there.'

I didn't have the faintest idea what practical use I could be, but I wasn't going to shirk my new responsibilities. After the initial bombshell it was rousing stuff, and I would most certainly be there for them. I looked back at Sarah. She was smiling now, albeit her eyes were redder than normal.

I had not taken one sip of my coffee.

5

Pretty soon it became clear that one of my new duties was going to be looking after David and Michael, at least for three evenings during the week, and some Saturdays and Sundays. This was no hardship for all concerned parties. The boys, now coming up to eight years old, and both passing five feet in height each with jet black hair, were great fun. We would watch TV and/or play games in the evenings. I would sometimes take them on day trips if we had a Saturday or Sunday together. As their godfather, it was a great opportunity to cement our bond. Having never had any paternal instincts before, it surprised me how much I enjoyed being with them. The white lie was Mum and Dad were working overtime on a special project, which was true I guess, and they were fine with that.

After the coffee shop meeting on the Saturday Sarah and Tom had approached their relative superiors and explained the situation. As they were both highly regarded, they were allowed free rein to work on their project around their regular duties and were granted access to all the facilities they needed. Some evenings Tom would leave his place and travel to Cambridge, so they could reconcile their progress and perform practical experiments. The only stipulation was they present all their work in progress to their respective superiors for analysis, which was not a problem for them. This pattern of living continued for just over five months. Sarah was receiving limited treatments. She resisted anything that could be debilitating such as chemo. Her thinking was that would be counterproductive. The good news was they had both been involved in related work in this field before, so they didn't start from scratch. The reason I mention that is so it doesn't seem that they achieved in just five months what countless teams of people had been spending generations to achieve without success. And I confess that although I had every confidence in their abilities and the strength of their resolve, I had my doubts over the months, that they would succeed.

But succeed they did, albeit while observing and monitoring the recession period. Naturally, Sarah was the guinea pig for the procedure once they were satisfied it was safe. It worked, the cancer was gone, and it never returned. Tom did try to explain it to me. Something about some colloidal particles delivering 'super' cells to the infected area. The eye opener apparently was that they only targeted the bad cells, which then linked up with the unaffected good ones to make the repair complete. The only drawback was the particles only attacked the local area it targeted, meaning if a body had more than one infected area, a separate particle insertion point was required. This wasn't considered a big deal as cancer was relatively easy to detect in the body. Getting rid of it had been the stumbling point up to now.

'So, the particles can't travel around the body like that microscopic ship with Raquel Welch in a bikini did in the movie?' I asked.

Reasonable question.

'No, Jack, unfortunately meeting the lovely Raquel's needs in that respect may be a leap too far for us presently,' Tom replied with a beaming smile.

'You're such a fucking cock, Jack,' added Sarah, before she gave me the biggest hug ever.

Needless to say, Christmas at Tom and Sarah's was the celebration to end all celebrations. I showed up with the best presents ... again. I tried not to, but I couldn't help it. It didn't matter though. Sure, I was still godfather, best friend and all that, but the dynamic had changed, once again. Tom could now stand proudly with his arm round his beloved Sarah, looking across at David and Michael with love and pride. At last, they were a fully functioning family unit. Although I couldn't quite get my head around the drama required to achieve that, I was genuinely delighted and relieved for them.

As goes with a breakthrough of that magnitude the shock waves around the world were immense. It was as if the last great danger to mankind had been overcome. Unfortunately, there remained far greater threats; we just couldn't see them at the time. However, this cancer thing was the biggest of big deals. Sarah and Tom's only stipulation with it all, apart from it being made available to everyone, not just those that could afford it, was anonymity. Consequently, the global reporting went along the lines that teams from London and Cambridge had combined to successfully produce a cure for cancer. All the plaudits went to their respective superiors. They were fine with this. They now had almost complete freedom within their organisations, who were prepared to provide them with whatever they wanted to keep hold of their services. Everyone within the scientific community knew the score, and they were inundated with requests for speaking engagements and articles in journals.

They were the darlings of science alright. If they had given the New Scientist their weekend shopping list it would have got published. This all provided a nice little extra income, but it was not of great importance. They contributed a lot of it towards assisting implementation of their cure in less well-off places, tying in with their desire for worldwide availability. They did the house up a bit. Nothing fancy. In truth, they didn't know what to do with the extra money. Their needs were otherwise. Tom asked me once if I needed any extra cash. Not being flash, just genuinely asked. If it had been anyone else, I would have taken exception, but this was Tom remember. I thanked him and said I was alright. Nice to have the luxury to be able to say that, ey?

6

It was my fortieth birthday when I first saw the Aja on one of those 'mysteries of the deep' documentaries that were always on tele. I was at Sarah and Tom's, and for a birthday treat they had prepared a lavish meal. Afterwards we watched a movie, and it was all nice as it always was with them. The boys were heading for their tenth birthdays and, in the cliched and somewhat condescending way people sometimes speak, were approaching the age when they got interesting. For me they had always been good guys to be around. I considered my role as their godfather one that had always brought me joy as well as giving me purpose. Kept me on the straight and narrow so to speak.

The movie finished, making it time for the boys to say their goodnights and march off to bed. Tom reset the tele to normal programs, finding this documentary featuring these guys in the middle of the Pacific diving down to the depths in submersibles, filming the creatures that inhabited a world where the light from the sun had given in many fathoms before. People had been making these shows for years and the amazing thing was they continued to discover new species. Of course, to some this was totally predictable, and they argued that while we continue to spend billions launching rockets into space, we had only explored one pico-percent of the oceans. And so on.

I learnt afterwards that the Aja were not actually new to this documentary. We had known of them for some time, yet we still knew little about them. They were most likely related to the squid or octopus family. If so, they were exceptionally large examples, being around nine feet in length fully grown. Their heads housed a large and forever opening and closing eye. The beak below appeared constantly wide open, presumably to ingest plankton and other small forms of life. It was difficult to gauge the colour of their torsos as they seemed to be constantly shimmering with all manner of colours. The narrator said this was presumably a form of communication, not unusual, and in line with their presumed relatives. What was different with these creatures was they could emit sonar as well, which vastly increased the number of their neighbours in the sea that they could talk to. Their bodies concluded with six large tentacles that they used to shift rocks in the search for food, among other things. They appeared graceful and intelligent.

There were other odd-looking creatures on show in this normally pitch-black wilderness. The narrator explained we were seeing spider crabs and fangtooth fish and other weird critters. The Aja dominated proceedings though. There were four of them on show and they were curious as to the nature of this gatecrasher to their remote world, namely the submersible. This provided wonderful film footage, all close-up shots of the creatures gliding up to the cameras and staring through the glass of the craft to see what was happening on the other side of it. It appeared that once they were sure they had an audience they retreated to what looked like ten yards from the front cameras and did something strange. The four of them began to swim from the left and right of our perspective, back and forth in opposite directions. The top one from left to right. The one below him from right to left and so on. I can best describe it as resembling a section of a large musical score albeit a moving one. It was performed immaculately and all the weirder for it. This lasted for a few minutes, after which they gave the cameras one more lingering stare, and they were gone. Soon after the program finished my eyes remained glued to the television, though they took in none of what was being shown now. It was Tom who broke the silence.

'Seen them before, Jack?'

'I hope not,' I said.

I looked across at Sarah. She was white as a sheet.

Maybe the Aja had been featured in documentaries many times before I first saw them, as I said before. Still, not much had been written about them up to that point, and I suspect they were still new kids on the block then. Didn't look much like New Kids on the Block I have to say. More like something The Residents would dream up. Over the years they began to be seen more and more, though. At first during deep sea dives, as when I first saw them. Then a few fathoms higher up and a little closer to land masses. They were spotted in the Pacific Ocean as before, the Atlantic Ocean and the Indian Ocean. Every time communicating through the altering colours in their skin pigmentations, as well as sending sonar calls through the depths. Naturally, the more we observed them the more we learned.

They seemed to have an extremely short gestation period making reproduction a slick affair. We didn't attach great importance to that at the time. A mistake. They showed absolutely no desire to surface from the water and appeared to have no need to. We didn't attach any great importance to that either, which really was a mistake. What we were extremely interested in was their feeding habits, or more accurately not feeding but digestion capabilities. As I mentioned before, they swam with their large beaks constantly open to take in plankton, small fish and the suchlike. Not dissimilar to whales and other mammals that deployed filter fishing techniques. Where the Aja differed was that as well as swallowing the food sources mentioned above, they seemed to actively seek out and digest non-food sources. By that I mean they targeted material unnatural to their surroundings. In short, our shite.

Large amounts of it. They were extremely proficient at it as well, and after some study, it was found their bodies managed to convert these materials, in the main plastics, into natural waste. An amazing achievement and a talent that over time caused the Aja to be namechecked in high places.

One further curious behaviour was being noted by observers of the world's oceans. On occasion when a group of Aja noticed they were being watched, they would put on a show for the cameras, in a similar vein to the musical notation dance I had seen on that initial documentary. That particular dance it would seem was an early one off. The new eye catcher involved seven or eight of them congregating into a ball shape of around twelve feet in diameter, always rotating anti clockwise, and always lasting for four minutes and thirteen seconds. After that time, they would simply disband and jet off into the darkness. This performance started to become more and more common, with sightings in all the oceans previously mentioned, and always the same rules. Seven to eight participants, twelve feet in diameter, always a rotating ball, rotating anti clockwise and always, always lasting four minutes thirteen seconds.

Naturally, Sarah and I discussed the Aja, although never with Tom unless it was a general kind of discussion. Our concern was that our view of these creatures may look like a secret that we had been hiding from him all these years, which it was really. So he may see it as a betrayal of sorts, which in fairness would be a natural reaction given our history. Tom was on the straight and narrow nowadays; the cancer business had enabled that to happen. But he was still the same person as before, meaning you had to treat him with care. Up to that point, he didn't need to be aware of what I believed to have been my previous encounter with these creatures all those years ago. If indeed they were the same creatures. From my description of the vision on the Downs, Sarah was pretty convinced they were, as was I. At this point in time, they were still curios of the ocean depths, with a lot to say, an understanding of the concept of measuring time, and what appeared to be a desire to clear up our mess. So far it seemed they had joined the party as unusual allies as opposed to a threat to humanity.

Part 3

1

Mum was two days shy of her eightieth birthday when she passed away. Time had marched on. I was by then in my mid-fifties. Craig contacted me first thing in their morning to tell me she had gone in her sleep. It was subsequently confirmed to be of natural causes. The news hit me hard. I was a mess for days after. Of course, we had kept in contact since she moved away all those years ago but that was it. Calls to each other occasionally. She had never returned to England and I had only ever flown to Australia the once to see her. My memories of her were largely idyllic childhood ones, which in some ways made it all the worse. I lost her in my teens, Dad's death being the catalyst. In truth, Craig had turned out to be a good man and a good choice. She had enjoyed a long and happy life with him, so I guess things had worked out for the best. It was just me feeling sorry for myself. Tom and Sarah said I was justified in feeling a little angry at being dealt a shitty hand as regards to Mum and me. They said I dealt with it all remarkably well. That's what friends say at those times isn't it, though I'm being unfair, as they were two extremely genuine individuals who were on my side. That's all.

I didn't fly out to the other side of the world for the funeral. Why would I? That world was not my world; it was alien to me. I would have struggled through the service, jet lagged to pieces, and would have left in a haze. Craig let me have a copy of the Order of Service and the timings, which allowed me to be there in spirit on the day, even though it was the middle of the night over here. The next day Michael and David came round to see me. Time had moved on. They were in their mid-twenties now, all qualified in the sciences following in the footsteps of Sarah and Tom. Now they could look out for me, and we proceeded to go out and get ourselves rip roaringly drunk. When you are mourning loss of a nearest and dearest, kindness from those now close to you can be a magical thing. I was lucky.

In a lot of ways Mum was lucky too. She died during a period of relative calm in the world's comings and goings. If she had held on another five years, it would have potentially been a much nastier ending for her. That's the benefit of my now having an overview of the key events during my lifetime. It ultimately doesn't make the pain go away. It just puts it all into perspective.

2

Didn't everyone love the Aja now. They were the eco warriors' bloody storm troopers. They had increased in numbers considerably during the years since the initial sightings. It was now fifteen years since I had first seen them on Tom and Sarah's TV. They appeared more and more in documentaries. They were by now inhabiting more hospitable parts of the oceans. So much so that dare devil divers could now swim alongside of them if they wished, watching them at work clearing up after us. I found the sight of that unnerving. Sarah asked me if I could maybe have a word in certain quarters as to the potential threat they may pose. I replied that my current professional life was one of zero kudos. If I did start spouting off about events of over thirty years ago that officially hadn't occurred, authorised by individuals either long retired or deceased, no good would come of it. I would just appear a fool.

Because of course the Aja were our friends. They wanted to help us tidy our mess. It is fair to say that over the years we had tried to put things right. We had initiated countless strategies designed to prevent an ecological global catastrophe. To be fair we were still here, as were most of our fellow residents on the planet. The problem was there were just so many of us, so that unfortunately, for every twenty or so good natured and willing hands, there would always be one dickhead who wouldn't think twice about lobbing a plastic bottle over the side of a boat, or leaving behind the detritus from their day at the beach.

In whatever way we behaved, be it well or badly, we just created so much shit. There were too many of us. There was too much rubbish, and no one really knew how to get rid of it all. There were container vessels stacked up with our waste, being refused landing permits at every port they tried to dock at with a view to negotiating some nefarious disposal deal. There were hundreds of these ships travelling the seas, effectively with nowhere to go. So it was, that having put up with valuable resources being deployed in this futile manner for so many years, the supposed greatest minds alive got together and devised a strategy to solve this ongoing problem. This was what they made happen. They instructed thirty of these vessels, as a trial of sorts, to converge in an area of the North Atlantic Ocean just south of the Labrador Sea. An area that had witnessed sightings of large numbers of Aja. Once assembled they were ordered to dump their entire 'payloads' into the sea. Naturally, the captains queried the sanity of this. However, after being assured the instruction was genuine, and originated in high office, they duly complied. It was a beautiful August day. I was approaching my fifty eighth birthday, blissfully unaware of this atrocity taking place, as virtually all of us were. The American president had this to say to a leadership gathering.

'It's a free lunch for the Aja. Let's work with our new busy friends. Everyone wins here people.'

This was never going to end well, was it? Even the dumbest of the dumb know there is no such thing as a 'free lunch'. The president was correct in one respect insofar as the Aja were busy, and to deal with this they needed to become a whole lot busier. Unbeknown to us, the ocean's version of the airwaves exploded into life. What had once been occasional chatter, whale song and organic light shows, turned a whole lot busier. Distress calls highlighting the outrage just south of Greenland, filled the seas. Warnings were issued to stay away! The Aja were alerted, but there were still too few of them. A plan was required, and so it was, that a number of the creatures were dispatched to the affected area of the ocean to begin clear up operations, leaving a larger number to engage in an aggressive breeding programme. Due to their extremely brief gestation period, this could manifest itself at pace.

On land our great leaders were untroubled by the fact that a greater intelligence than theirs was at work in the ocean, desperately attempting to clear up after the atrocity committed. They saw peaceful seas, and thirty freed up sea vessels and crews. To them the whole endeavour was an unqualified success. It would be a wasted opportunity not to repeat it. For that reason, in the following months similar waste disposals happened in the Indian Ocean, the Pacific, the South China Sea and the Arabian Sea. To sea creatures, it must have been the equivalent of how some nightmare nuclear holocaust would have been for us. The kind of scenario that had been predicted as a distinct possibility so often in history, and had somehow, so far, never come to pass. We would have visions of waking up to a destroyed world. The lucky ones, or unlucky ones, whichever way you saw it, being forced to scavenge for food amongst the rubble and the dead, while they waited for the radiation to pick them off over time. All this devastation caused by a handful of spiteful cylinders of horror, exploding on or above specific targets. Somehow up to this point we had resisted the temptation to unleash this hell on ourselves. Unfortunately for the creatures of the seas, we unleashed it on them instead, and in total ignorance of what we had done.

To say the effect on the marine life in the areas selected was anything short of catastrophic would be a massive understatement. Life down there was poisoned, suffocated, mutilated. The good news was mass destruction was averted. Extremely quickly, we are talking matters of months here, the Aja expanded globally, and began to repair the damage. It was an astonishing example of the planet deploying its natural defences to repair itself after an enormous disaster. Meanwhile, on the surface, the world's leaders were facing a backlash. This whole operation had been veiled in secrecy for obvious reasons. Public opinion would not react well to actions such as this. Unfortunately for our leaders, a fishing boat managed to sneak close enough to the vessels in the Arabian sea, and film the whole operation. This, despite all the bogus radio warnings of freak storms in the operation area. The horror film naturally went viral, and mass protests throughout the world followed thereafter. As always happens, selected talking heads attempted to excuse the inexcusable, and promised 'sweeteners' to appease the people. On some this tactic may have worked, however, there was an extremely vast global network of souls who despaired at the behaviour of our leaders. They made themselves heard through mass marches and civic disruption in capital cities. The world's media lapped it up. This time round it was peaceful.

Film was shown of the now vast numbers of Aja, busily at work consuming our garbage and converting it into their non-toxic waste. It was bad, but our friends the Aja could make it all better. Our leaders survived relatively intact. The only downside for them was that this whole sorry affair had created a political monster. The Aja. They were our superheroes now.

3

David was celebrating his thirtieth birthday with friends of his down at their place in the pretty Cornish fishing village of Mevagissey, when the first attack on a fishing boat occurred. David had, encouraged by me no doubt, developed a liking for all things cidery. That place was heaven to him. Lots of walks. Lots of drinks after. What's not to like? He was also the more outgoing of the twins. They had followed Sarah and Tom's lead into the sciences. They were now working alongside them with a view to eventually take over their work when it was time. Not for a while yet I hasten to add. David was the micro-biologist therefore he worked closer with Sarah, which could well have contributed to the slightly wilder way he carried on. Not that Michael was a stay-at-home reserved type. He was merely calmer, steadier, that's all. Also, neither had married or settled into steady relationships so far in their lives. Girlfriends came and went. I thought they missed out on a couple of good ones, but if your head isn't at the party maybe your heart must acquiesce. Or was it the other way round? I had never married. How the hell would I know? My only hope was that they had not adopted me too much as a role model. Even after all these years we were still close. Hmm. Brainboxes for Mum and Dad, and Sir Sidney Ruff Diamond as godfather. Maybe they were always going to be slightly off kilter.

As I was saying, it was David's thirtieth making it the end of May when the *Dirty Dancing* moored up at the jetty. It was not much after eleven in the morning. A particularly warm and sunny morning too, which made the crew's ashen faces stand out even more to those waiting, eager to discover the meaning of their anguished radio announcements earlier that morning. They were quickly ushered into the harbour master's cabin. The door shut, keeping out curious onlookers. This was a three-man crew, that had set off at three thirty that morning into the Channel, in search of precious sardines. They explained they were barely thirty yards from the *Scarlett* when it dragged its first net of the day in around seven. At this point Jamie, the new addition to the *Dirty Dancing's* crew, started filming from his phone.

You need to understand that these nets contained all the fish they had gathered, while being dragged along behind their respective fishing boat. The nets were of a size which meant they did not discriminate. Not all the fish they captured were desirable, such as dogfish. When the nets were pulled onto the back of the boat, the fish were then sorted, and the undesirable fish were then released back into the water. If these fish were lucky, they would have still been in one piece. Sometimes they were not so lucky. The process remained the same though, and they were thrown back into the sea. This did not happen on rare occasions. This occurred constantly, so much so that these unwanted fish had a name. They were called 'bycatch'. In fairness to the fishermen of Mevagissey most of the bycatch they captured were returned to the sea unharmed. The proper cruelty was dished out to dolphins and tuna amongst others, by the much larger fishing vessels operating out of the huge industrial ports located in South America, Asia, Newfoundland and so on.

It so happened the *Scarlett's* nets had acquired bycatch as normally happened that morning. The difference on this occasion was that once the net was dragged out of the sea, one of the things caught up in their net fought back, which was captured on Jamie's phone. His film began with the crew realising they had something larger than normal in there that was busily shaking the other captured fish off its shiny glistening torso whilst tearing open the net. Seconds later the huge lash of the first tentacle smashed the roof of the boat's cabin clean into the sea. Once on-board, it set about the crew, four on this boat. The phone camera footage was shaky for obvious reasons, yet it clearly picked up one member of the crew becoming entwined in a tentacle before the creature's beak decapitated him. The corrosive spittle did for another crewman, by which time the boat had capsized. At the end, only part of the deck was visible as it sank, taking the remaining two crewmen with it. As the sea slowly claimed the bulk of what was once the *Scarlett*, the creature was still clinging to it. It screamed that ungodly scream, first to the sky, followed by another scream in the direction of the *Dirty Dancing*. Unsurprisingly, by this time the captain was steering his boat in the opposite direction as fast as the engines could take him. Mercifully, the *Scarlett* eventually disappeared into the sea, taking the creature with it.

Cornish fishing villages are close knit communities. Well, the community that lives there all year are close knit. Something like that wasn't going to stay secret in the harbour master's cabin for long. Pretty soon it was the talk of every restaurant, coffee bar, ice cream parlour … everywhere. Also being as it was the start of the tourist season, word spread nationwide with great speed. David rang Sarah and Tom. Sarah rang me immediately. By the afternoon, the face of the apprentice on the *Dirty Dancing* was all over social media, as was his phone camera footage.

I must confess, to a massive temptation at this point, to climb to the top of the highest peak and shout out:

'They're not so fucking fabulous now, are they?'

4

The first time Sarah rang was to tell me to get onto any news feed to see what had happened, to which I explained I had already. An hour later she rang again.

'You in?' she said.

'Yes Sarah.'

'I'm coming round. Do I need to bring any booze?'

It would seem I had no say in the matter.

'Don't worry. The fridge is well stocked up,' I said.

'Good. See you in five,' and with that she hung up.

Sarah hadn't visited me on her own since we'd been seeing each other. That was almost thirty years previously.

The doorbell rang, I opened the door and let her in. To me she looked no different to the young lady who graced my living room all those years ago. OK she now had a couple of age lines on her face that made her stare a little more intense. The rest was as it was. Punky tufts of hair, almost a Mohican. Deep set brown eyes, subtle traces of lipstick and powder. Graceful neckline. She was most certainly still a stunner, standing as she was in my front room. I am ashamed to admit I was clearly seeing her in a different light than I would have had she been with Tom and/or the boys. Maybe it was the location. Maybe because we were alone in my house. Whatever it was, feelings buried during the previous years were resurfacing within me.

She said 'hi' and we headed into the kitchen. I opened two bottles of Rattler, and we sat down at my breakfast bar which I had hoped we would. It was just more relaxed and less formal than the sofa for some reason. She took a long swig of Rattler and began.

'Stroll on Jack. You must be wanting to hammer your fist on a few stuffed shirts' desks, surely?'

'They wouldn't listen. It's so long ago, and it'll all now be filed away in the 'Didn't Happen' tray. They'd think I was a madman. What does disappoint me is I was almost glad to see that footage.'

'You'd begun to doubt yourself?' she said.

'Yeah, maybe. Those wretched creatures have in their own way been a large part of my life. But just my life, no one else's. It makes you feel alone. I know you believed me, and you still are the only one I've told. We all require proof of sorts, don't we? That's simply our nature. I could never accept that you totally believed, if you know what I mean. But it's out there now. They've shown their true colours, lots of them as it goes.' I laughed at my little joke.

'Of course, the immediate concern is what will happen next? I cannot believe they're only off the coast of Cornwall. When will the next attack occur? What will our great world leaders do? Let's be honest their recent track record is not great. This isn't going away.'

I then did something slightly risqué. I took hold of her arm, smiled and said:

'You're still looking fantastic by the way.'

I smiled so it was OK. Serious face would have been creepy. She looked back at me, welled up and then stopped. Gran would have described Sarah as a lady with all her chairs under the table. She did not enjoy losing control.

'Oh, Tom was all over it straight away. In his world there's always a solution. I sometimes think he views life like one of those stupid Crystal Maze things that hipsters and the like used to love so much. He lives for it. Solve this poxy puzzle and move onto the next room. Life isn't like that though. It's a constant struggle. It's the ability to view the whole picture, not just the next challenge. You must look up, look around. Try to understand what's really going on and make the best decisions for you and those you love, based on what you think is the best thing to do. It's not always just about successfully moving on into the next room.'

She was clearly quite uptight as evidenced by her quickly dispatching her bottle of Rattler. I brought another two out of the fridge and opened them.

'That approach served you well as regards to the cancer business,' I said, feeling I should defend Tom's corner.

Sarah had never spoken about him in this way before, and it was a shock.

'Yes. I fully realise that when Tom and I combined our efforts to beat it, we were probably the only two people on the planet who could have done so. We probably wouldn't have succeeded on our own if that had been the case. Yes, we achieved something miraculous, not just for me, but for the whole of humanity, and our coming together was maybe divine providence. OK. I didn't love him any more as a result, even though I at least half owe him my life, if you know what I mean. I still loved him for sure, but he was still Tom. I mean, after that we became scientific superstars. We still are. We get flooded with stuff, even though we requested anonymity. It's all requests, suggestions, crazy ideas. Would we like to sit on some stupid panel on some Saturday night TV show, judging stuff, because well, we've been there and done it and that gives us the authority to pronounce, "Yeah that's great and you're great, or no that's shit go away?" I mean really?'

'Tom though, he feels this obligation to make it all right. He's given the recognition therefore he has a moral duty to. I don't. We cured cancer. If it weren't us eventually someone else would have. That's what we do for a career. We are scientists, and I see it as our job to try to make the world a better place and living more bearable. But it's a job, not a quest for the Holy Grail. Tom just doesn't see it that way.'

'He hasn't agreed to appear on any TV shows yet though, thank God,' she added.

'Are you OK Sarah?' I said, genuinely.

I had never heard her talk like this before.

'Yes, I'm just upset. Get me another Rattler, will you please? I treated you in such a shitty way.'

I got her another bottle, and she continued her remarkable outpourings.

'I thought I had you sussed. I figured we were in love, but I thought it was one of those wild short-term love stories. Even after the Downs I thought you would, after a while, dust yourself down and get back on the treadmill. Tom oozed that innocence and vulnerability that some women adore. I fell in love with that. I could care for him and keep the demons away. It was a disaster that you were both as close as you were but sometimes you just cannot help that. You meet people through people, don't you? Sometimes it's good and other times it can be unbelievably painful. Don't get me wrong, Tom has been a wonderful companion, and I love him to bits, as do the twins. He's been as good a role model to them as any man could be. And I know he loves us all unreservedly. It is really, all good. What I wasn't expecting, was you would stick around. I hate blowing my own trumpet, but it must have been painful for you at the beginning seeing me with your best buddy.'

In fairness to both they had never played up in the affectionate sense when I was with them. They had always observed some decorum which I took as a compliment.

'People are weird, aren't they?' She continued.

'You see the thing was I was broody. You're a lovely man, but you're hopeless at spotting things like that. You were with me anyhow. And I'm sorry to say I didn't see you as the fatherly type during our time together. That isn't misrepresenting your requests for birth control. I believe that was fuelled by the nightmares the creatures gave you, as you eventually explained. No, you just didn't seem to me to be that type, and of course Tom did and was. And then blow me, over time you turn into the best godfather ever. Reliable and kind. Maybe that was inevitable. And you stuck around. I just didn't see it, Jack. I guess I didn't really understand until I saw that fishing boat today with my own eyes. As you said, I think, getting a bit pissed here, it makes a difference when you see it with your own eyes. It affects you, and you were, what, mid-twenties when you faced those horrors? At least thank God you got through it. Your Italian buddy didn't manage to, did he? How can people send people to do things like that? And I guess your mum and dad had in a way abandoned you before all that. I had no way of

94

seeing into what was driving you, but still I insisted on making my judgements and believing I was right. What an awful arrogant cow I was. I'm so sorry.'

She then grabbed my arm. She was looking at me with great sadness in her eyes. They welled up again with less control from her this time.

All you can do in situations like this is listen. I had no words of wisdom.

She pulled herself together as she always did, wiping a couple of tears away, slightly smudging her eye shadow in the process.

'Whoa, Siouxsie Sioux,' I said trying to help lighten her mood.

'I wish,' she said and smiled.

That was enough of that. We talked mostly run-of-the-mill stuff the remaining time she was there. Around nine she ordered a cab.

'Hey, at least we went out with a bang so to speak,' she said smiling, by way of a parting shot.

'Yes, and none of my irritating precautions that time eh,' I said, trying to finish with a light-hearted comment.

'No Jack. There most certainly weren't, were there?' she said, straight faced. Fixing my stare until we heard the cab outside.

With that she got up, kissed me on the cheek and left.

5

The Mevagissey happening may well have been the first recorded sighting of the 'Angry Aja' for the world to see. Nevertheless, it was not the first occurrence by a long stretch. As a result of their recent population explosion, they began to get caught up in nets everywhere. From Chimbote to North Sumatra, from Vladivostok to Pago Pago. Pretty soon similar horrors were being reported from all over the planet. The ships being attacked were now the big boys: three-hundred-foot-long factory ships operating multiple trawls. There were films uploaded and sent out to the watching world, showing two or three of the creatures being hauled onboard these ships. Every time the same outcome. The crew violently attacked, the ship destroyed or at the absolute best laid to waste. Within a matter of days, it had become a global crisis. All other government business appeared sidelined. The attacks on the fishing vessels took centre stage.

Submersibles were dispatched after the attacks to observe any alteration in the Aja's behaviour. To try to understand what had turned what were supposed to be our friends, against us. These vessels didn't go unnoticed, but the Aja did not attack them. They simply gathered around seven or eight strong as always, in full view of the submersible's observation platform, and began the anti-clockwise rotation dance which ceased after exactly four minutes thirteen seconds. Once completed some would swim away, others would remain staring at the crew for a few seconds. Not in a threatening manner though. Crew members recounted later that they looked more like they were trying to understand us. Their large single eyes switching their gaze from the individuals in the crew to the apparatus surrounding them in their observation platforms. After a fashion they would also swim away into the darkness, maybe gulping down a discarded plastic bottle or two for the cameras.

Unsurprisingly, fishermen soon began displaying reluctance in wanting to go out to sea. Different regimes around the globe devised different strategies. Some offered their fishermen arms to defend themselves. Others threatened to kill their fishermen if they didn't go out. That always seemed quite counter-productive to me. The problem was, even if a couple of the crew of the boat were armed and ready as the nets were dragged out of the ocean, the Aja reacted so quickly and violently once out of the sea that even a couple of well-directed shots didn't always stop them. It made them angrier if that was possible. Their screams alone were enough to drain any courage remaining in the marksmen, and any hesitation always proved fatal. Some crews got lucky and returned to their ports unscathed, but they were an exceedingly small minority. And of course, many countries simply did not have the ability to offer their fishermen any form of protection. In these cases, they simply stopped operations, with the prospect of disastrous consequences for the fishermen.

Worldwide debate raged on. The world's leaders gathered in Zurich to formulate a plan to combat the Aja. Nuke them. Poison them. All options were on the table. Unfortunately for them the world's cameras focused on the tens of thousands gathered outside the conference building. These people anticipated the extreme measures our leaders would consider in getting the global fishing industry back on track. Not difficult to work out as heads of the industry had also been invited to the talks. The many people gathered had a totally different take on the current crisis, as had millions around the world. They had viewed the mass dumping in the oceans a few years previously in horror. They viewed the Aja as the guardians of the oceans. As well as clearing up our mess they had now been forced into extreme action to protect the rapidly diminishing fish in the seas, not to mention the cruel maiming of unwanted bycatch. To these people, the actions of the Aja made total sense. It was our responsibility to work with them, seek alternative food sources and employ our people accordingly. The thought, to these people, of measures possibly being considered to wipe out the Aja was too much to comprehend. They were prepared to take action, violent action if necessary, to prevent it. Make no mistake, this group was large and growing larger by the day. There were gatherings worldwide, and they were coordinated and organised.

My point of view at this time was naturally affected by my previous encounters with our new ex-best buddies. I certainly didn't view them as guardians of any sort, in the same way as I didn't view their attacks on the boats as a strategy in any way. The four minutes thirteen seconds thing: not a clue. For me, all that seemed apparent was our complete reluctance to contemplate the bigger picture once more. We seemed to approach each crisis point as a separate individual challenge, just like Tom did. Sarah was right. There was a need to take a step back and ask the real questions, such as how did we get ourselves into this mess in the first place? Not how can we use/kill these damn creatures when the circumstances suited. As I have suggested before, a holistic approach would have been a breath of fresh air. We wouldn't ask these questions though, would we? We may not have got the answers that we wanted to hear.

The pressure to resume fishing was huge, though. Just bear in mind that by the time this crisis came to a head there were over five million commercial fishing vessels registered worldwide. That is one massive industry. To our leaders its decimation would be a disaster they would struggle to recover from. They had a responsibility to act. If they did not, the consequences, well certainly for their positions of power, would be dire.

6

The summer was now well and truly upon us. Despite constant reassurances that there would be no food shortages, apart from the countries that never had enough food, civil unrest and panic remained and gradually grew. By August, Peru was under martial law. Countries such as China, Indonesia and the Philippines had started using explosives to literally blast fish, and everything else, out of the water. This did not sit well with the environmentalists. Protests soon turned to rioting which pre-empted draconian measures. It's never good news when a state starts executing its own people. Thankfully, back home in England the situation was contained, though only through mass bail outs from the government to the fishing industry to keep them 'afloat', while a solution was found. This could only last for so long, what with economic pressure increasing by the day, and people grumbling about the lack of their traditional Friday night fare.

I had a landmark approaching too. It was August, and on the 17th I was going to retire at the grand old age of sixty, when my covert government intelligence pension kicked in. Hoorah! I was well looking forward to the prospect of self-isolation at home, no longer having any direct involvement in this global nut house. I knew I wouldn't miss work and I certainly wouldn't miss grinding my way into London every day. The world was going down the tubes, but I was alright thank-you very much. I was mulling this very thought over on my penultimate Friday afternoon in Whitehall when Tom rang.

Let me just say the days of Tom and me meeting for a beer after work in London were well behind us. I saw Sarah and him at their place on occasions. That was it. We were still close I would say, but our bond was mature and measured now. Tom had become full on dedicated to his work, as Sarah had alluded to, so I think he probably found me a frustration. I was not seeking the Holy Grail. My life had no tangible purpose, and I probably still drank a bit too much. That aside we were still big buddies and each of us would have been the first person for the other to call in a crisis. When Tom spoke to me that afternoon it was not because there was a crisis. Sadly, it was not an invite for a beer either. He asked if I may want to nip down to the London Aquarium and meet him when I finished work. He had been working there for a couple of months and he had something he wanted to show me which could possibly be of some interest. That last statement of his would I have to say turn out to be one of the most outrageous understatements I had ever heard. Of course, at that stage I had no idea. I told him I would be knocking off work in around an hour. As the journey involved little more than crossing Westminster Bridge, and being as it was a glorious summer afternoon, I would come by foot. He seemed happy with that. There was excitement in his voice, which meant to me that this was clearly going to be much more than the unveiling of some new soppy particle. I was intrigued. He told me to just mention his name at the customer service desk in the foyer when I arrived, and they would direct me as to where I needed to go.

Naturally, when the time came, my leisurely stroll from work to the aquarium was not straightforward. I had elected to walk down Horse Guards Avenue so that I could approach the bridge from Victoria Embankment, thus taking in the pleasant vibe generated by the various craft sailing up and down the river. As soon as I caught sight of the bridge, I could see trouble. An army of angry fishermen had organised a protest outside parliament that afternoon. In the light of recent events not wholly surprising. Whether their initial approach had been noisy but essentially peaceful was by the by. The environmental gang had turned up, whereby it had all kicked off. You can imagine a group, largely made up of vegans, clashing with a group of distraught fishermen who had been taught to fish by their dads, who in turn had been taught to fish by their dads and so on, were not going to find any common ground. And as always occurs in these situations, the element of agitators in both groups would see that noisy debate upscaled to 'full on' violent confrontation. I was still a hundred yards away and I could see police in full riot gear dragging protesters from both groups into their waiting vans. I could smell what I imagined to be the last swells of tear gas drifting away into the summer sky. By lucky chance this was the final clear up. The protesters had now either been arrested or had scarpered. Westminster Bridge, which had been shut when events escalated, was open again. I walked now with purpose and took the left turn onto the bridge making sure I kept looking straight ahead, fully aware that any prolonged eye contact, however innocent, could land me in trouble. There was still, even in the aftermath, a lot of adrenalin still pumping throughout the immediate vicinity.

I crossed the bridge without further incident, reaching the end with St Thomas' Hospital on my right and the County Hall hotel on my left. As the aquarium occupied the left-hand side ground floor of the hotel, I climbed down the steps at its side and walked along the Embankment until I arrived at where I wanted to be. There was a queue to get in; there always was. I incurred a lot of harrumphing when I sidestepped it and spoke to an employee, who then gestured me into the building. Once inside I did what Tom told me to do and approached the customer service desk located on the left of the lobby area. Once I had established who I was with the lady on duty, she directed me to a door behind her to the left with a 'Cleaning' sign on it. She gave me a key to open it and told me once in to follow the corridor in front of me until I came to a large steel door. Once there I would find someone who would direct me onwards. "This was all very cloak and dagger," I thought. "What on earth have you got involved with now Tom?" I thanked the lady and headed towards the door, imagining myself as Richard Burton or Michael Caine in one of their fabulously unglamorous cold war dramas. I unlocked the door and hit the light switch on the wall to my right before I quickly shut the door behind me in true covert style. The corridor lay straight in front of me. At the end, around thirty yards further on I could see the large steel door with a suited individual standing guard to the left of it. As I walked towards the door, I spotted cleaning mops and brooms. There were cupboards and unlit storage rooms too and I saw shelves with bottles of disinfectant and bleach. Was it all part of the subterfuge or was it simply where the aquarium stored their cleaning gear? I was loving this and I was going to have a field day when I finally met up with Tom. What with the initial kerfuffle on the bridge before, now a world of smoke and mirrors. Len Deighton, eat your heart out. When I had arrived at the large imposing door, the suited man asked me for some ID which I duly produced. I would say he was in his early forties, dark hair and dark rimmed spectacles. Nothing remarkable. He was a blend in with the crowd type. Once he was satisfied that I was who I claimed to be, he pulled up a lever on the door until it clicked and then slowly pushed from the side so eventually it slid open. It was a heavy steel door and he struggled a bit, although he did his best to hide the effort it took him. He made the comment after it was fully open that an automated mechanism would not go amiss. I smiled at him. Whatever he was, he didn't seem a bad bloke.

I walked through the door into what appeared to be a submersible base. There was a pool, the size of two tennis courts, currently housing five such submersibles. Difficult to judge their size but I would say they were roughly the same dimensions as an articulated lorry. The pool I assumed led straight out into the Thames. The wall to my left dropped below the waterline along which the vessels would presumably depart. There was equipment set out on the ground in an orderly fashion. Diving kit, ropes, chains and the suchlike. Nobody about. The walls around the pool area reached up high, to forty foot or more maybe and were constructed of brick. It looked quite old brick too making me think this place could have been here for a long, long time, maybe as a base for subs during the war or for some totally different reason. The brickwork made the sounds echo, although the only sounds were that of the water lapping against the moored-up vessels and my footsteps. Oh, and condensation drips falling from the ceiling into the water giving the place a cave like aura, or like those large Roman baths maybe. I started to make my way along the walkway to my right, and away from the pool, remembering I was here to see Tom and he clearly wasn't in this bit. The walkway quickly expanded briefly into a courtyard leading towards a large opaque glass wall ten yards away and the right-hand side of this wall revealed the walkway again though somewhat wider this time. Now I could see Tom, just past the wall, sitting at a simple desk with three laptops in front of him. Beside the desk was a large metal box, six-foot square, with pipes protruding from the front and back. I was still familiarising myself with the scene when Tom looked up and saw me striding toward him. He stood up sporting a big old smile on his face, and met me with an old-fashioned hug. He thanked me for coming and asked if everything was OK getting into this place. At this point I was going to give him a ribbing about all the cloak and dagger business.

Yet I did nothing of the sort, as my field of vision gradually revealed the other side of the large opaque glass wall. It was a giant tank similar to the ones in the actual aquarium, though this seemed much larger than I remembered them to be. It stretched up to the ceiling, so forty feet high, and I would say it was thirty feet across and a little less than the two tennis courts wide due to the larger walkway here. It had the rocks and vegetation you would find in a normal tank in these places, to allow the dolphins or sharks or whatever some soothing memories from home. It was clearly lit from lamps attached to its roof. And it had two inhabitants, though these were not dolphins, or sharks, or whales. These were two Aja.

'This is your latest project then Tom,' I said.

My previous script had gone by the by. The tone of my voice was not complimentary, and Tom instantly picked up on this.

'You don't like these creatures, do you Jack?' he said slightly defensively.

Remember, Sarah had never let on to him the story of my previous encounter with them.

'They're causing a global catastrophe,' I said mentioning the previous riot in Parliament Square.

I stood and watched them for a while. This was the nearest I had ever been to them, alive that is. I hate to admit it, but it was difficult not to be fascinated by them. They were beasts, all three yards of them, but they were so graceful in the water and seemed not the least bit bothered by being enclosed in a tank. They continued to swim, sometimes together, sometimes separately, seemingly following patterns, like one of their dances. Their greeny brown skin colouration was constantly changing to waves of blue and red and yellow. It looked random, yet you got the distinct impression it wasn't. No four minute thirteen second thing though. There weren't enough of them for that. They called to each other too. Some clicking sounds and long drawn out wailing.

'Watch this,' Tom now said.

I think he had seen my initial hostility had morphed into curiosity. He pressed a switch and one of the pipes from the big metal box pumped some stuff directly into the tank. I saw some small fish, a few small eels I guess they were, and several plastic water bottles. The Aja saw it was an unscheduled feeding time, turned and swam through the assortment delivered through the pipe. Their beaks wide open so they could devour their meal, plastic bottles and all. Once that was done, they reverted to their previous dance.

'Their excretion is a colourless paste,' Tom said. 'I've managed to grab some of it from the tank and study it. It's completely non-toxic. In fact, I dropped some of it into a tank with assorted fish swimming inside and some of them consumed it presumably as nutrition. That is remarkable. They can turn a discarded plastic bottle into a meal. I concede that we are still in our infancy as regards studying these creatures, but I cannot believe that there are not opportunities for us to work together somewhere further down the line. And I don't mean like dumping all our garbage on them like those fools did a few years back. We can learn a lot from the Aja.'

'How did you get hold of these?' I said.

I was playing along with it now. He smiled.

'The bottom of this tank can be opened so it flows out under that little courtyard affair into the pool you saw when you came in, then into the Thames. They're in the Thames now. I've been on this for a while now and we've swapped them around a few times. Partly to see if there are any differences in individuals, partly to avoid keeping them prisoners for too long.'

'I had no idea this place existed,' I said.

'Neither did I. We'd get shot if we made it public knowledge. Literally. I vouched for you and in fairness you're considered a safe pair of hands by our superiors.'

'OK. I accept all that you say Tom. I trust your judgement. The problem is they're causing riots around the world, and all that's going to happen is it's going to get worse. People are taking the law into their own hands. They miss their cod and chips, their Sushi bars and all that. They have a dark side these Aja. You do accept that, don't you? I admire your hopes for us all to get along. I'm sorry, I just can't see it happening.' I'd said my piece, hadn't I?

Tom looked at me. He had a glint in his eye. I had the uneasy feeling the show wasn't over yet.

'I accept what you're saying, and from your perspective it's perfectly reasonable,' he said. 'Let me assure you I've been doing things other than watching them eat plastic water bottles.'

He then turned towards a dial on his black box beside him and began slowly turning it.

'This will blow your mind.'

It became clear after a short time that Tom's actions with the dial were causing the water to slowly empty from the tank. He then hit a switch on his console, and I could hear a faint hissing.

'That's my air replacing the water,' he explained.

The 'my air' comment resonated some. I stood motionless watching the tank, glancing at times across at Tom. He showed no emotion; his expression was one of complete concentration on the task in front of him. He kept focused on the tank while he manipulated the dial. I guessed the dial was in place to keep control, so he could stop instantly if he felt he needed to. He didn't stop though, and the water continued to empty. The tank was half full now which was enough to allow the Aja to remain submerged. No dramas so far, but it wouldn't be long until the creatures had to raise their heads and breathe in 'the air.' It goes without saying that I was becoming more and more agitated the nearer that moment came. The glass seemed thick and robust, but would it keep those things in when they started going nuts? Would their lethal bile corrode the glass so they could smash through it? Tom was one amazing scientist, probably one of the best if not the best in his field in the world and I trusted him implicitly. He was my lifelong friend too. But this was hardcore. I caught both the creatures staring at us through their huge eyes when the tank got to a quarter full. If they had an expression, I would describe it as one of curiosity. Why would we do this?

It now came to the point where they could remain underwater no longer. They looked at each other, squashed flat almost by the receding water's depth, flashed an array of bold vivid colour through their skins ... and stood up. I didn't mean to, but I took an involuntary step back at this point. Tom looked at me and smiled, saying nothing. I now waited for the fury, and the screams, and the violent contortions as they attempted to force their escape. None of this happened. They both stood up in the tank next to each other, water dripping off their metal-like skin, staring at Tom and me. Same expression. "What are you guys doing here?" I looked across at Tom.

'Your air,' I said.

'Yeah, that's about the size of it. They won't attack us. I accept they would probably prefer to be underwater, but we've done this a few times now and they remember that we'll fill the tank again shortly. They are highly intelligent creatures. We're only starting to understand just how intelligent.'

'OK. You've put something in the air that apparently calms them––"

'No, Jack. I haven't put anything in the air in that tank. I have introduced no new particles of any description. It's what I've taken out that's making the difference. Watch this.'

With that he walked down to the right-hand corner of the tank where I could now see lines in the glass and a small device waist high attached to it. He pushed some buttons in sequence and the lines in the glass became a door frame which he now pushed open, quickly shutting it behind him. I watched him thinking, no, knowing, that I had never seen a ballsier dare in my life. Tom, my buddy Tom. The introvert. The pacifist. Before I wouldn't have credited him saying boo to a goose and here he was walking into a cage occupied by two Kraken. Astonishing! My fingertips tingled. Adrenalin was sending my heartbeat crazy. I had a pounding in my head, but I couldn't take my eyes off him. And he carried on walking until he was no more than three feet from where they were standing. He staring up at them in wonder and they both staring down at him, in silence. Even the light show had calmed down now. Maybe they understood the colours would mean nothing to Tom so what was the need? A few minutes passed at which point one of the Aja took their eye away from Tom and glanced through the glass towards me. He then looked at his buddy, shot a shimmer of dark blue through his skin, followed by his buddy shifting his stare to me. Tom broke the silence.

'They want you to come in too,' he did not quite shout but had to say loudly due to the glass between us.

This did not seem to bother the creatures one bit.

'I bet they do,' I cursed to myself.

The last thing I wanted to do in the world was to go inside that tank, but it's not always about what you want, is it? And so I walked towards the door repeating in my head the words to the song, one of Mum's she gave to me: 'I'm not here. This isn't happening.' Over and over as I opened and closed the door behind me.

The Aja slowly turned their gaze my way as I walked towards Tom as calmly as I could, desperately resisting the urge to violently raise my arms and scream. Keep repeating, 'I'm not here...' And so on.

After a couple of seconds, we were in our places, whatever they were supposed to be. I was standing next to Tom and we were both facing our respective creature. Tom understood I was probably in a heightened state, so he broke the ice.

'You see they can breathe the air without reacting in the hostile manner that we've seen before, and we can breathe it. We can breathe it too Jack.'

I swallowed hard and built up the wherewithal to speak:

'You didn't introduce anything to the air. You simply took stuff out?'

It was not quite how I wanted to say it. I think it made me sound like an idiot. Tom was cool with it thankfully.

'You see I am aware we are currently at crisis point with these creatures, and it scares the shit out of me to consider what our great leaders will dream up to find a solution. So, it would have been a pointless exercise creating air that the Aja could breathe OK but suffocated us like Mustard gas, to get old school on you. Therefore, I hit on the idea of removing rather than adding. If you think of rust on a piece of metal, I have removed the rust. Clearly, this is early days. We need to look at any long-term implications for us and the Aja. Also, there is the rest of the animal kingdom to bear in mind. Will there be any unpleasant effects on birds and mammals and ...'

I stopped him there. 'And bees maybe?' I quipped.

'Goes without saying.' He looked at me and smiled. 'But all that aside what do you think?'

I never answered his question. The Aja, hearing us communicating appeared to conclude it would not be bad table manners to have a little banter themselves. They diverted their gaze from us to themselves at which point the bright colours began again to shimmer through their skins. No vocals. We stopped talking and watched the show. A bright yellow snake moved from the head to the toe of the one facing me, which received the reply of several flashes of blue and orange and indigo from Tom's one. This carried on for a couple of minutes and then something remarkable happened. The light show receded and they turned their gaze back to us. At this point I became fascinated by their tentacles. They seemed so agile and free flowing in the water. In this state they had become as rigid as they had to be to support their large torsos. It was some transformation and made me wonder why they had become so adaptable. I didn't see the need. Even the bottom of each tentacle bent slightly forward to create a foot of sorts. Anyway, I digress. So, the light show calmed down and they turned their gaze back to Tom and me. It was then that the Aja facing Tom raised a tentacle, just slightly, and moved it across to touch my Aja's right tentacle. Followed by a little light show, soft pastel colours this time. The tentacle then wrapped itself once around my Aja's tentacle. They looked at each other then they looked down at us. I looked across at Tom. He was transfixed by what was going on. The cancer cure had been his great triumph in that it saved Sarah's life and sealed his, and her, scientific reputations for life. This moment was up there for him. His expression was that of a small child seeing snow for the first time. I marvelled at how he had achieved this. I couldn't believe there was anyone else alive that could have created the scenario we were now witnessing.

I would never have mentioned to Tom, at the time, what I am going to say next. It was his moment of wonder, confirming all that science and hard work could achieve. It was not for me to put a dampener on his moment of triumph. What I will say now is I believe the Aja's expressions changed while this performance was being played out. Now I'm not claiming to be an expert on judging their mood or anything, but it did seem to me that whereas their initial expressions underwater and directly after were ones of curiosity, it appeared to me as they stood facing us 'holding hands' that the eyes were giving out a different story. If I wasn't mistaken, I would have sworn they were looking at us with pity.

7

A week later, my retirement bash. Could you possibly have had two more contrasting Fridays? Naturally, I didn't ask for it and I most certainly didn't want anything of the sort, however Charlotte was most insistent. Yes, Charlotte was still running the show and I kind of admired her lack of ambition, or whatever it was that had kept her in that position. I had initially had her down for one of those flakey types who made their way up the career ladder ruthlessly using jobs such as hers, and her people, as a stepping-stone, nothing more. Clearly, I was wrong. Still dreaded the damn thing mind.

I took the train in that day. Work fizzled out not much after three. Charlotte gathered everyone together and made, I have to say, a nice little speech. I then got up, thanked her, and rattled out a few pre prepared harmless anecdotes. She presented me with a watch, we scoffed down the cake and made for the pub. Relatively painless. Our chosen boozer had a function room which Charlotte had reserved for us as well as laying on a buffet. I didn't pay for a drink all night. I was determined not to go nuts resulting in leaving with a sour taste. I couldn't see the point of that. I didn't really have anything in common with any of my colleagues. I didn't like most of them, but why spoil it all by getting smashed and spouting some home truths? No, I behaved. When they asked me what I was going to do with my freedom I replied that I may have a go at writing a novel. When they asked what it would be about, I replied it may well include them so they better be nice to me on my final evening with them, or they could be portrayed as right rotters. This got me a few laughs and a few drinks. If I ever had written a novel, I didn't as events overtook that potential path; none of these goons would have had a cat in hell's chance of being in it. Hey ho. I accepted the drinks.

This was the pattern for most of the evening and in fairness it was OK. Nothing earth shattering, just meaningless chit chat. My plan was to make an exit around ten, and if it wound up sooner more's the better. My work colleagues didn't get out much, and there were people from other departments there too that I hardly knew, making the whole gathering upwards of forty men and women. It soon became apparent that it was not going to wind up early, not because of my landmark I hasten to add. By nine o'clock for the majority it was an official piss-up. Around half nine I started to distance myself from the increasingly loud conversations in progress, in preparation for a discreet getaway. It was at this point Charlotte grabbed me and guided me away from the throng into the front bar of the pub. We both had a drink, so she led me to an empty table, and we sat down.

'Thanks for the dignified way you've behaved this evening, Jack. I get the impression you were probably dreading it.'

'It's been OK, Charlotte. Thanks for putting on a nice send off for me,' I said.

She had put some effort into it though, and I have to say, she was looking foxy that evening. She was only a few years younger than me, but like Sarah she had aged well. A couple of lines below her eyes had made her more alluring in the mature sense. As I said when I first met her, I had her down as a potentially fun girl when she dropped the guard from work. She still had that, combined with a look that told you that she knew what she wanted as well. It was a good look. Her outfit matched the look perfectly. After work she had changed into a black top, dark blue jeans and thin black leather jacket. It was summer. Her red shoes were the only acquiescence to flash, though her now dark hair dropping gently over her shoulder and her light red lipstick gave her whole look a sense of balance. What I would say is she had had a few drinks, and I could sense this getting me away from the crowd was leading somewhere. She wanted to bare her soul. In fairness, having technically reported to her for thirty years, who was I not to let her have her say? To let me know she was not the old battle-axe everyone thought she was, and so on. I was in no rush; besides, I was enjoying sitting talking to her.

'I always wondered what was going on in your head Jack,' she began.

'I'm fully aware my department is considered a refuge for people who weren't suited to their original roles and thus farmed out to me. I'm OK with that. Personally, I love what we do. Maybe I'm weird but it's the truth. That's why I've never moved on. Why would I? The pay's great. It's not hard work by any stretch, besides, I don't want to be competing with the bulls and the bastards. I've had a crack at marriage. It didn't work out, so be it. I'm civil with my ex and there aren't any children involved. I have a nice house in Clapham and I have a nice life. That's me Jack. If I meet someone new, then great. If not, I won't shed any tears. When my time to retire comes in a few years, I'm going to buy a nice big rucksack and travel round the States for a year or so. Can't wait. You, though, Jack. Sorry about prattling on about me. What about you? I just don't know. No one told me anything about you, you just appeared one day looking lost and a little scary. All I had was an email from one of the top boys, similar level to your stepfather. It hinted you were precious goods, not ballast, excuse the phrase. Christ, you could have been James Bond for all I knew. Shall we get another drink?'

With that she went to the bar and ordered a glass of wine and a bottle of cider for me. I watched her explain to the barman she had a tab next door and after checking he smiled and accepted her word. She carried the drinks over, sat down and carried on. I couldn't wait. I'd never been compared to James Bond before. If I were in a fortunate enough position for her to be working her magic on me, bring it on. She took a swig of her wine and, bless her, asked if she was going on too much.

'Not at all Charlotte. I'm enjoying listening to you,' was my predictable reply.

113

She continued, 'I watched you over the years, Jack. The work was clearly beneath your abilities, but you persevered with grace and consummate professionalism. You didn't even let the mask slip when I had the ghastly duty of informing you of your stepfather's passing. What class! You must have been in such pain. He was much respected I believe and a great loss to us. God only knows how you must have been feeling.'

Well, she clearly hadn't met him, had she? And as for the great respect, you only had to be at his scantily attended funeral to understand just how much of that he generated. Far be it from me to rain on her parade though. This thing we were having was a triumph of supposition over truth. We were both embracing the illusion, why destroy it? It was clear to me after a time that Charlotte had an agenda which seemed to be me. She was an attractive woman and it was the end of our working relationship. Let's rock!

'I'm not trying to pry into your past, Jack,' she continued. 'It's none of my business. All I would say is I'm glad whatever occurred enabled you to land in my team. You've helped me more than you realise. When things got tough between Dan and me towards the end, I used to look at you and think whatever I was going through, the chances were, you had gone through worse. And you always held it together with dignity. In some ways you were my salvation.'

And with that she moved towards me and we kissed. It was one of those kisses that divinely last just too long. Not a hello or goodbye or thank you kiss. This was a this is only the start kiss. I put my arm around her shoulder, and she nestled her head into my neck. To her credit she clearly didn't give a damn if anyone from work saw us. I would say we nattered away for an hour with small talk, favourite holidays, embarrassing moments, all that kind of thing. Just enjoying the simplicity of each other's company along with the physical closeness. It was around midnight when she sat up straight.

'Right, Jack. Let's get a cab.'

I wasn't going to argue. While I finished my bottle, she got up and went next door, presumably saying her farewells and settling her tab. All done in what seemed like a flash. Before I could catch my breath, we were smooching in the back of a London cab on the way to Clapham.

She was apologetic that she had to throw me out at two the following afternoon. She had arranged to meet a friend, who she explained wasn't coping with life quite as well as her and she dare not let her down. She even explained to me that she wasn't looking forward to it due to her concern that the state of elation she was currently experiencing would be difficult to hide from her friend. Blimey! State of elation! Bring it on. I had a spring in my step too. She walked with me to the station. We kissed, then kissed again. The train arrived, and we kissed for a final time. I got on the train, found a seat, and spent the journey home trying to work out what the fuck happened there.

With a smile on my face.

8

The first three weeks of retirement were great! No alarm clocks. No ball-ache trawl into London and back every day. I got up when I wanted, and I went to bed when I wanted. Did I adopt gardening as a hobby? No. Did I visit the pub more times than would be considered healthy? Yes. Did I watch hours of nonsense on the tele? Most certainly. I had no plans, well maybe the England cricket team tour of South Africa. Charlotte rang. She was off to Italy with her 'troubled' friend for an extended break. Last minute thing and I wished her a safe trip.

I would never see her again.

On the Monday of my fourth week of idleness Sarah messaged me.

'Tom's going to ring you. He's in a right flap and he is massively getting on my tits.'

Oh God, what was coming? True to her word, under an hour later Tom did ring.

'They're going live with it! It's not fully tested! It's not finished yet! They're going to blast it into the atmosphere! It's not ready I tell you!'

I had never heard him like this before. No introductions. No how are you doing. Straight into it. There was panic in his voice. I was at a bit of a loss.

'Are they really?'

'Yes! Yes! They're setting it up now. I've been pleading with them not to be so hasty, but they're not listening. These are desperate times they're telling me. My solution is their best shot. My guess is it'll happen before the end of this week. I don't know what to do, Jack.'

For a bit of an explanation here, Tom had been working on a solution to the fishing conundrum with the Aja, as had hundreds of teams around the world. Due to the importance of the work, their results were fed directly and dynamically to their respective leaders. Now, the only leaders in the world who by this stage realistically called the shots in global terms were the leaders of the United States, India and China. Subsequently, these guys had filtered the results of all the teams and settled on Tom's. An easy decision to make as it was the only one that appeared to work. And he had form.

'They're going to set off fission bombs high up in the atmosphere that will blast my air against the current air we breathe. I've put in a little add-on to enable a chain reaction to kick in, allowing my air to alter the molecular make-up of our regular air on contact,' he said.

'Will that work Tom?'

'Yes, it should,' came the reply, 'If they do it correctly. It's not the point though. It's not ready. It's too risky!'

And so on and so on.

He hung up. There was fear in his voice when he did, which I felt unsettling. He was at the aquarium when he rang, and he said he was off to try and dissuade his people from this action. I didn't hold out much hope as regards that. Even if he convinced his immediate superior, that fellow would have to convince our leaders, causing them to lose face in trying to convince the big three, who had probably made their minds up anyway. Face it, it was going to happen.

Tom was right about the imminence of deployment. The bombers took off from their respective airstrips the following Thursday, five of them with precise co-ordinates for bomb release, calculated to complete the spread of Tom's new air. When they were in position, they released their payloads into the upper atmosphere then got the hell out of Dodge. The bombs all exploded as planned. No hitches. Knowledge of the whole operation was restricted to a need-to-know basis. The remaining population of the planet had been thrown into a gigantic laboratory experiment they remained in blissful ignorance of.

On the ground, testing stations all around the globe had been set up to detect when the new air had taken. The

Singapore station was the first to report positively, just ten days after the event. The rest soon followed. Next stage now. See if it had been worth it. The Peruvian navy were the first ones off the mark. Peru remained under martial law but still there was civil unrest all over the country. Reports of shootings were rife. They were keen for it to end. There were upwards of thirty marksmen on the deck of the Peruvian frigate which netted its first Aja, ready to hit it with everything they had when it came to the surface. The winch on the hastily adapted ship seemed to take forever only heightening the tension onboard. When the creature did eventually emerge, the combined sighs of relief when it remained passive were profound. They hauled it fully into the air filming the whole thing so everyone could see it was a genuine Aja. It was moving, colours flashing across its skin, clearly in some distress as you would be if caught in a net, but by no means behaving in the aggressive way it would have done a few weeks ago. When everyone was satisfied with what they saw, the net was lowered, and it was released back into the ocean, with much celebration and relief from those onboard. This was the green light, allowing all the major ports in the world to embark on a similar test run to convince their fishermen that it was safe to go back to sea. All were met with similar results to that of the Peruvian frigate. Back in England the newly commissioned aircraft carrier HMS *Jean-Jack Burnell*, sailing in the English Channel just south of the Solent, managed to drag three of the creatures onto its deck. Several brave seamen released them from their nets so they could stand upright, next to each other. They stood a while in the same spot gazing around at their surroundings, appearing to take in all they could see. The fighter planes taking on fuel, the gun turrets; it all seemed of great interest to them. As confirmation of this there was the flow of colour coursing over each one's skin. When they were satisfied they had seen everything they needed to, they gave each other a glance, and headed for the side of the ship and back into the sea. This was followed by a loud round of applause from all on board. The crisis was over at last.

The entire operation had been an overwhelming success.

9

Slowly things returned to normal again and in time fish was back on the dinner table. I contacted Tom to congratulate him on his success. This was a mistake.

'They're really pleased with themselves, but they have no understanding of what they could be facing. I only really tested it on us and that was massively incomplete. What about the animal kingdom? The birds, the insects? Even the plants. We have no idea how they are going to react,' he said.

'What, it's going to be like a scene from 'The Birds?'' I said glibly.

'Jack, don't come out with such stuff. You're better than that. This could be serious, and I am going to go down in history, if there is any, as the architect of Armageddon, and I don't want that, do you see?'

There's no history if there's no one to recall it. Blimey!

I had never heard Tom talk like that. It was completely out of character, particularly the part when he discussed his potential legacy. He had always distanced himself and his achievements from the actual work. The work was paramount, everything else was an irrelevant distraction. At this point I wasn't sure if I was more concerned about him, as opposed to what he was saying, even though what he was saying was quite alarming.

'Come on, Tom. Your record speaks for itself. You're up there with the top scientific brains on the planet. There is a possibility that you've got it right. Knowing you as I do, I would be more surprised if you hadn't. That would be a first.' As you can see, I was trying.

'There's always a first time. Yes, I've had a good run I'll grant you that. I'm not confident this time though. Not confident at all. This is ... well it doesn't get bigger than this does it. Oh, what have I done Jack ...?' He broke off and I could hear him quietly sobbing while presumably attempting to cover his phone.

'Tom, let's meet up,' I pleaded. 'Face to face would be better for talking this over.'

'No time, Jack. I've got too much work to do. It's not ideal but if I can continue the research and the experiments, I may be able to head off the calamity if indeed it comes. Look Jack, enjoy your cod and chips tonight if you have it. I'll speak to you soon,' and with that he hung up on me.

I sat down again after I had poured a drink and dwelled on that conversation. Tom and I had known each other from schooldays. We were, and always had been, best friends. And I would say we had been through a lot over the years. The friendship had remained strong throughout. Now though, well it was like he didn't want to know me anymore. The enjoy your cod and chips crack sealed it. It was like I was being lumped in with everyone else, with all the shallowness and laziness and impatience therein. I was now just another ant obeying my pre-programming with no ability for rational thought or understanding of cause and effect. I had history of setting the self-sabotage button, and all the misery it brought. I could see it happening now with Tom. In my experience it took time to resolve, also meeting Sarah helped me at the time. Sarah. She was not particularly impressed last time we spoke. I couldn't see things being any better now. I resolved to meet with her, so I messaged her and as luck would have it, she was in town and could meet up around two.

It was early November now, not raining but an evil cold wind. I grabbed my best coat, it was Sarah I was meeting, and headed to the coffee place in town that we all liked. I do try to defend my hometown, but I must concede that it was not a pretty place in November. As I walked up Church Street the Priory Church on my left looked physically angry, as if it were about to declare abstinence for all and pronounce the delivery of fire and brimstone to any transgressors. Pretty strong stuff for the C of E. Crossing the street and walking into the shopping arcade that many had written off for demolition over the last fifty years, did nothing to relieve the gloom. Shop open, empty shell, shop open, empty shell, and so on. The upside of all this, rather wonderfully, was that once you got out of the cold and damp and went in somewhere, the mood was lightened by it simply being indoors. As I entered the coffee place it felt like I was walking into an American sitcom equivalent. Everyone chatty and happy and beautiful. An illusion, and it didn't last, but it was nice while it did. One of the regular Polish lady baristas served me, smiling as she always did while doing so.

'No, I didn't want a muffin thank you. I am meeting my friend. Can you put a coffee in for her as well?'

'Of course, sir. Sit down. I will bring it over when she arrives,' she said.

Yes, lovely lady. We had used that place a lot over the years, and Tom and the twins as well. I grabbed a seat in the corner as I usually did when there was serious stuff to discuss. Sarah arrived a few minutes later. She was always punctual. She looked at first glance particularly driven on this occasion. I stood up and we exchanged the greetings kisses as the nice barista lady brought Sarah's coffee to the table. Sarah took off her coat, we sat down, and she hit me with it straight away.

'I'm moving out, Jack. I'm leaving Tom and I'm moving out of the house. I've found a flat to rent, just round the corner from you, and I can move in next week.'

'Oh my God, Sarah!' I said in genuine shock. 'What's happened?'

Naturally, I had an idea what had happened, but my first instinct was to attempt to dissuade her from doing this. They'd been together so long and yes, they were good together. And there was David and Michael to consider. As was often the case she was way ahead of me.

'I've spoken to the boys. Naturally, they are deeply upset. They have both spoken to Tom in the last few weeks and the conversations did not go well. They're sad for me, but they do understand,' she said.

'Yes, but I just spoke to him Sarah. He didn't mention any of this. Does he even know?' I said.

'He knows. It says something that he didn't mention it. It's probably of no importance to him. Maybe he thinks he'll be better off with me gone,' and with that she began sobbing gently. I got up and pushed a chair next to her and put my arm around her shoulder.

'That can't be the case Sarah,' I said desperately trying to find the right words. 'He's very worried about that thing with those damn creatures.'

'I begged him not to get involved with all that. I told him it wasn't always his job to save the world. Superman struggled with doing that. But no, stubborn Tom had to take it on full throttle as always.' At this point she rubbed her eyes, sniffed and wiped her nose. Poor woman. I imagined she was dying inside.

'I told him of the risks. I told him that he would be closely watched, leaving open the risk of any progress getting hijacked and deployed without any due diligence. And what happens? Exactly that! So now it's all his fault if something horrible happens. He's overwhelmed with guilt and consequentially obsessed with putting it right. It may not need putting right, Jack, he may have got lucky.' At that point she paused briefly. 'Science takes a dim view of relying on luck though.'

'OK. It sounds bloody awful. How have you been coping?'

'If the truth be told I haven't really seen him. Since he began working on this, he was either at the aquarium or fannying about with his fucking bees when he wasn't there. He slept on the sofa, that's when he did sleep. The brief occasions we got to talk soon became arguments, sometimes escalating into full on rows. Your wonderful friend can be a cruel man when he wants to be. It goes without saying that this behaviour escalated once they went atomic on him. Nothing else matters now. He has been awful speaking to the twins; really shocking some of the things he's come out with. Personal hygiene has gone out of the window. He looks ghastly, unkempt hair and a dreadful apology for a beard. And he smells awful, like makes you feel physically sick awful. I can't be in the same room as him. I imagine they just leave him alone at the aquarium. They called him a hero for a couple of days before he shouted them all down with insults both professional and personal. So, yeah, they probably leave him alone now. I imagine they keep him on working there as a sort of insurance policy for their own reputations. I don't know.'

She was still sad as she spoke. Thankfully, that was it, she was not defeated or desperate. She was a tough old nut. I wouldn't tell her that though. By that time, any efforts of mine to encourage a reconciliation would have fallen on deaf ears and would maybe have been offensive, implying I hadn't been listening or worse didn't believe her. I asked her what I could do practically to help.

'Be there, Jack. That's it, just be there. I've got help moving my stuff out. Involving you in that would be insensitive, I think. I'm going to Mum's for Christmas. It'll be the first one since Dad passed so she'll welcome the company. After that I don't know. Maybe time will heal things. Part of me still loves Tom you know. Maybe ... just maybe ...' she trailed off, her eyes looking far away from where we were sitting.

'If you see him, let me know please.'

A faint twinge of guilt in with the sadness.

'Of course I will, though I don't know when that'll be,' I said trying to reassure her.

With that she reached across the table, gave me a kiss, then got up quickly and left, putting her coat on as she did. She had begun to well up again.

10

I didn't meet up with Sarah again before Christmas. She obviously had a lot on her plate, so I let her get on with it. We spoke on the phone a few times. She liked her new flat and sounded almost upbeat at times during our conversations. I think she understood that quite rightly I didn't want to take sides in all of what was going on. No good would come of that. The last time we spoke before she left for her mum's I wished her, and her mum, a Happy Christmas. Naturally, she returned the compliment. As the conversation wound down, she asked me if I had seen anything of Tom. I told her I had only yesterday.

This was true. I had been a bit sneaky actually and tracked Tom down when he was away from the house with his bees. He reluctantly welcomed me while grabbing me a protective suit. This suit worked on all sorts of levels at this time. While protecting me from bee stings, the suits also worked in keeping us isolated from each other, even when we were talking face to face. Tom seemed more at ease with this situation. I have to say Tom's suit also served to keep any stink away, if what Sarah had said was accurate. Tom was also relaxed due to the fact he was with his beloved bees. He asked if I had spoken with Sarah. I replied yes, a couple of times and told him I was sad about what they were going through. He stopped working for a moment and stood still. I could see his face inside his headgear and Sarah was right. The beard looked ridiculous. His hair was not great either, but his eyes still looked sharp and he sounded more with it than he had before on the phone. Not his old self quite but still redeemable. He expressed regret as to what had happened. Blamed himself, naturally, and even betrayed a hint of optimism as to the outcome of, well everything really. The bees were doing very well he told me. I said that was great but I wasn't there to talk about them. He smiled and thanked me for coming. We talked some more until I detected he was bored, and really wanted to get on with what he was down there to do. I wished him Happy Christmas and after disrobing myself of the protective suit drove away. He had seemed relatively OK, but he always was when he was with his bees.

I gave Sarah a carefully edited version of our conversation. She thanked me, telling me I was a good soul. A smart one as well; meeting him with his bees was inspired thinking and she laughed; the first time I had heard her laugh in a while. We signed off promising to meet up when she returned from her mum's in the New Year.

Christmas without Tom and Sarah. That was going to be a first for bloody years. I sent the boys gifts as they did me. I didn't really want to get involved with talking to them about their parents. I didn't think it was my place. I did remind them, though, that I was still their godfather and if they needed anything from me, they just needed to call. I thought that was about right.

So, Christmas without my lifetime companions, well half a lifetime in Sarah's case. What to do? It could have been grim. As it turned out it was a rip roarer! I reconnected with some buddies I used to drink with in the Victoria. Guys I had shamefully neglected in previous years. As with everyone their lives had changed since we last spent time together, but everything goes out of the window at Christmas, well it surely did this one. The owners of the pub loved us. We were in there constantly. I even had Christmas dinner in there. It was ridiculous. By the time New Year came round my internal organs were pleading with me to give it a rest.

Sarah returned to Dunstable on the fourth and we met for coffee. It was a more 'light-hearted' affair this time. The break had evidently done her some good. Her mum was still in relatively good health for someone in their eighties. They had gone for short walks and talked and talked. On her last night Sarah told me her mum had explained that she had been dreading Christmas without her wonderful husband. Sarah being there had, not to put too fine a point on it, saved her. Sarah had then hugged her while crying and smiling at the same time. She had a tear in her eye while she told me.

11

It was the last Saturday in January when I next spoke to Sarah on the phone, and it was weird this time.

'How are you feeling, Jack?' was her opening gambit.

'Fine thanks Sarah, I think. It's still early,' I said. It was just gone eight in the morning. 'Thoughtful of you to ask. Any specific reason?' I continued.

'Headaches? Have you thrown up in the last couple of days? Going to the loo a lot? Anything?' her questions continued.

'No. None of that. What are you on about? Are you OK?' I said.

There was always purpose behind everything she said. She was like a movie insofar as every scene, every detail however small, has a function within the story. The trick was to spot the key bit of detail and work out its function. Like with the movie.

'I'm going to Cambridge in an hour. I'll probably flop down on a friend's couch so I can spend more time working and less time pissing about travelling. You won't hear much from me for a week. If you have any odd symptoms please call me, any time. Between you and me, I'm a bit worried. I think something bad may be coming, but I need to know more before I start sounding the alarm.' She sounded business-like more than panicky, which was a relief of sorts.

It was early so I was not at my sharpest, if indeed I had a sharpest, making my responses damn limited.

'What can I do to help?' I said, guessing there was bugger all I could do.

'Do everything you would normally do. If you were going for a beer later still do that. Eat everything you would normally eat. Go to the gym if you were thinking of going. Don't alter your routine in any way. When you wake up, do the coffee followed by your ablutions as you always have. If you are smoking currently, it's difficult to keep up with you, carry on doing that, or don't if you aren't. You can help by being my guinea pig for a week, but it will only work if you carry on as normal. As I said earlier, should you experience anything out of the ordinary in the way you feel, contact me immediately. Can you do that?'

'Yes Sarah. I'm sure I can manage to do that.'

'Thanks, Jack. Maybe I'm wrong. I'll speak to you in a week if not sooner,' and with that she hung up.

I went and had a shower, her words running riot in my mind. She was thinking there was something up with the air, wasn't she? I wasn't an idiot. I was capable of working some things out on my own. If she was on to something, then what was happening in Tom's world? I dare not imagine. Now was certainly not the time to pay him a visit. No, do what she said. It wasn't exactly difficult to keep doing what I normally did. Only problem was apart from the coffee and ablution thing I didn't really have a routine, certainly not since I had retired. Yes, sometimes I went to the gym, sometimes I read or watched tele, or listened to tunes. It was decided by how I felt on any given day really. I could have gone to watch a local rugger game being as it was a Saturday. The weather was diabolical though, so sod that. After some thought I opted for a trip to the supermarket followed by any sport that was on the tele. Crazy rock 'n roll lifestyle me.

The supermarket was busier than it normally would have been at just after ten on a Saturday. There were queues and some shelves seemed a tad depleted. Last weekend in January: a lot of people would have been paid for the first time since before Christmas, would probably account for that. I finished my shopping which seemed to be dominated by booze and savoury munchies, then headed back home. And due to the weather never improving it was TV, booze and unhealthy snacks for the rest of the day. January sucks!

Wednesday was the first day I thought I needed to report in to the boss. I'd been to the gym, just for an hour. I didn't do anything crazy, but after showering I had to race home, which I didn't manage to do fast enough because I threw up all down my front door after I'd got out of my car.

Sarah thanked me for calling. I think she was glad, not necessarily to hear from me but to speak to me. She even made a sort of joke implying I may have overdone it in the gym. But I was right to contact her.

That was the last visit to the gym that week for obvious reasons. My front door didn't need another coating. In addition, I was disinclined to do so due to an overwhelming lack of energy. I even took to taking a nap in the afternoon on the Thursday and Friday. For heaven's sake I was sixty, and I think a young sixty. What was that all about? I passed all this on to Sarah which she thanked me for, while informing me she would visit on the coming Saturday morning.

Have to say she still looked sharp when I answered the door to her just after eleven. Brown top and light blue jeans. She did have bags under her eyes, though. Tough week I imagined.

'Yeah, Jack. It was. Got any booze?' she said matter of fact.

'Bit early,' I said.

'I couldn't give a horse's arse,' she said. Proud to say she got that phrase from me.

I reached into the fridge and took out two bottles of Rattler. Goodbye Saturday.

'Thanks.' She took a long swig devouring nearly half the bottle.

'You look like you needed that,' I said.

'Quite so,' she said finishing off the bottle. I produced another from the fridge and opened it for her. I had hardly started mine at this point.

'Right.' She took a deep breath. 'This is how it is.'

'Go on,' I said.

'Have you been out much this week? I mean other than your gym experience?' she said with a poker face.

'Once or twice. Just into town, nothing special. A drink or two,'

'And?'

'Nothing out of the ordinary that I can think of. Lot of babies crying,' I said.

It was true. Every baby I had spotted seemed to be crying. There were normally one or two hollering and annoying all in the immediate vicinity. Thinking on it, Friday was horrendous. The town had sounded like a nursery from hell.

'They're hungry, among other things,' she said. 'Anything else?'

'There was a scrap in the Vic last night. That's unusual. I suppose thinking on it I should have told you these things, shouldn't I?'

'Doesn't matter. I know what's wrong.'

'Oh yeah.' By now I had kind of figured out she had a clue of what was going on.

'Ever heard of protein poisoning?' She walked to the fridge and grabbed another Rattler. I was still halfway through my first.

As it goes, I had. 'It's sometimes called rabbit poisoning? The body receives too much protein and not enough fat and carbs. Knackers the kidneys and liver among other vital organs. Bloody hellfire. It's not that, is it?' Saying the words was starting to bring this home to me. I too grabbed another bottle.

'That's correct and, for some weird reason, that's what this is. We've done thousands of tests this last week. All the teams around the globe have been testing and we all agree. The symptoms are always the same. Sickness, diarrhoea, headache, weakness and fatigue, food cravings. Slow heart rate, low blood pressure and mood swings. All in the early stages but still detectable, along with the blood and urine and heaven knows what we've been testing. Everything confirms this is protein poisoning. We organised a conference call yesterday. Over twenty countries have been working on this. The US, China, Germany, Sweden, Brazil, you name them. They all agreed unequivocally that this is what we are up against.'

'OK Sarah.' I was desperately trying to keep up. 'We're not all just eating rabbits though, are we? I mean, our diets across the globe haven't changed in the last month, have they?'

Obvious questions I thought.

'Doesn't matter what you eat. Our bodies are only absorbing the protein and rejecting everything else. You could eat a bowl of breakfast cereal, a bowl of pasta or a fry up. The results would be the same. Your body would recognise the protein and everything else it would consider waste.'

Come on, Jack. Think man!

'Right. If this is indeed what you say it is, then what percentage of all these thousands of people you tested came up as positive? Like, how many tested as having this protein poisoning?'

'One hundred percent. Everyone we tested, everywhere in the world we tested, was suffering from it.'

I took a minute. 'That's impossible. I understand outbreaks and pandemics and all that. They spread quickly and you must isolate those infected and so on until you find a cure. Maybe on occasions when the virus is particularly nasty everyone must go into a form of lockdown until it passes. And yes, a lot of people can become infected and a lot of people can die, but not everyone surely.'

Sarah came back straight away. 'What if it isn't a virus in the conventional sense?'

'Well, if it's not a virus then how can it ...?' And that is when I remembered last week's conversation.

'Oh yeah. It's the air, isn't it?' Wake up man!

'We still have some work to do to tie the two together, but yeah, it more than probably is the air.'

She sounded particularly sad when she finished that sentence, which made my next question a painful one to ask. I had to ask it though.

'Have you spoken to Tom?' I made the facial gesture as if in pain as I asked.

131

'We're not exactly on speaking terms. I have left messages, but he hasn't replied. Colleagues have reported conversations they've had with him though. They said he sounded disorientated and defensive. We've not proved beyond all doubt it is the air yet, to be fair to him. It is though. They did get confirmation from him that he was on board with what was going on and was working with a view to finding a solution. That's it I'm afraid. He will most certainly have taken this personally and will be devastated. No point going home. He won't be there. He'll be living in his lab now I would imagine. It's a bloody nightmare.'

'Is there a cure yet?' I had a feeling there wouldn't be.

'Currently no,' was the curt reply.

'Therefore, all life on the planet's going to die?' It was a statement and a question I was throwing in there, I guess.

'I don't think so,' she said. 'We've tested some animals, mice, frogs, the usual victims. They show no symptoms. Although we haven't focused on the rest of the animal kingdom, or insects for that matter, the consensus from my colleagues around the world is that at present the only inhabitants of planet Earth currently falling victim to this are us.'

I thought on this for a while. There was an irony at work here if this was true. Ever since mankind had mastered his surroundings, this planet, it seemed he had, whether deliberately or not, tried at some point to blow it up, boil it, smash it and poison it by increasingly ingenious methods. And when that became hard work, he had built machines and artificial intelligence to do it all for him, while he sat back and treated the place like some enormous khazi. The rest of life on Earth could now be forgiven for metaphorically, and in unison, enjoying a collective moment of schadenfreude. The dogs would miss us. That was about it.

Sarah's eyes were now bloodshot. She was slurring a little and her voice had got louder by a few notches. I figured the weight of all this on her shoulders, in addition to the four bottles of Rattler drunk on a Saturday morning, was getting to her. She was a tough nut alright, but if our bodies were weakening ...

'How long have we got?'

'It's extremely aggressive. The old and weak will start dying in a matter of weeks. The rest of us ...' she broke off and let out a long sigh. 'Five, six weeks maybe. Society will have totally broken down long before that happens mind you.'

She continued, 'I've been summoned to Whitehall, your old gaff, Jack, on Monday morning. All my colleagues have been summoned to meet with their respective governments' decision makers. We present our findings. I imagine they then hold their crisis meetings, and we'll see. It's a couple of weeks since this thing reared its head so I would be surprised if there aren't plans afoot as we speak.'

'Five, six weeks!' I said the words, but they had no relation to the reality. They were not enough. No words were enough. 'What do we do in the meantime?' I said.

Part of me still did not really believe all this. I suppose it's a survival mechanism. I looked at Sarah. She believed it. Every expression she pulled, her body language. The lot.

'Play a tune, Jack,' she demanded.

'What?'

Part of the attraction with Sarah was you just never knew what was coming.

'Jack, the fucking world's ending. Play a damn tune!'

With that she staggered to her feet and stared impatiently at me, deadly serious.

Think fast Jack and get it right, you will not get a second chance at this. Joe Jackson, yes, he always told it like it was. I put on 'A Slow Song', which gave me seven minutes and three seconds holding her in my arms, as we danced slowly in my front room. The singer pleaded for resolution with all his soul. Her head on my shoulder, holding me tightly. Was she clinging to me or clinging on to life? Both, I imagined. It was a sad, surreal and beautiful moment.

The song finished. We held each other for another minute or two before Sarah disentangled herself from my arms and gathered up her possessions. She knew she didn't need to tell me to keep all we had discussed to myself. Trust in shared secrets can be a wonderful thing. And rare!

'I'll call Monday night. I'm going home to bed now.' She gave a resigned smile as she said it.

'Speak Monday then, Sarah,' I said as I shut the door behind her. I sat on my sofa gazing blankly out of the front window. As sometimes happens in these moments, the most inappropriate song came into my head. Bloody REM. If this was indeed the end of the world as we knew it, I certainly did not feel fine!

12

Sarah rang on the Monday evening around seven. The meetings, yes in plural, had been intense and lasted all day. She told me she now had a new role in all this, acting as a conduit between her science community, who were now focusing almost entirely on a cure, and Whitehall. She would be staying in London tonight, returning to Whitehall tomorrow for further crisis planning. She couldn't really say much more. I had the impression she didn't trust her phone network. She told me she would ring around the same time tomorrow evening, wished me well and hung up.

I hadn't ventured out all weekend or Monday for that matter. I wasn't feeling too bad yet, though having easy access to a loo was becoming a comforting thought. I could feel myself becoming more lethargic as well and yes, constantly hungry. There hadn't been anything directly pertaining to the oncoming health crisis on TV yet. Of course, there were mutterings and conspiracies on social media, some of them almost hitting the mark. The only thing that made the TV news was that supermarkets were struggling with an unprecedented demand for certain items and were having to limit the numbers individuals could buy at a time. Toilet roll was one such item. Always toilet rolls.

It was now Tuesday and I needed food shopping, so I opted for this Italian mini-supermarket come deli in town. It was more expensive than conventional supermarkets. Their stuff was ace though, and they were more civilised in there. I figured whatever I ate was going to kill me so I may as well go down eating quality food. I don't think I had fully absorbed the gravity of the situation at that point, but my logic was spot on. Maybe it was paranoia at work but there seemed to be more drones flying about than there would normally have been. The delivery drones' numbers were constant but there were certainly a few more 'bizzies' in the air. Bizzies was a throwback name, and not a complimentary one, for the police. The modern-day version was a drone with distinctive yellow and black markings, that in the main served as a surveillance tool for law enforcement. However, if any individual decided to play up and ignore them, they would begin by barking instructions such as 'Stop what you are doing and move away!' or 'Remain where you are. Do not move!' depending on the severity of the individual's actions. If said individual continued to ignore these instructions the bizzie was equipped to strike them with tasers, accurate from twenty feet. That swiftly ended that argument.

As I walked back home down the slight hill, the church lay on my right. I stopped briefly to take in the sight. It had stood in that same place since 1185. The West Front of the building would have watched over the Peasants' Revolt, The English Civil War, industrialisation and all that came to pass after that. I had no intention of stepping inside. For me, if you feel God inside you, go to church if you wish. If you do not, then so be it. There was no way I was wandering in now, giving out some schtick concerning the current predicament we were in, and just by the way God would you mind making it all better, please? No way. I simply stood where I was and stared at it, and as it would have done for anyone over the hundreds of years it had stood, it just stared back at me.

Sarah rang as she promised, just after four in the afternoon. It was all cryptic. She explained that there was a lot happening. Busy. Busy. Also, she wouldn't be able to ring again this week due to an imposed lockdown on all communication outside her new inner sanctum. She assured me she was fine and enquired after me. I reassured her I too was still doing OK. The conversation was stilted on her part, so I figured she had accepted that it was being monitored now. She left the show-stopper until the end. I had been summoned to Whitehall on Friday morning, at eleven for a meeting with a Mr Brown. She did not/could not elaborate, but she assured me that it would all become clear during the meeting. The following instruction was given with the utmost urgency.

'Don't be late, Jack! Whatever you do, do not be late!' With that she affectionately signed off.

Mr Brown! Who the hell was Mr Brown? So many questions.

I drove down to London on the Friday morning just because it was easier, and the possibility of train cancellations was a real one. I could still use my old work car park even as an ex-employee. It was a dead handy privilege as it turned out. I arrived with half an hour to wander about aimlessly before the eleven o'clock meeting with Mr Brown. At ten to eleven I was in the reception area I knew so well. I was guided up to Office 1001 on the third floor, where on arrival I sat in a chair and waited. The receptionist said she would buzz upstairs to confirm my arrival. Just after eleven a tall man, who turned out to be Mr B, came out of the office and turned to me.

'Please come in, Jack. Did you have a good journey?'

'Yes, fine, thank you sir,' I said. The 'sir' was my attempt to get him onside. He invited me to sit opposite him, then pushed some of the papers on his desk towards me, gave me a pen and asked me to read and sign. I did begin reading but soon I could see he was getting impatient, fidgeting and a bit of tutting, so I reverted to type and just signed the damn things.

His office was not unlike other offices I had been in over the years in that building. Roughly thirty feet square. High ceiling, bookcase, filing cabinet, yes, these places still had filing cabinets. No picture on the wall, view of the adjacent building out of the window, wooden desk with neatly folded papers on the left as I was facing. He sat with his back to the wall. It was one of those offices that didn't really belong to anyone. These rooms got used when the need arose.

Now for Mr Brown. He was over six foot tall; six two or six three I'd guess. He didn't appear to have an ounce of fat on his physique. Not due to the current situation. I was sure he was built that way. He possessed inquisitor's eyes. His lips were thin. My initial suspicion was that he was a man who was frugal with language, and he did not disappoint.

He opened. 'You are aware, Jack, that we are currently in something of a predicament.'

'Yes,' I said. 'I am sure you are aware that I have been given some insight.'

I couldn't see anything to be gained by playing dumb. They would know I knew Sarah and they would know we would have discussed … things. It would just insult his intelligence to act any other way. And possibly would have riled him which, as I still had no idea why I was here, could be hugely counterproductive.

'Thank you for being honest, Jack. Yes, we are well aware of your long friendship with Ms Milhaven, as we are of your lifelong friendship with Mr Day.'

He said this with absolute zero emotion. He was impossible to read. And of course, Mr Day. Tom. Where did he fit into the agenda of this meeting, if at all?

He continued, 'What Ms Milhaven has told you is all true. If we do not find a cure for this thing inside six weeks humanity will be wiped out. There are teams around the globe currently working on a solution, but every day all these individuals become weaker and weaker which naturally impairs their ability to focus on the job in hand. We are not, at this stage, confident that they will indeed discover a cure, certainly not within the time frame they have been given.'

'That's quite shocking. Is that it then? It ends here?' It's fair to say the realisation of our impending doom was properly sinking in now.

'I'm afraid so, Jack.' I could feel he was building up to something. I was not sitting here just to have what I already knew confirmed to me. There had to be a plan.

'As it appears inevitable at this current time that the surface of the planet will not support human life, there are to be evacuations to a safe place, with a view to preserving the human race until a time, hopefully, when a return to the surface is viable.' And when he finished he sat back in his chair and stared directly at me looking for any reaction.

'That's a lot of people to evacuate,' I said.

'Just over ten billion people,' he said. 'If we save ten thousand it will be a monumental effort.'

'My God!'

'Yes, well we're in his hands now, aren't we?' As he said this, I got the sense he wanted to wind this meeting up. I imagined he had other people to see. It was time to get to the nitty gritty.

'Jack, you have the good fortune to have been selected as a participant in this evacuation.' He sneered as he said this.

'Do you wish to be part of this evacuation?' He phrased the question deliciously. I could see in his expression he wanted me to consider what I was doing by saying 'yes'. I would be condemning one of billions of people who deserved this opportunity far more than me to certain death. Nurses, humanitarians, religious folk. It could be any one of them. I got away. They died.

'Yes, I do,' I said. I wasn't going to say no, was I?

'I see. Be at the aquarium at five tomorrow evening then. If you are late, forget it. Pack clothes for three weeks maximum. Laptops are allowed but they will be given a full diagnostic so you may want to remove anything you don't want to be made public.'

Nice touch Mr B.

'I must inform you that if any of the conversation we have just had gets out …'

'Yes?' I said.

'If you give me any reason to believe you may not be able to keep all this to yourself, any reason, then I am at liberty to use this.' And with that he pulled out a handgun from his jacket pocket. A Glock. He then pointed it in my direction.

After he was satisfied that I was sufficiently startled he directed my eyes to the papers he had rushed me to sign. I stared at him in a state of shock. That was the first time anyone had pulled a gun on me.

'We're not fucking about here. Just remember that.' Those clipped tones now had a sinister edge to them.

He continued, 'A fifty litre capacity rucksack or equivalent. That's it. Any further questions?'

'I'm going to an undersea base then, I take it?' I said, voice cracking a little.

'It will all become clear tomorrow. Now, if you excuse me, I have some more scheduled meetings. Good morning Mr Lee.'

Ooh Mr Lee indeed. I had got to him. Or maybe it was the situation. Or maybe 'Jack' went out of the window when firearms got involved. Whatever. The good news was he hadn't seen reason to use it on me. I got up and shook his cold bony hand, thanked him for his time and walked out of the office. I smiled and said goodbye to the receptionist as I passed her and walked out into the grey cold early February gloom. It was there that it hit me. That business up there wasn't personal at all. He wasn't invited, was he?

It wasn't raining so I opted for a stroll before heading back home. One final wander along the capital's arteries before I headed away. I couldn't overcome the feeling that this was like checking out of a hotel, but still afforded a day at the beach before the plane was due to leave for home. It can be considered a bonus, a 'free' day, but all you are really thinking about is going home. That was how this felt. As I walked down Whitehall Place and then into Northumberland Avenue before the massive exhalation of breath when you hit Victoria Embankment and it all opens out into view, I tried my utmost to take it all in for one last time. But I just wasn't there anymore. My mind and I suppose my spirit were elsewhere now.

I persevered and continued walking towards Blackfriars. There were crowds, of course there were crowds. It was lunchtime and people would be escaping their workplaces for food and the outdoors. As I looked around it was noticeable that it was considerably quieter than it should have been, even for early February. That could only be down to sickness I figured. That was the only visible sign that gave the game away, otherwise it still appeared business as normal. Sure, there was a palpable tension in the air. The killer did not appear to be manifesting itself in the open just yet.

As I walked into Blackfriars station, a slight break in the cloud allowed a speck of blue sky to appear in the south. I walked across the bridge heading to the South Bank. When I was approximately halfway, I stopped and looked out across the Thames and down to Tower Bridge. Stationary trains were blocking my view the other way. I saw St. Paul's on my left, and I remembered the photos of it during the Blitz. It had survived that. Now it was facing a new threat, more a threat of abandonment this time but a threat, nonetheless. And I fixed my stare beyond Tower Bridge, to the skyscrapers, some constructed as long ago as the previous century when they smashed the docks and built their New Jerusalem.

When I reached the other side of the bridge, I walked down the steps out of the station, passed the coffee bars, and headed to the Founder's Arms, a fifty-yard walk. I could have walked further and visited the New Tate. However, this wasn't a day for Dalí. It was time for a pint though. Inside, the pub was one long bar with wooden benches for furniture. All minimalist. The selling point was the tables outside and the view of the river, and all that was going on, on it and around it. Mum and Dad had brought me here when I was a kid, as part of one of their day trips up to London. We would sit outside. Mum would smoke a fag and sip her gin and tonic while watching the river. Dad would have his pint and watch the river. They always produced sweets for me at this point which was great and eased the boredom. I would have been nine or ten. Rivers are boring at that age unless you can go swimming in them and you didn't want to go in this one. It looked like shit!

I gathered my Guinness and grabbed a bench inside. It was too cold to sit outside, last visit or not. Indoors, you could smell the coming apocalypse. It smelt of disinfectant and bad breath. Everyone looked gaunt, and grey. Their skin beginning to sag against their bones like a postman's linen parcel sack. I counted twenty or so punters and two bar staff. They all gave out the same waves. It was a depressing sight, so I drank my Guinness and got up to leave. At this point I could feel my resistance to the effects of alcohol was not what it had been in the past and I must confess I staggered a little. 'Get a grip, Jack, you've got the drive home in front of you,' I thought as I steadied myself.

There was a crowd of twenty people or so between the pub and the station, hanging around by the stone wall that prevented them from falling down to the riverbank. They seemed quite animated and at first, I couldn't see what about. And then I could. In the middle of the river between its two banks, two Aja were rising out of the water, putting on a light show for a few minutes before they dropped back into the water out of view. They had just appeared again, and the crowd were applauding them. Really? Applauding these bloody creatures, the architects of our impending demise. It was like giving racing tips to your executioner before he removes your head with his blade! How I wished to tell them the truth of the Aja. How they were not the plastic bottle munching saviours of the human race. They were devils! They were abominations upon the planet. They would soon have the blood of billions of innocent souls on their hands. The Guinness had sure got to me.

I could stand it no more, so when I noticed the discarded cola can by my right foot, still unopened, there was but one course of action to take. I bent down and grabbed it, and before they descended once again, I threw it as hard as I could at the creature nearest to me. And what a shot! I got it right in its evil eye. Disappointingly, there was little reaction from the creatures. As the can bounced off my target and fell into the river, they both just slowly turned to face me, the perpetrator. And again, the same expression in their eyes that I had spotted in Tom's aquarium ... pity. I felt a bit cheated by their apparent lack of interest in my actions as they once again dropped down into the river. I got a reaction from the crowd though and it was not a good one. A lot of booing, a lot of swearing, and threatening and pointing at me. So, when a sweet young girl, early twenties I'd say, long blonde hair, wearing a 'Save the Planet' T-shirt, marched toward me and on arrival aimed her right knee expertly into my groin with speed and force, there was a loud cheer and much guffawing among them. I immediately doubled up in agony. But I needed to get away from there pronto. If Mr Brown, or 'Shooter', or whatever you wanted to call him got wind of this, I'd be off the programme tout-suite. Suitably humiliated, I scuttled off toward the station still slightly hunched forwards, making sure I gave the crowd a wide berth in doing so. I could still hear them laughing and cheering as I entered the station and relative sanctuary. As I walked across the bridge heading back to Whitehall, I looked down at the river once more. The Aja did not reappear, and the crowd was now dispersing. They had a good story to tell now about their time by the river. Shame they only had a month or so to tell it.

As I drove home, I repeatedly shook my head in disgust at my thoughts and behaviour during the whole incident. My thoughts more so. A fine future carrier of the torch for humanity I was.

13

I had packed everything I needed by nine in the morning. Unsurprisingly, my previous night's rest had been erratic, probably only getting two hours of actual sleep. I watched some TV for a while. Outbreaks of civil disorder were sprouting up worldwide now. The governments had gone on record as accepting there was a virus sweeping the planet. Miraculously, there was now a vaccine and mass inoculations were being prepared for everyone. The advice in the meantime was if you were feeling unwell stay at home and keep hydrated. This was a massive lie. The inoculations were placebos. It was a delaying tactic, delaying mass panic and chaos, nothing more. I turned off the TV and went and had a shower.

It was another cold grey day as I left the house just after eleven for my final trip into town. There were people around me going about their business. They did not look well, and they looked scared. And anyone who didn't look scared looked angry. I wandered into a newsagent just short of the centre of the shopping precinct and bought a couple of cricket magazines. As I was leaving the shop a lady grabbed my left arm just above the elbow.

'We're going to hell for what we've done, aren't we?'

Her words hit me like Morrisey's ten-ton truck.

'Not sure I believe in the concept of hell,' was my somewhat inadequate reply.

It wasn't a lie though. I did have faith of sorts yet these literal manifestations, the 'Interventionalist God' and suchlike, I struggled with. Besides, I really did not want to lie to this lady. She had the look of someone who had been let down by people, men possibly, all her life. Men like me, I guess. And she was strikingly attractive. Her eyes tore into your soul with the ferocity of a cocaine rush. She let go of my arm.

'I'm sorry,' she said as her eyes began to well up with tears.

I wanted to hold her close to me and tell her it was going to be alright. But it wasn't going to be alright, was it? It was soon going to be the fucking polar-opposite of alright, and again I did not want to lie to her. I had been in her presence not much more than two minutes and during that time I'd felt like I was on the edge of an abyss. It was as profound as it was frightening. I so wanted to take her with me, to sanctuary maybe. Why, oh why had I not met her until now?

'Come on! We need to go!' came the shout from outside the shop.

'I've got to go. I'm sorry,' and with that the spell was broken.

On leaving the shop, a large lady, a friend I guessed, who had shouted to her, seemed to be admonishing her for talking to strangers, or weirdos, or whatever she had me down for. I hoped to catch 'my' lady's eye again, but they were off sharpish, leaving me standing at the doorway, rooted to the spot.

When I left the newsagent, I could hear a commotion coming from the centre of the precinct just on my right. God, and the smell was overbearing! There in the paved area sometimes used by people trying to flog supposed cheaper electricity or something like that, stood Martin. He was a big old unit and a regular around town. He had some form of learning difficulty which made his age tough to pinpoint. I would guess late thirties. He had always seemed harmless to me, though he could be loud on occasions. This time he was standing in the one spot bawling his eyes out. He had soiled himself, which explained the smell. Passers-by were cursing him and calling him all sorts of names. OK, they're in pain themselves, but people can be so cruel. It wasn't his fault. A lady who I had down for one of his carers was trying to coax him away from the crowds.

I walked further on heading for one last cup of coffee in my little place. Ten yards further on from the shop was the High Street from where I heard an extremely loud sound of a car skidding followed by the dull thud of a collision. At the crossroads at the centre of town a convertible had gone into the side of a larger estate car. The convertible had not come out of it well, the front completely crushed with the force of the impact. And to make matters worse, from the position the cars were in it looked as if the estate driver was at fault. Both drivers had got out of their vehicles, seemingly unscathed and were now going at each other hammer and tongs. This caused all traffic waiting to use the crossroads to be blocked from doing so. At first car horns were sounded and when these proved to have no effect, some of the drivers got out of their cars and headed for the arguing crash drivers. Soon punches were traded and within seconds a proper fight broke out, anyone invited. The initial crash had not happened five minutes ago, and now I counted over ten men giving it what for. Even the sound of police sirens did not curb their enthusiasm for violence. Naturally, this all changed when the bizzies arrived on the scene and started barking instructions. Unfortunately, in these highly charged times some individuals were of a mind to ignore the threats and continue fighting. Not a good move. I watched three of them getting zapped. Their screams as they dropped to the ground were enough to discourage any further punches being thrown.

I had seen enough and headed into the coffee place. The lady baristas had popped outside to see what all the fuss was about, but they were back in place now. They looked at me almost with relief in their eyes. I sensed they'd had a tough morning, and I was the proverbial sight for sore eyes. I was always well behaved and never played up. There was some mopping up after 'accidents', and a lot of air freshener being sprayed around the place. I smiled at the ladies. They probably wouldn't be going to the promised land. The thought made me incredibly sad. All they had got wrong was their timing. If they had come into this world fifty or sixty years sooner, they would have been spared all this. I didn't really know them, but I couldn't see them as being bad people. They just didn't deserve what was coming their way.

I said thank you and took my coffee to a corner table. For a Saturday it was quiet, only another half a dozen people in there. I opened one of my magazines and tried to read. Nothing sank in. All I could think of was the lady in the newsagent. I wondered where she and her friend were going. Maybe they were headed for a nearby bar or another coffee place. I considered seeking them out, then I came to my senses. In a couple of hours, I would be leaving my hometown, probably for the last ever time. What good would catching up with them do? Her friend looked a bit frightening, the brief glimpse I got of her. I felt helpless. I so wanted to somehow make it better for her. How could I, though, in this poxy shit situation?

When I had finished my drink, I folded up my magazine and left the building, bidding slightly over the top fond farewells as I did. I walked back past the shops, retracing my steps from earlier. Martin's poor carer had self-evidently had some success being as he wasn't anywhere in the arcade anymore, though his aroma did linger somewhat. I exited the shops and crossed the road. Once again as I walked down the slight incline that was Church Street I looked across to my right at the West Front of the church, and once again, same as before, it stared right back at me.

14

It was just after half passed three in the afternoon when I parked my car in the Whitehall car park and began the walk to the aquarium. My last cold grey February afternoon in London. I had my rucksack strapped to my back and to shield myself from the populace I had the hood of my coat up and over my head. I kept my head down as I strode, avoiding eye contact with every passing soul. A mixture of guilt and fear at work there. I reached the bridge without incident. As I walked across, I saw beggars sitting on the pavement looking for handouts. Slim pickings today. I gave one all the change I had in my pocket. He thanked me as he looked up, his sad and grateful eyes staring into mine. At that moment he probably thought I cared. That I sympathised with his plight, the tragic series of events that had generated the downward spiral dumping him where he was now. Maybe I empathised. And as I walked on I considered that was ultimately the most tragic thing about him, as he sat *'among the fetid breath of living Death'*. His world was dying, and I was leaving him behind, with my miserable coins in his hands. I couldn't get off that bridge quick enough.

I was an hour early but I was still allowed through the 'cleaners' door on entering the aquarium. This was good news as I had one last stop-off before assembling beside the indoor pool. I explained this to my new buddy guarding the large entry door to the off-limits area, and he was fine with it. As I made my way inside there was what looked like a submersible just leaving. I watched the sheen of its hull disappearing into the water and heading out into the awaiting river. There were people hurrying around, clearing up bits and bobs, possibly preparing for the next sailing, my sailing maybe. I introduced myself to one of these men explaining who I was and why I was here early. My guy was fine with my explanation but he stressed the importance of punctuality. I told him I would be back in good time. I then turned to my right and headed back towards the big tank that had been giving me nightmares since my last experience here all those months ago.

I didn't know for sure that Tom would be there. I thought there was a reasonable chance though, and he did not disappoint. As I approached, he looked up from the same desk he had been sitting at previously all full of excitement and wonder. This time it was a different story.

'Hi, Jack. Bless you, thanks for coming.' His voice seemed deeper now. He got up from his chair and approached me. He'd had a haircut and a shave and fortunately a shower too. I imagined he'd been told to.

'How are you, old buddy?' I said, attempting a connection that I feared may have long gone.

'I'm good. There's progress being made here. We're not quite out of the woods yet but I'm fairly sure you'll be buying me a pint pretty soon and we can sit and wonder what all the fuss was about.'

To be fair it wasn't a bad pitch, and if it hadn't been for the look in his eyes, I may have believed him. He was standing motionless in front of me now waiting for a reaction, waiting for my sharing in his enthusiasm. I just looked straight back at him. He returned my stare, then looked away to the side, then back at me. It takes a minute or two sometimes to see these things properly. His eyes now seemed pitch black. He had lost weight, a lot in his facial features, making his gaze almost skeletal. His eyes now sunken back into his skull accentuating this illusion. I could read no emotion behind them. No inquisitiveness, no spark. No soul.

'I'm glad you're making progress.' I had to break the silence between us. He knew I was stringing him along albeit not maliciously.

'It's an interesting problem you see. The challenge is in effect isolating the component parts and then re-assembling them all in a way ...' He couldn't complete the sentence.

The mask had slipped, and he now bore the look of a man who knew the game was almost up.

'I'm so sorry, Jack. I am so sorry. I'm trying so hard to put this right. I cannot imagine what you must think of me. My God, I'd make all the monsters in human history blush if they could see what I've done.'

'You didn't let off the explosions.'

'I gave them the hope though, didn't I? Then their hope turned to expectation. Listen, I'm not concerned with my legacy. That doesn't matter. I simply want to put it back together like it was before. It's just so hard. It's so hard to focus. I go to sleep hoping, praying it will all be solved when I awaken. But it isn't, is it? I could have had this licked in the old days but now ...'

Again, he couldn't finish the sentence. What could I say to him? I was thinking I just wished he had listened to Sarah, and not tried to save the world every time it needed saving. Unfortunately for him the belief that he could, which was an arrogance of sorts, had directly led to his, and subsequently to our downfall.

'I try,' he said, 'I work on established principles. I study my notes again and again, but nothing works. Nothing works. Then it gets foggy and I get annoyed and I can't think straight. So, I get up, and I walk about to try and clear my head. But it won't clear. I can't get out of my head what I've done, so I self-medicate and try to start again.'

It didn't bear thinking about what 'self-medicate' consisted of.

'My mind drifts to the consequences of what I've done. I can't bear it. It's just too much.'

He looked back at me, then down at the ground. When he looked up again, I could see tears in his eyes. This man had been acclaimed by his peers. He had possibly been the possessor of one of the finest minds the world had ever seen. He had dealt with all the praise with humility and grace. He had adored his family. He had been selfless. And he had been a wonderful friend.

That man had now left the building. What was left was a broken shell, the lifeforce now sustaining him not much more advanced than that of a zombie. I thought of all the leaders. Of all the captains of industry. All the movers and shakers who were only concerned with their own self-serving. And then I looked once again at this once beautiful man, now a bedraggled, broken, walking corpse whose spirit had been taken from him by men not fit to tie his shoelaces. With that I too welled up. He saw my reaction and we embraced for one last time.

'I'm glad you got the chance to start again. Look after Sarah and the boys, won't you? I know you will. They love you.' He hesitated for a few moments. 'I love you. Now go, you don't want to be late for the pre-embarkation briefing. It's quite a speech I've heard.'

With that he disentangled himself from my arms and headed back to his desk to continue with his work. As he seated himself down, he looked up at me one last time attempting a smile. Sadly, it came across not so much as a smile, it was more a look of longing for the torture to stop. I could bear it no more as I turned and headed back towards the pool.

It was now a quarter to five and a crowd of around thirty had assembled between the large steel entrance and the pool which now contained a submersible currently refuelling. There was a lot of activity around the pool which I imagined was preparations for the sub's departure with, once again I was supposing here, us onboard.

A shortish man appeared in casual clothes. Thick spectacles, not quite 'Magoos', did blur his eyes somewhat. He appeared to be double checking the numbers. He then made his announcement.

'Good evening. I am pleased to say you all appear to be here so we can begin a little early. The first thing I am going to ask you is to place all your baggage against the wall next to the large steel door. Secondly, can you please empty your pockets and place the contents in the blue trays on the table to your right. You will be scanned as well so please treat this exercise the same as you would at any airport checkpoint in the world.'

There followed ten minutes while everyone complied with his instructions. None of us was saying much. The one thing I did notice was that all my fellow passengers appeared to be at least thirty years younger than me. There were ten or so Asians, several Afro-Caribbeans. Three or four appeared to hail from the Far East. I heard the American twang from four young men and women. The remainder looked like they were from the UK, but it was difficult to say for sure. It appeared an even split as regards boys and girls. I wondered if they were thinking I was a head of state or something, due to my advanced years. Now was not the time to explain to them that the only reason I was here was by virtue of being the proud possessor of a Willy Wonka Golden Ticket. That wouldn't have gone down well.

Once he was satisfied we had complied with his instructions, Mr Magoo led us through an open door in the direction of the pool's exit into the Thames, which revealed a small room with seating for all of us, facing the wall backing onto the great outdoors. Our man stood facing us and once we were all seated, he began his address.

'Let me begin by telling you that my welcoming speech will take little more than ten minutes, after which there will be a brief Q & A. You will then leave this room and collect your personal belongings before you embark. If any baggage is still by the pool it signifies that something contained within it has been deemed unsuitable for the coming journey and has been removed. Also, if the tray you placed your personal belongings in has a red sticker on it that too indicates that an unsuitable item has been removed. If this is the case with any of you here, you will then be given the choice of continuing onward without said item or items, or, if they are just too precious for you to leave behind you may remain here, but naturally in the process forfeit your place in all this. Don't worry, there will be plenty to fill it should you decide to remain. Does everyone understand what I've just said?'

A consensual 'Yes' resonated around the room.

'Good.' He continued. 'As you will by now be aware, humanity is facing a crisis, one that it may well not recover from. You are a part of the fortunate few who have been selected to work to maintain our presence on this planet. You are a small part of a percentage of the total population I am sad to say, making your involvement in all this critical. You have all been selected for your skills and aptitude and perhaps more importantly, your potential.'

Yes, I admit I did look down at my shoes at this point.

He continued, 'You are travelling to a New World. You may have already guessed that your transportation is moored outside this room, in the pool. It is a specially adapted submersible, adapted to transport you all to your new home ...'

He paused for a moment as all good orators do, striving for the maximum dramatic impact.

'Your new home. At the bottom of the ocean.'

Again, he paused waiting for a reaction. I'm sure we were still being assessed even this late in the day. An involuntary gasp of horror or any slight hysterics from any of us would result in our expulsion from the programme, for sure.

Silence!

That hurdle negotiated he now gave us a brief description of the life we would all begin to lead in just a few hours' time.

'Your new home will be the ultimate controlled environment. CCTV will monitor your movements at all times. There will not be money as such. There will not be wealth. Private property will not exist. You will have no personal data. This is the most important project in the history of humanity. It is not a holiday. Your participation in this is a privilege and a life commitment.'

It was Thomas More's Utopia without the slaves, though, in this realisation set underwater. No pubs or bars either if so! Magoo wasn't wrong. This was no holiday. With that, he announced he was done and threw open the floor for questions, though he emphasised there was little time set aside for them.

'Where is our new home? On the map I mean,' one of the American sounding girls said.

'Your Captain will explain that en route.'

'How many of us will be living in this base?' one of the Asian boys said.

'Initially just over a thousand,' came the reply.

'Are there other installations such as these around the globe?' an English girl said.

'My information has it that there are three more undersea worlds. There will also be subterranean communities scattered around the planet, and of course there are our colonies on the Moon and Mars. Will we hear any more from them? I think we have said our final farewells to the space explorers for sure. As for the others, I really couldn't say. Now if you will excuse me, we have a schedule to keep I must wind up this part of the programme.'

With that he beckoned us out of the room and back onto the concourse outside. All the baggage was gone. That was particularly good news. First and foremost because all my stuff had passed muster, laptop and all. Secondly, it meant for no last-minute dramatics from anyone. Most of our personal belongings from our pockets had been given the green light too. Phones. I was surprised at that in the light of our previous lecture. One individual did have a red sticker on his tray. One of the American boys. I overheard his conversation with the men of authority as we began boarding. A packet of cigarette and a lighter. Astonishing! Sheepishly, he rejoined the line of boarders. Guess a packet of fags was not a good enough reason to stay and watch the world die a slow horrible death. Some stared at him disapprovingly on account of his stupidity. A good time to quit I'd say fella.

Once inside the vessel we took our seats. There were five rows of six seats each with a walkway down the middle, much like the set up you would find in an aircraft though obviously much smaller. Some of the rows of seats didn't have a window. The windows were mainly at the front and I was sitting aisle side next to two Asian girls at the rear of the seating section. I got the impression that these subs had been built for scientific exploration, making the section I was sitting in probably where equipment and diving gear was normally held.

Once we were all settled a voice came over the intercom.

'Good afternoon ladies and gentlemen and thank you for travelling Nemo cruise lines.'

A titter of nervous laughter.

'My name is Captain Kirk. Yes, really, and I shall be transporting you to your new home. We are heading for the upper edge of the Bay of Biscay, one hundred and seventy-miles due west from Brest, ta-da, and just under six thousand feet below sea level. I estimate the journey to take somewhere in the region of six hours. There are toilets at the front and the rear of your seating area. Unfortunately, there will be no buffet service, and I'm afraid there won't be much to see outside, so I suggest you spend the journey reading a book or maybe having a nap. My second in command Henry is sitting next to me up here in case he is needed during the trip. I sincerely hope he is not, ladies and gentlemen. Thank you.'

Give him his due, he tried his best to ease the palpable tension. I smiled at the girls sitting next to me. I didn't really want to engage in conversation at this point. No one seemed to want to. I felt the engines kick into life, some shouting outside before all the hatches were closed tightly shut, followed by a shudder as the sub began its forward descent. After the initial dip down, so that we were fully submerged, a sharp right into the Thames, and we were away. The captain wasn't lying. The view out of the windows was gothic darkness.

I slipped on my headphones, as had everyone. I also had my magazines, but it was extremely difficult to concentrate on the words inside. My thoughts were dominated by our destination. Our new home under the sea. Would it be like an underwater city with monorails connecting the buildings? Or would it be one of those scientific outposts you see explorers camping in at the North Pole. A series of Jerry huts, extremely robust Jerry huts, scattered randomly. Maybe it would be one large construction. This was where it got scary, as I imagined some giant rust yellow cylinder on the ocean bed. The kind of place where you lived on top of each other and quickly developed all the symptoms of claustrophobia as well as other related conditions. That would be the way of things until you all went nuts and started slaughtering each other in a frenzied bloodbath until the screams subsided and the ocean claimed its vanquished invaders.

I looked at the girls sitting next to me and they smiled back at me. Hopefully, it wasn't going to be like that.

After a couple of hours, a steady procession to and from the toilets was in full swing. Fortunately, that was the only activity to speak of other than sleeping or reading. I noticed the little Asian girl sitting next to me was reading the novel *Dracula*. I looked up at her.

'Let's hope we've left those dudes behind, eh?' I said, and then directed my gaze to her book.

She removed the headphone in her right ear. 'I'm sorry?' she asked having not heard me properly the first time. The moment was lost. 'Just joking.' I replied rather gormlessly. She smiled and carried on reading her book. Keep up the illusion, Jack. This girl could most likely wipe the floor with you so just leave it alone.

I closed my eyes allowing my thoughts to wander. Straight to Tom. What was to become of him, I wondered. I thought back to our last embrace, where I had been conscious of not hugging him too hard. He had been all bones and I imagined that those bones were more like breadsticks, liable to snap and crumble if not treated with care. I hoped he would find peace somehow, though while he was alive, I could only see that happening through total mental collapse. Sad, sad thoughts. It must have torn poor Sarah apart seeing him towards the end. She was tough, though, and pragmatic. I wondered if she would stay up to greet me when we arrived at whatever we were arriving at, assuming she was there already. Had she managed to negotiate David and Michael a deal? If she had been behind me being onboard, which she almost certainly was, surely, she would have worked on getting them down there as well. Also, they had the desired skills, I would have thought.

Yes, the boys. I thought of them for a while. Hmmm ...

By this point I was starting to feel a little drowsy. I attempted to lighten my mood by picturing in my head the night of my retirement bash and its alcohol-fuelled coming together of Charlotte and myself. That was it. That was my last 'wild' night in the world I knew, other than the massive Christmas piss-ups in the Vic. Wow. It wasn't a bad story to drift off to and within five minutes I was away.

I was woken by a commotion at the front of the sub. People in that seating section had spotted something out of the windows to the right. A few behind them had got up to try and catch a glimpse. It was a small bright dot many miles away that we were slowly descending towards. For the first time since we had left London, the Captain made an announcement over the intercom.

'Ladies and Gents. You may have noticed the bright speck below us to the right. It is indeed your new home which we are approaching. Arrival approximately thirty minutes from now. Thank you for your good behaviour so far. It has been a pleasure bringing you here. Hope you like it.'

With that he signed off while he concentrated on guiding us toward our home. The speck gradually became larger, and larger, and larger. Fifteen minutes away it was assuming a form and it was at this point that something rather wonderful happened. By now it became clear that it was not a collection of hap-hazard underwater encampments or some nightmare cigar shaped aquatic hell chamber. It was a giant dome. Or rather a giant dome with several corresponding giant domes attached to it. It was the Eden Project only on a much, much larger and grander scale. And of course, at the bottom of the ocean. At this point it became clear that I hadn't been the only one on board who had had misgivings concerning our new home during the journey. The sense of relief within our little sub was palpable and all thirty passengers, now smiling with pure joy, spontaneously broke into a round of applause. For me, it embodied all that was good about us. We needed to make this work. Despite all previous crimes, the flame of humanity did not deserve to be extinguished just yet a while.

Part 4

1

When the airlock door opened, allowing us to exit the tunnel connection between the sub and our new home, the sight was breath-taking. I can only compare it to the experience a sport star would have when he emerged from the darkness into one of the great sporting theatres of the world. Or it could be likened to entering a magnificent New Age Cathedral. The dome itself was enormous. Two hundred feet high I later discovered. There seemed to be over a hundred tables and chairs arranged across the floor. It was midnight I remembered. The lights were low, and it was clear that not many were still up and about, because you could make out individual footsteps on the shiny floor. In the middle of all of this were steps leading up to a second level, though the lack of illumination meant I could not see what was up there. Also, and importantly, the outer skin of this dome that was protecting us from the ocean depths was opaque. We could have been anywhere. On land, in space, anywhere. The more I became acclimatised with the surroundings, the more apparent the low-level hum became. This, I assumed was the sound of what was keeping me alive.

If the initial vista had been one of wonder, our assembly point was a hilarious contrast to that, comprising as it did three large tables arranged in an 'L' configuration and manned by three men and one lady. It reminded me more of the set-up when you go to register to vote, without the voting booths. As I was to discover there was no voting to be done down here. The first man we were directed to had the easy job of ticking off our names. These were at the bottom of the list, on his last page of lists. We were the last arrivals of the day. The man standing next to him had the tougher task by far. He had a cardboard box in front of him in which he instructed us all to place our mobile phones. I had wondered when this would happen. Now, you must remember, I must have been among the brightest individuals the planet had to offer, hence them being there.

I therefore couldn't help smiling to myself at the reluctance of some to comply. The list man had to help his colleague, more as back-up than anything else. We had it explained to us where we were. Connection with the surface was impossible. The wi-fi as it was didn't work on our phones. They were of no practical use to us, and handing them over was an instruction, not a polite request.

'Will we get them back?' an Asian chap said.

'Probably not,' came the reply from the guy manning the box.

'What about all my personal stuff?' a young English girl said.

'This was explained to you before you left. You have no personal stuff down here. If it helps, no one is going to delve into the secrets that may be contained within. That isn't because of data protection or any security protocol. It's because we've all got better and more important things to do down here. This will become apparent to you all after a few days in your new home.'

He wasn't lying. I saw boxes of them a couple of weeks later dumped in a corner of one of the hospital rooms. Apparently, the micro-chips had been removed along with the batteries. Those were of value.

At first the box man had been directing his answer at the English girl. He concluded by addressing all of us. These people were probably temporary volunteers for this work. Maybe they were scientists when not having to perform this chore. The whole reason this set up looked the way it did was because it was temporary too. Pretty soon the arrivals would be zero. It was a sobering thought, and I don't think I was the only one having it. One by one the phones went in the box until our hosts were satisfied they had everyone's.

We were then directed around the tables to the third man and the lady. The man gave us all what appeared to be a bespoke iPad and the lady gave us all a wristwatch. It was explained to us by the pair that we were always to wear the watch. They were waterproof so they were to be worn

161

during showers, baths, everything. The iPad was our guide to our new home. Contained within were explanations of everything we needed to know, including the idiosyncratic properties of our 'watches'.

Having achieved all they needed to, as regards our checking-in, our hosts gathered our stuff up, while directing us to a seating area at the far side of the dome. As I walked with my fellow passengers, some still mumbling about the phone thing, I caught sight of Sarah sitting alone at one of the smaller tables. Wow! Was I glad to see her! I quickened my step as I approached, deviating away from the others. She got up and on contact we shared an extremely warm embrace like that of two people who had not been certain of ever seeing each other again.

'Thanks for staying up, Sarah. My God you're a friendly face in a strange world. When did you get here?'

'Wednesday, around midday.'

'You're looking well,' I said genuinely. She was looking well. As I said this the guys who had been processing us began to bring over plates of food and a bottle of juice of some sort. Mine arrived, appearing to be pasta with a Bolognese accompaniment.

'You not eating?' I was extremely hungry but I still had my manners about me.

'Not hungry. Besides, I'm not ill. Tuck in.'

Due to the sparseness of people her words appeared to reverberate off the walls. The build-up of chatter coming from the other tables gave off eerie echoes in the air. I demolished my meal in under five minutes.

'That was great. They've got beef down here?' I was surprised.

'It's made from plants. Good, isn't it? Get used to a pescatarian diet from now on. Can't see that bothering you much.'

'Guess we're OK for fish,' I joked, and we both smiled, both relieved to see each other. 'And the air's OK down here?'

'Yes, Jack. The air is good. In a couple of days, you should be back to normal health thankfully.'

So many questions.

It was at this point I suddenly felt my insides churn with guilt. The boys. I had been so involved with filling my face I hadn't asked the most important question. I looked at Sarah, feeling like the most selfish and uncaring shitbag alive as I asked her.

She smiled at me understandingly. 'They're fine. They came down with me, which was ideal. Don't worry, you'll meet them tomorrow. And Jack, this has all been very traumatic. I think we can be forgiven for having slightly muddled minds.'

It certainly had been unsettling times, though I knew full well where I would rather be.

'Look you'll have to excuse me,' she continued. 'I know you've got a zillion questions, but I've had a long day and tomorrow will be a long day as well, so I'm going to have to call it a night. I'll walk with you to your living quarters. It's not far, and I'll explain the important stuff as we go. As for tomorrow, for you it's all about getting to know this place while you're eating and drinking the right things. All the instructions will flash up on your iPad, so always keep it with you. It will also answer a lot of your questions when you delve into it. It's a good bit of kit. Oh, and never, ever take your watch off. If you do, they'll think you've died or gone rogue, and they'll be all over you within seconds.'

'They?'

'It's all in the iPad.' She was tired and she certainly didn't wish to get into all that malarkey at that time of night.

We both rose to our feet, with Sarah leading me to the left side of the dome as you would see it when entering from where I had originally. There was a door I had not spotted before marked 'Accommodation Dome A'. Sarah motioned me to raise my left hand to the door when we were directly in front of it, and it opened for us.

'Your new watch does a shit load more than just tell the time.' She grinned as we walked through. We entered a corridor that appeared to follow the outside of this new dome we were in. On the right of us on entering was a set of stairs.

'They go up to the first floor. And there are stairs up to the second floor for the poor unfortunates who have to lug their arses' up there. We're on the ground floor. A benefit of seniority.'

I noticed a sign on my left as we started walking. 'Avenue A1'. As we walked, we began to pass apartments on our right, 'No 1 AA1' followed by 'No 3 AA1' and so on. Upon passing 'No 7 AA1' there was a gap allowing for a dissecting path and I noticed this had a sign up saying 'Alleyway A1' and the first apartment on this path was marked as 'No 2 ALA1'.

'Avenues and Alleyways. Outrageous. If it was a Tony Christie fan who designed this, I'll go with it no worries.'

'That's good,' came Sarah's somewhat uninterested reply. 'I'm sure he'd be over the moon to hear you approve.'

We walked on further along the curved path or avenue. Sarah stopped at 'No 61 AA1'.

'This is you, Jack. Straightforward little journey, wasn't it?'

'Yes. I don't think even I could manage to get lost.'

'Don't worry, you will. Everyone gets lost at first. Keep your iPad on you and you'll be fine.'

'Where are you? Have you far to go?' I said, trying to appear a bit chivalrous at least.

She smiled, 'No. I am at No 252 ALA1. Sounds miles away. It's actually just round the corner from you. David's next door and Michael lives opposite. All very cosy. Now I will bid you goodnight. Breakfast starts for you at nine tomorrow morning in the main dome. Don't worry, your watch will wake you in good time.'

It was at this point I noticed the CCTV camera pointing at my front door. How could I have missed them? There was one pointing at every door.

'There's some inside your apartment as well. You're in the Truman Show now my love.'

Hmm. OK. 'One final question then I'll let you go, and I can't begin to show my gratitude.'

'OK. Last question.'

'I think I counted seven of these domes on the way down. Is that right?'

'There's ten, and another two currently under construction.'

'Wow!'

'Goodnight Jack.' And with that she gave me a peck on the cheek, and she was gone. Down the avenue to her alleyway.

I raised my left hand to the door, and it did indeed open for me, the lights automatically turning themselves on albeit low in brightness. My new home. I plonked my rucksack down on the floor. On first sight it was not dissimilar to holiday apartments I had stayed in. Bathroom on my right as I entered. Living space in front of me: sofa, coffee table then a door on my left leading to the kitchen. On the right of the kitchen a door to my bedroom, which was the only room I'd mutter about if I were on holiday, as it was small. There was just enough room for a wardrobe, small chest of drawers and a single bed. I wasn't on holiday though. And as Sarah had warned me, there was a camera in the far upper right-hand corner of the front room, one in the kitchen and one in the bedroom. There were also curtains in the living room and on the back wall and in my bedroom. I opened them both, revealing black screens, which was a bit disappointing. What did I expect though?

At this point it all caught up with me and I felt the immediate need to sleep, so all I unpacked was my toiletries. Piss, brush teeth and bed. The toilet light came on automatically and it was bright. There was a shower, no bath; otherwise all was as it should be.

That done I wandered across the living room to the door to the kitchen and bedroom section, noticing that the lights turned off behind me as I moved. When I entered my bedroom the kitchen light turned off. All clever and efficient. I undressed and got into bed wondering if the same would happen, and indeed it did. As I settled myself in the bedroom light slowly faded to darkness. I lay still for a while contemplating the circumstances, where I was in the world, what was outside. A little like the first night on holiday, when you lie in the darkness and consider that you are now in some sun kissed hedonistic hotspot, looking forward to all the debauchery that may well be coming your way. As comparisons go that one may have been way off the mark, but the thought sent me off to sleep in a calm haze of memories gone by.

2

A gentle vibration in my left wrist. That is all it was. The source of my wake-up call told me it was eight o'clock. I sat up and the vibration ceased. Breakfast, I was told, was at nine. I was now awake at exactly the time I needed to be, yet I'd set nothing up for this to be so. Interesting.

I wandered into the kitchen and looked around searching for my immediate needs. I found the kettle, filled it with water from the sink tap and switched it on. Next stop, the cupboard to the left of the sink. A fresh jar of instant coffee and a pressure jar for brown sugar. A nice coincidence or someone had been doing their homework. Limited cutlery was in the drawers next to the sink and I had a nest of brightly coloured mugs standing on the work surface below the cupboards. I opened the surprisingly small fridge which stood on the work surface against the wall facing my bedroom door. There was not much at all inside. All I was concerned with at that moment was the unopened container of milk. By the time the kettle had boiled I had everything in place to start the day.

I stood with my back to the sink taking my first few slurps dressed in nothing but my boxers. I wasn't cold, the temperature inside was fine. There was no need to fiddle with any of the appropriate controls. I wandered over to the curtains in the front room and opened them. The screen was now a light grey. The same effect when I opened the bedroom curtains. So many questions. One thing I noticed missing in the front room. No TV. I finished my coffee considering if I was being dumb thinking there would be one, even if it were just a screen with announcements on it. I couldn't decide so I dropped that thought, washed my cup and spoon up and made for the bathroom.

I had to chuckle to myself. After the bathroom visit, which was all in order, I unpacked a few things. I got dressed, set my laptop up on the coffee table and just wandered about the place checking on this and that. It was only then that I remembered the CCTV cameras in the front room and in the bedroom. I checked both. The power lights were shining so I had to assume they were functioning. The odd thing was they didn't bother me at all.

It was five to nine, time to go. I took one last look in the bathroom mirror to make sure I was presentable. I had chosen to wear a polo type T-shirt, jeans and brown brogues, as I was not aware of any dress code. I thought that was safe. I opened the front door and as I did, the watch started vibrating again. What was that all about? Ah, the iPad. Always have it with you. I walked back into the front room and picked it up off the coffee table where it was sitting next to my laptop, at which point my watch stopped vibrating. With everything in place I left my apartment, turned left into Avenue A1, and began walking back to the entrance to the central greeting dome, or whatever it was called.

As I opened the door leaving Avenue A1 behind me the first thing that hit me was the sound of hundreds of people talking, the moving of chairs, the clinking of cutlery. It was not abrasively loud, more like the bustle that you'd hear in a large restaurant with an extremely high ceiling that added the echoing effect. After the noise came the smell, which was awesome. It smelt of every dish in the world. There was the smell of fried onions, of curry, of noodles. I just had to turn my head and another aroma came into play. I looked around trying to absorb it all. Directly in front of me were all tables occupied by people, eating, or drinking coffee, or just talking. Some with their open laptops in front of them next to their iPads. Following the scene to the right I saw the Heath Robinson welcoming point I'd negotiated the previous night. The other side of that were more tables occupied by people sitting and eating, the same as this side of the arena. What caught my eye, was the wall panels that side of the dome looked like they were full of announcements, like a massive platform display at a railway station. This display was floor to ceiling from the welcoming point to the other side of the central staircase to the upper level. It stopped around ten feet short of the bank of food serving outlets that dissected the entire width of the dome at that point.

This was where all the varieties of food were dispensed, and was split into individual 'huts' for want of a better word, all with their own style and their own particular dishes. For example, the Caribbean hut was all yellows and greens. It had that ramshackle look about it and naturally had handwritten signs announcing today's 'Hot Reggae Sauce' on specials. Next to that was what I figured to be a Chinese place due to the brightly coloured lanterns hanging from its roof and the dragon design on the front of the counter. I figured behind these were kitchens, or one massive kitchen sectioned off into individual ones. As it would have accounted for a third of the floor space of the dome, it would have been a big old kitchen.

There were large plants scattered around, housed in concrete supporting flower beds, giving the place that wonderfully artificial home from home feel. It looked great to me. I wasn't standing on ceremony.

I had to see what these messages were on the far wall. The rest of the building's 'skin' was now displaying the same light grey as my bedroom window, causing this board to stand out more. As I headed round to the front of the building I noticed some more new arrivals enjoying their first sighting of the interior of their new home. I smiled at their collective look of wonder and out of badness considered hanging around to eavesdrop on the impending mobile phone performance. I thought better of it and crossed to the other side of the dome, allowing me now to stare directly at the notice board, which was exactly what it was. People's personal notices to each other. There was a 'Harry, I'll be in the viewing arena at three this afternoon. Joni x,' followed by some emoji I didn't know. There was a 'Band practice in the Gardens. 19.30,' with another emoji attached. New ones kept appearing, all in bright neon. There must have been over a hundred messages and there was room for hundreds more. This was most certainly something that required further investigation, however, now was not the time. I was hungry.

By following the wall round the building, I was now at the beginning of the 'wall of food'. I walked along taking in the various outlets until I came across what looked to me like a regular breakfast servery. Steel lids covering steel pots of hot goodies.

'Just arrived buddy?' came a voice from behind the counter.

'Yeah. Last night. I'm a new face I guess.'

'And your watch has an amber tint,' he said. 'Goes green when you're gainfully employed. Today breakfast is on the house. What you fancy bud?'

My guy was a tall, dark haired, good looking American, mid-twenties I would say. He had a big smile making him a positive introduction for me to my new co-inhabitants.

'Um eggs?'

'Fried or scrambled?'

'Scrambled please. Toast?'

'White or brown?'

'Brown please. You got any veggie sausages?' I said.

'Sure. Couple OK?'

'Fine thanks. Beans?'

'Beans. Hash browns?

'Yes please. Don't suppose you have any mushrooms, do you?'

'How will these little beauties, do ya?' And with that he opened a pot of beautifully browned button mushrooms.

'Fantastic. Thank you so much. My name's Jack by the way.'

'Hi, Jack. I'm Ben. pleased to meet ya. Cutlery is on the table over there by the wall. Tea and coffee dispensers are everywhere, and always free. I'll see you 'round.'

Sorted.

I sat myself down at a table facing two Indian gents who I assumed were Sikhs due to the turbans. Could have been Shias or Sufis maybe. I didn't have a chance to find out as they comically got up to leave as I sat down.

'We're so sorry, sir. We must go to our work. The world of medicine calls us. Please forgive our rudeness.'

'Of course,' I said and smiled. 'Next time maybe. My name's Jack by the way.'

'I'm Damanjeet and my friend is Dilsher. We'll look out for you.'

With that they headed off in the direction of the notice board, eventually locating a door between the board and the food wall. I would have walked straight past it before. The food was hot and delicious, made all the better in the knowledge that I was now properly digesting it. That prompted a thought for the poor souls above.

'Well ... how did I get here?' To quote a great man.

I didn't eat alone for long. A gent not much younger than myself asked if he may join me. He was carrying a breakfast like mine.

'You're more than welcome,' came my genuine response. He sat down opposite me. There was a distinct American twang to his voice.

I would have had him around five foot nine or ten. Brown hair that he had let grow to his collar. Touch of grey. Pretty unremarkable in appearance but he had enquiring eyes. I stiffened up a bit for fear that this man had the ability to allow me to bare my soul to him and I didn't want to do that. I still felt a bit of a fraud for being here. Hanging on in the way of the worthy. He took a couple of bites of his breakfast, let it digest and then he looked up at me.

'How are you finding it here, Jack? It's a bit mind blowing at first, isn't it?'

He knew my name. That was unexpected.

'Well, I only arrived last night so I'm still acclimatising.' I had the suspicion he knew that too.

'So far, everything's good thanks,' I said playing a straight bat.

'There's a lot to take in but there is no need to rush. We all acclimatise at our own pace, don't we?'

'Of course. It generally takes me a while to adjust but once I'm there, it's there for good.' Was that gibberish? 'If you see what I mean,' I added hoping for clarity.

He smiled. A warm and reassuring smile I was pleased to see.

'I know exactly what you mean. Maybe you and I are the same, or maybe it's the years behind us, eh?'

I would have loved to have known how he had spent the years behind him. The impression I was getting was that it would have been something remarkable. We both took a few more mouthfuls of food.

'I think you'll be OK here. I've a feeling you've got an important role to play.'

Was this an interview?

'Really?'

I had the impression this guy was on my side, but I still had to be defensive. I'd finished my meal now.

'If you remember back to the work you used to do. The real work! And then imagine the absolute opposite. That is why I believe, no, I know, we know, you'll work out fine. I am sorry, I didn't introduce myself. My name's Aaron.'

'Pleased to meet you, Aaron. It would appear you know my name already.'

'It's my job.' With that he smiled and caught me with the look of a benevolent tormenter. Aaron was clearly enjoying himself, though I had the feeling he wanted the best for me. Maybe I was tired and disorientated therefore succumbing to his will too easily. And what was that crack about my 'real work' all about? This was a bloody weird conversation. No mention of the horrors above. It was almost as if I were being seduced. Sod it! I went for broke.

'What is it you do down here then?' I politely enquired. What did I have to lose?

'My base is the dome through that door.' With that he pointed to a door to the right-hand side of the notice board, leading round to the entrance.

'In your current mindset you would call it the leadership dome, as opposed to the hospital dome, or the accommodation domes etcetera. We drop the 'dome'. It is just the hospital, or the gardens, what have you. By telling you this I have created an impression in your mind. You will be viewing the word "leadership" in a sinister light. You will be viewing me in a similar way. Now you must trust me, Jack. This view will change over a period, I hope, and when that time comes, I will invite you inside for a little tour. We have absolutely nothing to hide.'

He continued, 'I've been involved with this place for a long time now. Its purpose has altered, evolved, however you wish to describe it, many times in that time. Originally, it was built for scientific research which makes sense. From there it grew into almost a resort, then an indulgence, and now it is transitioning into its most important purpose. Not for the best of reasons, it must be said. What we are about to do is so important we cannot afford ourselves the luxury of dwelling on the past follies of humanity. If this sounds harsh and inhuman, maybe it is. I make no bones about it. We all have a huge responsibility to make this work. It is not just about keeping the power generating, keeping the place secure. Those things are important, granted, but it's also about us. How we interact with each other. How we grow together. What we share.'

With that he paused. For breath as much as anything else. As he did this, I once again became aware of the many people around us, the chatter, the going about their business. I had been so caught up with his words. With him, his whole aura of purpose, I had quite forgotten we were among a crowd and not in our own private bubble.

He sat back in his chair. He had finished his meal too by now.

'You cleared your plate. That's good. Every bit of food is important.' And with that he reached over and gently grabbed my arm, I think attempting reassurance. I wasn't saying anything. This was listening time.

'Haven't I prattled on? Look, I have to get back and you have a hospital appointment in five minutes.'

'You know everything, Aaron.'

He smiled with that teasing look again. 'Not everything. Your iPad just flashed it up. I enjoyed our chat. I hope I didn't overwhelm you. We'll talk again. It was good to meet you, Jack.'

With that he got up and headed off in the direction of his place of business. I looked around; no one batted an eyelid. In my head, I had just had breakfast with royalty. For everyone else we had merely been two older guys having breakfast together, talking about this and that.

I looked down at my iPad. It was indeed informing me that I was due for a check-up in the hospital.

I got up and headed toward the appropriate door, somewhat pleased with myself that I knew where I was going.

3

The hospital was a scream. Not a scream, bedlam like; it was hilarious, or as hilarious as those places could be. It was so higgledy-piggledy. All signs and arrows and long corridors snaking off as far as the eye could see. All the departments seemed to be present and correct. I saw signs directing me to 'Emergency' and 'Cardiology' and 'Neurology' among others, and I'm sure it all made sense to the individuals who put it all together as well as to the good people who worked within. To me it was the familiar maze I had negotiated in all the hospitals I'd ever visited. Maybe this was deliberate, I wondered. A ploy to reassure folks with a sense of 'home from home.' I must say it worked for me. The only perceptible difference from the hospitals I had visited before was that it wasn't busy, and the individuals I passed, who I guessed didn't work there, didn't look in poor health. There were no stretchers or drips, that I saw, and it was quiet. There was not the bustle that you would normally find. No porters focused on delivering their patient to wherever they need to go, scattering anyone blocking their way through sheer force of will. None of this. It was not a ghost town, but it was a noticeably quiet day for admissions.

My iPad directed me to my destination which was a smallish unit with four chairs backing onto the left-hand side wall. There was a room on the right facing the chairs with the door open. I knocked on the door and stuck my head inside.

'Jack, is it?'

'Yes, sir,' I said.

'Good. Come in. Close the door behind you and take a seat. My name's Dan.'

I walked in and duly sat down at the side of the desk he was perched behind. The name plaque on his desk read Dr. Simmons but it was all informal. All Dilshans and Aarons, and now Dans.

'How are you feeling?' he opened with. Fairly obvious opening question. If he had wanted a full answer to that question I could have rambled on for a week.

'I don't feel too bad, Doctor. Head's a bit all over the place. That's to be expected I guess.'

'Good, and yes, it is to be expected. Unfortunately, these are difficult times we are living in. The good news is, you look well. Are you up for producing a urine sample?'

I nodded. With that he gave me a glass cup and pointed me to a curtain the other side of his surgery.

With that done I passed the full glass back to him. Sitting on his desk he inserted a glass tube into it, waiting ten seconds or so. The tube slowly began to glow light green.

'Green is good. May I take some blood now?'

'Sure.'

Cue another glass implement, this one resembling a large pencil in size. He found a vein in my arm and positioned one end of his instrument against it. I felt a small jab, watching the glass inside fill with my blood. Again a few seconds wait before some numbers started to appear on the glass. He studied these for a while. Once satisfied he placed the tube carefully into another glass on his desk.

'Blood's fine. You're well on your way to a full recovery from the sickness.'

'Thanks. That's good news. Particularly in the light of the limited time I've been here.'

It's true I had no idea how much I had been affected by the sickness. In truth, I hadn't experienced a lot of the symptoms many people complained of in the preceding days, so I didn't have a point of reference as such. Maybe I was just more resilient. What did I know?

'I think you got out just in time. Up to now no one I've seen down here has appeared to display any serious or permanent organ damage. Kidney and liver functions have all recovered. Sadly, I don't think this will be the case by the end of next week unless we find a cure.'

The bedside manner mask had slipped at this point. He was genuinely disturbed by his words. The enormity of them. The tragedy.

I tried to be positive. 'Maybe they'll find a cure, Doctor.'

'Yes, maybe.' He had quickly gathered himself and the mask was back in place.

'Your friends are working upstairs around the clock on that. If we don't find one it won't be for want of trying.'

I had not even noticed an upstairs level or levels on my way in. So that's where Sarah and the boys were working.

'Right, Jack. That's us done I think. I'll see you again in a week and if you're all good then it will be every six months.' And he reached out to shake my hand at which point I hesitated.

'Anything wrong?'

'No, no. I am just surprised that's it. I normally get blood pressure checks. Stuff like that, that's all.'

He smiled and sat down again. 'I've got all that,' and with that he pointed at my watch.

'Your relationship with that little device will define your time here. If you find it invasive you may struggle. Embrace it. Its function is to keep you in good health and on the right path, both literally and spiritually. It's an astonishing piece of kit, totally tuned to the person it serves. It wants you to have a healthy and fulfilling life here. If you accept that you won't go far wrong.'

He continued, 'As you will have seen already this hospital section is quiet at present, and we want to keep it that way. We want the busiest bit to be the maternity wards in years to come. It is all about proactive and preventative care. It's an opportunity.'

At that point he stopped, maybe sensing he had said more than he needed to. This time I accepted his handshake and bid him farewell.

I retraced my steps back through the maze, locating the door to the social 'dome' or whatever it was called, without incident. As I walked back in it was still busy and bustling, although it looked more like a working environment now. Lots of little meetings, laptops open in front of the delegates. Some studying alone. It was approaching eleven. What to do now?

I stood in front of the giant message board with a view to understanding the messaging style people employed. I read a few when, ooh, there was one for me.

'Hi, Jack. Meet you in here for lunch at one, with David and Michael. Study your iPad in the meantime. Love, Sarah.' The message concluded with an emoji of a lady with a spikey bit of blonde hair Mohican style. That had to be her, didn't it? It was typical Sarah. Don't bug her with endless questions. Find out yourself.

I grabbed a coffee and sat myself down at a vacant table placing my iPad in front of me. It opened conventionally enough with a main menu, no password protection or anything like that. As with conventional iPads you simply touched the glass against the desired sub-section, and it displayed the detail held within. I hit the first sub-heading, 'About your new home' and it opened to a map of all the domes. The best way to describe the set-up would be to imagine a block of nine discs set up in a three-by-three formation. The three on the left were all marked 'Accommodation'. The middle three in descending order were 'Workshop', 'Gardens' and 'Social', where I was sitting currently. And on the right, again from the top were 'Farm', 'Hospital' and 'Control'. Now taking your thought of the block of nine discs and giving it a more accurate picture, you needed to push the three middle discs up effectively by the length of each one's radius and bunch in the two outer columns, to accurately portray how they sat. By doing this you could see the forecourt entry point to the 'Social' dome, between the first accommodation dome and the control dome, as well as appreciate the greater connectivity between each individual dome. Honeycombs came to mind. Yes, Tom would have approved of the design. The tenth dome was marked as 'Worship', and it was attached to the right-hand side of the hospital and farm domes. As a footnote there was mention of the two further domes Sarah had spoken of the previous night that were currently under construction to the north of the third accommodation dome and the workshop dome.

Each dome was two hundred feet high and five hundred and fifty feet wide, constructed in the main using steel and concrete. The skin of the domes was constructed in a similar fashion to that of the Eden Project in Cornwall insofar as it consisted of a collection of hexagons made of super toughened layers of ethylene tetrafluoroethylene. There were also toughened glass sections for use as viewing platforms. That was a thought. I hadn't seen one fish since I had arrived.

All the domes had multiple levels. The farm had loads, and appeared to grow every crop imaginable, from wheat and corn to rice and soybeans. And potatoes obviously. There were animals and insects. Cows and chickens for milk and eggs, nothing more. There were beehives at the rear of the farm and the gardens, for pollination and honey. In fact, the gardens contained many of the insects you would expect in an English garden. No wasps though, which was good. The workshop contained the means to build tables and chairs or hexagonal panels for future domes. It was mind blowing reading, and when you factored in that this was at the bottom of sea, even more so.

The 'history' tab mirrored what Aaron had told me this morning. Construction began forty years previously, originally just two linked domes designed for teams to stay for six-month periods of scientific study. Further domes were constructed in the following years and yes it spent time as a vocational retreat for the wealthy and powerful. People like US presidents. The worship dome was the final one to be completed, just over five years previously. The text did not say specifically but it was clear to me that by that time, this whole set-up's purpose had once again shifted to that of 'sanctuary'. Give Aaron his due. He and his group were given the gift of foresight for sure.

The next tab in my iPad's menu was marked 'actions', and I noticed within this was a set-up guide for the message board. Quite simple really. You just created your own signature and having done that you simply started typing your messages. You had to be careful with your first practice message as everyone would see it. I played safe. 'Hi Sarah. I'm sitting at a table near to the stairs.' Safe if boring. And up it popped in bright green neon on the board, bearing my signature for identification. Awesome. I was now a member of a massive WhatsApp group, of which I currently knew only a handful of members.

The time had flown. I spotted Sarah and the boys' entrance prompting me to check my watch. It was indeed one o'clock. They located me with little bother even though the place was filling up again as it was lunchtime. I got up from my seat and embraced the boys as soon as they arrived at my table. We had a little chit-chat, the three of us. They seemed fine considering. Sarah then sent the boys up to grab their meals while we held the fort.

'All OK at the doctor's?' she said.

'Fine thanks. He seemed a decent enough bloke.'

'So, what have you been doing in the meantime?' That question signified that if I had replied something like 'oh you know, just people watching' she would have kicked me in the shin.

'I've been getting jiggy with this here iPad.' I replied with a 'have some of that' twist to my words.

'Good. It's better if you try to pick it up yourself. And you know what a cow I can be.'

I smiled and directed her gaze at the message board.

'Well done. Just why have you signed yourself "Jack" with a germ emoji?'

'In-joke I had in a previous group.'

This was true. I had got it muddled up with a caterpillar much to the members' bemusement.

Sarah gave me that look women give men when they cannot be bothered with the nonsense they're hearing. The boys returned, prompting Sarah and me to go and grab a meal. When we returned the boys were discussing a group of ladies sitting two tables from us.

'That one with the short dark hair. I think she's French. She's so hot!'

Clearly it had not taken David long to adjust. Sarah looked at him with a mixture of disapproval and resignation.

'I don't think your love 'em and leave 'em tactic will go down very well here, David.'

'I'm just saying, Mum,' he replied giving out the mock shock look. Michael was giggling to himself, before he stopped and smiled at all of us.

Good for them. The business with Tom must have been killing them inside and they were putting on a brave face. Attempting to avert a reflective pause I quickly summoned up a question.

'Why grey?' I said, looking up and around at our external skin's colour scheme.

Michael jumped in this time. 'It's February. It'll change into varying shades of blue in a month or two. They try as much as they can to maintain the illusion of seasons here. The thinking is it's good for our mental health and in addition it assists in growing stuff. Guess they want us to have seasonal fruit and veg.'

'OK. I understand that. So how come I haven't seen anything of what's outside yet?'

Again, Michael replied. David was still focused on his French Mademoiselle.

'You can upstairs. There's a viewing lounge opposite the cinema and shops.'

Cinema and shops. Blimey. Now he mentioned it I had noticed some people taking their meals upstairs.

He continued. 'As regards restricting the view outside do you really want to wake up in the night facing a shark staring at you?'

Fair comment I thought. Or one of those bloody creatures. I didn't think it was appropriate to bring them into the conversation yet, so I changed the subject.

'What is it you guys are working on at present?'

Sarah jumped in immediately.

'A cure.' And with that she rose from her seat having finished her meal. The boys followed her lead. 'Time for us to get back to it. We'll see you down here at six.' With that they were gone.

After I had finished my millionth coffee so far that day, I tidied the stuff from our table and headed upstairs. My initial gaze was to the right and to a row of shops which I began to investigate. The first shop on the row to the left appeared to be a bookshop and seemed as good a starting place as any. I bid the middle-aged man behind the counter good afternoon and he returned the compliment. I was currently his only customer.

'Looking for anything in particular, sir?' he said, in exactly the same way as he would have done had the shop been in London, or Oxford, or anywhere.

'Not really, just browsing.'

'Feel free, sir. Just arrived?'

'Yesterday evening. I'm on the learning curve. Have to say I am surprised there's a shop like this here. It's great mind you. I'm just surprised. My name's Jack by the way.'

'Johann,' came his reply.

'Ah. Dutch?' I thought I had detected an accent.

'Yes. From Arnhem. Lovely place. You ever been?'

'I have actually. Yes, a beautiful city. We went to see the bridge primarily, but there was much more to enjoy, and the people were lovely.'

He smiled. One of the best compliments you could pay anyone, anywhere, was admiration of their home. I had made a friend.

'Of course, you are English. You would be drawn to the John Frostbrug. It has historical importance for both our nations. And you Jack, war historian. What is your hometown?'

'Dunstable, Johann. Not famous for much. The Priory Church and Henry the Eighth had some history. Roman crossroads. The Downs. That's about it.'

I was a long way from that church now.

'I would have thought these iPads would have had a selection of books in their memory,' I said.

'They do. Some people just prefer the feel of an actual book. This place works more like a library really in that people buy their book then often return it for a refund when they have finished it. We cannot really call it a library though. The range of books is limited. There is truly little reference material in the shelves pertaining to the period we were discussing for instance. Most of the books here are fiction.'

'Maybe there is concern with potentially flammable material,' I suggested.

'Our history is constantly flammable,' he said.

'My point exactly.' And with that I bade him farewell. I didn't really want to get tied down in political discussion on my first day. I was just trying to absorb as much as I could, to save getting moaned at by Sarah more than anything.

Johann smiled kindly as I left, so I couldn't have been rude I hoped. Next shop.

This one was difficult to pin down. It was a mix of ornaments, potted plants, keepsakes and cleaning products. There were a few customers busy looking for bargains, so I didn't engage with anyone. The final shop I visited was a clothes shop. Bear in mind none of these shops had signs or anything outside. There was no brand as such. Again, I looked around. Brightly coloured shirts and jumpers. Plain versions. Some with designs and some without. Brown shoes, black shoes, trainers, the lot really. Jeans and chino affairs. Everything you would expect to find. No maker's labels though, like Levi's or Adidas, plus I struggled with the fabric.

'Hemp, sir,' came the voice of an assistant.

'Most of our clothes are made from it. It's used for loads of things here. One of our most valuable crops. Not allowed to smoke it though I'm afraid if you're that way inclined.' He laughed at his little joke.

That was about it. The most noticeable thing? No food shops. With that I thought back to my kitchen and thinking on it I couldn't remember a cooker in situ. I was sure all would be explained in time, though it was odd. At the end of the row of shops, of course, a cinema. Amazing! Like all conventional cinemas it had a list of current movies showing next to their corresponding show times. There were some that had still been showing in all cinemas up top. *'Move – And You're Dead'* and *'Planet Claire',* being two such examples. Bollywood and Asian movies were also listed. There was a selection of oldies too and my eyes fixed on one of my favourites of all time, *The Invasion of the Body Snatchers*. That film was a hundred years old yet did it for me every time. I possessed it among Gran's archive stuff, but it would be fun to watch it in a proper cinema with a contemporary audience. One to pencil in I thought.

The viewing lounge, as Michael had referred to it, lay opposite the shops and cinema, the other side of the stairs. It seemed it was located behind a black plaster wall that sealed the entire section of the dome off from all outside. That seemed strange but there was a large entrance door which I approached as a lady opened it to leave. I entered once again to what seemed like a hundred tables and countless chairs. And the view! Wow! The entire section of outer skin was toughened glass, the view enhanced by powerful lamps on the outside shining into and illuminating the watery abyss. It was now clear the wall's purpose was to enhance that view, and there was a lot to see.

The place was empty, due to it being afternoon and people being at work. I grabbed yet another coffee and sat myself down facing the seabed. I detected incredibly soft music in the background, ambient music, designed to enhance the experience. It was hypnotic, like the most far out aquarium you had ever visited. You must understand we were at the bottom of the ocean; therefore, it wasn't all enormous schools of small fish. It was less densely populated but the population here was some of the most extraordinary creatures on our planet. There were giant eels. Some of the fish looked terrifying. Humpback angler fish I think and if so, it wasn't difficult to understand where they had got their name. There were giant crabs scuttling along the ground and multi coloured squid floating above them. Every now and then some weird looking thing grabbed another weird looking thing for food. There were these transparent creatures down here everywhere and if they got close enough to the window you could see the goo of microbes they were consuming as a meal. It really was extraordinary and what a panoramic vision. Every now and then everything would have to shift out of the way as a sub moved across the view. And yes, the Aja were down here too, all different colours everywhere. I spotted two, with what appeared to be a baby one in tow. I must admit, they were once again very graceful in their movements and the way they kept a protective pattern around the young one was quite moving. They had to be careful. There were sharks about. I had spotted two already, and while I wouldn't bet against the fully developed ones in a fight against anything, the young ones must have still been vulnerable, as they always are in all life.

I must have been gazing at this scene for over an hour and it got to the stage when I thought I'd better do some homework, or I faced a grilling from Sarah. There was a subsection in my iPad's main menu called 'philosophy'. This may be interesting, so I touched the glass against the word.

There was actually not that much. It was all about sociability. Ultimately, everybody here would eventually know everybody. Well, that was the aim. One big happy family I supposed. All meals were to be taken in the social areas downstairs and upstairs, where I was currently, or in the garden. That was it. The reasoning behind this was it again provided an opportunity for friendly discussion and introduction, plus we were guaranteed the correct amounts and balanced meals. That answered the lack of food stores mystery. It went on. 'Once the individual family structure begins to develop, meals within one's apartments will also begin to happen for obvious and practical reasons.'

Dr. Simmons's words from the morning began to have some resonance. Your relationship with your watch will define your time here. How did these gizmos exert an influence over portion control though?

And families? Please. No sinister breeding programme!

It finished with a spiel concerning the importance of what we were working towards. The impression I got was that this was the last chance saloon and renegade gunslingers were most certainly not welcome.

They didn't even mention the CCTV cameras all around. I took that as an attempt not to insult our intelligence. Present company excepted, this place was inhabited by the best of the best, salvaged from a dying world to prolong the species. We were being watched for our own good, weren't we?

I decided to put the iPad down and knock the conjecture on the head for the final hour until I met up with Sarah and the boys, once they had clocked off for the day.

The boys didn't hang around. They were off to the movies.

'What you going to see?' I was genuinely interested.

'*Our Man in Havana*, Jack.'

'Wow. That is one old movie.'

'Yeah. Still good though.' Michael being a bit defensive in his reply.

'For sure. Great movie. Great book too,' I quickly came back with, not wanting to cause offence.

The boys finished their meals and headed off, wishing us a pleasant evening.

'Graham Greene had some controversial opinions for his time, didn't he, Jack?'

'He did.' And considering her question I wondered if our powers that be fully understood the message behind that movie I had spotted earlier.

Sarah suggested we spend some time in the gardens. She explained that they could be accessed through doors either side of the wall of food; therefore, the nearest one to us was the one on the left. We passed through the door and entered a brightly lit corridor veering to the right. I imagined behind the walls the kitchens to my right and maybe the second accommodation dome to my left. We walked between fifty and a hundred yards or so and then came upon the big entrance door at the top of five concrete steps, bearing large green lettering announcing 'Gardens'. The door was quite thick and produced a low-pitched hiss as we opened it. As it closed behind us the first thing that became apparent was the temperature in here was a few degrees higher. Not tropical but warmer, humid even.

This dome initially appeared to be an indulgence. It was Eden, or near to the image of Eden that we carry in our heads. There were trees and plants and borders of tulips and daffodils. There were orchids and all sorts, as well as large areas of luscious grass for picnics maybe, dissected by streams and babbling brooks. There were fish in these streams. I saw carp, I'm sure, and many smaller ones I couldn't identify. There were pathways, some leading up almost to the top of the dome where vantage points had been designed enabling you to look down on this creation. The colours took your breath away. As I looked deeper, I saw that this place had a function too, for there were apple trees, orange trees, lemon trees. I could see what looked like a cherry orchard in the distance. There were benches and wooden tables scattered around. To my right was the dining area comprising of fifty or so tables quite close together and full of people eating and talking. The outer skin of the dome was covered with climbing plants which dampened the sound of their chattering. There was also the low hum of insects. This place wouldn't work without them. Huge lamps at the top of the dome provided the 'sunlight'. Unlike the other domes I had seen so far, this one just had the one level although, as I said, there were pathways built on large rocks leading upwards towards, presumably, further plant life.

Sarah looked at me and smiled. 'It takes your breath away, doesn't it?' she said. She would have been in here a few times already but was clearly still in awe of its magnificence.

It was at that point I noticed a wooden sign on my right bearing the request, 'Please do not take any of the fruit. Everything within here is for our kitchens. Thank you.'

'We don't want to be picking any of this stuff then,' I said as I smiled at the symbolism of it.

'No. We don't want to get thrown out a second time, do we?' We both stood giggling at this for ages. We were all in need of some light relief.

We followed a pathway intersecting all manner of bedded plants until we came to a little wooden table with a bench beside it, not far from the centre of things. Next to us was a little rockpool fed by a passing stream. I gazed in.

'There're crabs and all sorts in there.'

'Not sure if they're farmed for food. Haven't seen any on the menu yet,' she said.

I grabbed her arm. 'Thanks for what you've done,' I said as I looked directly into her eyes. I could feel myself welling up a little.

'They didn't take much persuading actually. The boys were an easy sell but don't do yourself down. They like you.'

'Can't see why,' I said. I was honestly trying not to be gauche but I was damned if I could see what I brought to the party.

'We'll see.' She paused. 'Up for starting work tomorrow?'

'Of course.'

'Good. You'll be working in my team. I've got loads for you to do.'

'Excellent. I'm looking forward to it. And thanks again, Sarah.'

'You may not be thanking me this time tomorrow.' She smiled as she said it. 'Now, tell me about your day.'

A bee was busy at work among a bunch of yellow freesias in a flower bed behind where I was sitting. Its buzzing made me look round for a moment. This really was idyllic. Sarah, the surroundings, everything. I felt pangs of guilt for feeling as I did. Seeing the bee reminded me of Tom.

I told her about my doctor's appointment, my little chat with Johann in the bookshop. I told her of the wonder I felt in the observation lounge. I also mentioned I had spent time studying my iPad. Oh yes, and my breakfast conversation with Aaron.

'You had breakfast with Aaron Des Moines?'

'If that's his full name yes. He works in Control he told me.'

'He's the man! I'm impressed. What did he have to say?'

'Oh, this and that. The importance of what we are doing here. He told me I could have a little tour round the control dome when I'd found my feet. He's been here for a long time you know.' From her words and facial expression, I had the distinct impression I had a little 'one up' on Sarah by way of all this, so I spoke in an offhand manner to gently tease her.

'Well, if he's invited you for a tour, you'll have to take him up on that offer. Blimey. You don't hang around, do you? He's been here from the very beginning. Made his money by his mid-twenties I'm told. Makes him a bit older than I bet you thought he was. He was one of the "founding fathers" of this place. You see. I told you they liked you.'

I think she was quite proud of me. Well, there's a thing. I gazed around some more. So much to take in.

'What's that set up over there all about, Sarah?' I said having spotted a small shack at the far end of the dome, overhanging branches from trees either side of it giving it the appearance of how I imagined Hansel and Gretel's cottage would look.

Sarah smiled. 'I wondered how long it would take you to spot that. It's a microbrewery and cider press if you must know.'

'Nooo!'

'They are aware we're not machines. We need quality time and the means to relax. You won't pick the apples now, will you? Now you know there's a pint at the end of it.'

She laughed as she said it and her face lit up framed as it was by this beautiful backdrop. That would have been a picture you would keep on your mantlepiece forever. And what a tale that picture would tell. With all the dramatic twists and turns our paths had led us down. Would it have been better for me to have turned away from her and not engaged in conversation when we first met at the bar of that 'sort of' pub? Never! No way! I'd probably loved her from soon after we first met, and I loved her as much now. Besides, we would possibly both be dead by now if we'd passed each other by. It's all about the long game, I guess. Sacrifice and salvation.

Now I looked at her inquisitively. 'Well?' I said.

Again, she smiled. 'Our watches wouldn't allow it. We're still recovering. Our bodies won't be able to safely process alcohol for another week I imagine. Oh, cheer up. I'll buy you a drink next weekend maybe.'

I hadn't expected to have a drink again in my lifetime so I could live with waiting a week. Her crack about the watches intrigued me though.

'They glow red and you won't get served if they glow red. In essence it means you are attempting to put something in your body that would be harmful in some way. The same principle applies to quantity too, so I'm sorry but it's not going to let you have ten pints and a kebab straight after.'

'That isn't good for you?' I said.

A long sigh. 'Apparently not.'

She continued. 'I've seen them in action while I've been waiting to be served food next door. A Chinese girl was putting stuff on her plate and I saw her watch glow red when she put on, sweetcorn I think it was. The guys serving immediately removed it and her watch reverted to green again. Presumably, she has an allergy to sweetcorn that even she wasn't aware of. Whichever way you look at it your watch is designed to keep you healthy. Its purpose is benign.'

We talked for a while longer and then sat in silence for a while. The seating area was almost empty now. There were a couple of gatherings of people at similar little tables to ours within the grounds, but they were also starting to leave this wonderful place.

'There will be people here again in the morning when the night shift clocks off. Sadly, it's time for us to leave now. It's nearly ten and we've got a busy day ahead of us tomorrow.'

'Well, I hope the boys enjoyed the movie,' I said.

'Yes. I suspect they weren't too bothered one way or another with it. They're good lads. They knew we needed to spend some time alone. We can get together with them after work tomorrow. Maybe David will attempt an introduction to that attractive French girl, eh?' She smiled again although this time it was a maternal smile.

We left the dome taking care to remember the steps outside and walked the corridors back to No 61 AA1.

'Oh Jack. I almost forgot. I have something for you.' With that she rummaged through the bag she was carrying and pulled out a light brown satchel affair. 'It's for your iPad. Lots of people wear them. Men too.' It was her turn to tease. 'You're never too tough to carry your stuff.' She giggled after she said it.

'Thanks. And thanks for this evening. Oh, what time tomorrow?'

'Nine OK?'

'Of course.'

'See you at nine then. Your iPad will lead you to our bit. It was a nice evening. Sweet dreams.'

And with that she kissed me on the cheek, same as last night, and headed back to No 252 ALA1.

4

I thought science was supposed to be exciting. All explosions and cries of 'Eureka!' Seeing things wriggling around and multiplying or doing something crazy through the lens of a microscope. Sarah had me staring at a screen and making a note of the numbers displayed as every minute passed. After an hour of that I was measuring temperatures in various flasks and by the afternoon I had progressed on to releasing droplets out of various pipettes on to Petri dishes. This was more interesting work due to the different reactions from dish to dish. Some produced a little bit of smoke. Some went weird colours, and some smelt funny. I'm not selling it very well, am I? The guys I worked with seemed happy with my efforts though, and I was contributing which was the important thing. Every so often Sarah would come over and see if everything was OK. Doing her mother hen bit I suppose. As first days go, I'd had worse.

Just before six in the evening a new group appeared in our surroundings above the hospital. These were the night shift. I saw Sarah having an involved discussion with, I assumed, the head of the new team. A handover, I guess. He was tall and blond, with a blond beard. He looked Norwegian to me which Sarah confirmed later that evening. A good guy apparently. Once they both appeared happy that they were on the same page, we all packed up anything that needed packing up, said our goodbyes and headed downstairs for something to eat.

We all ate together that evening, all eight of us, including David. Michael sat on another table with all his particle physicist buddies. Everyone was friendly. They asked me about my life, and I gave them a brief and unspectacular synopsis before asking them about theirs. The bulk of the conversation as the evening wore on, though, was way over my head. I wasn't going to interrupt them mind you. Mighty things can emerge from relaxed post-work conversations, and if there was ever a time in human history to allow that to happen it was then.

People started wandering off to their apartments just after nine. They were all currently doing twelve hour shifts seven days a week. They needed their sleep. Pretty soon it was just David, Sarah and me still sitting at our table. Sarah looked at me.

'Sorry, Jack. That was probably hard going for you tonight.'

'What? An evening with "The Big Bang theory"? Whatever makes you say that?' I said.

David laughed out loud at that.

'Twat!' replied Sarah with her serious face.

'It was fine. They're a good bunch. So seriously, are you making progress?'

She sighed. 'We're making progress, sure. At some point we'll crack it. It's just when, isn't it?'

At that point, a new set of arrivals were making their way from the entrance to the assembly point. Maybe my eyes were playing tricks on me, that or I was tired. I had only been here a couple of days, but these young people looked a lot scrawnier now. Their skin looked blotchy and unhealthy. Nowhere near concentration camp horrors yet, but they didn't look good. The doctor had said yesterday morning he thought the tipping point would come in a week. This was the visual evidence. That thing was kicking in now for sure and it didn't bear thinking about what was happening up top. I thought of Hogarth's gloomy paintings. Rake's Progress, and Beer Street and Gin Lane immediately came to mind. Women abandoning their screaming babies, squalor, deprivation, all of that. These were not good visions, and compounded by Sarah's doubts about the cure, the reality of my situation as a new recruit at the lab seemed all the more absurd.

'I'll come in earlier tomorrow, Sarah, if you need me to.'

She smiled wearily. 'Thanks. Don't worry, nine is good. Gives us a chance to set stuff up. You did well today. Everyone likes you. You're a valued team-mate, believe me.'

'He was a bit of a lummox with the pipettes though Mum,' David said.

With that they both laughed out of tiredness more than anything else.

I looked at them both and they laughed again. 'You were fine, Jack. Now come on. Let's call it a day.'

That was Sarah calling the shots. I was in her world now, and she was the boss. We got up and made our way to the exit door, and then it was the final stroll of the day, negotiating the avenues and alleyways.

I think it was the Friday. Nearly a week had passed by. The team were having their evening meal, Michael had joined us for this one, and the conversation was, as normal, science based. I was joining in a bit more now and fair play to my colleagues, they encouraged me to. So, there had been something that had been bugging me and I couldn't see anything about it in my iPad. At the risk of appearing dumb I came out with it.

'We're working, aren't we?' Simple question.

'Yes.' In unison.

'So, to get these meals and things we get paid I guess?'

'Yeeeas.' They were encouraging me to stick with this.

'So how does it work? How much do I get paid? Do I see what I am getting paid? Is it money, or beans or something? How do I know how much I have in my account? Do I have an account? Can I afford a new shirt maybe? How do I budget what I've got? What happens if I'm halfway through the week and I've blown it all without realising? I mean I'm sure you guys, and girls, get more than me and quite rightly so. You're the experts. You know what you are doing. I'm the home help and I'm more than happy to be that. I enjoy working with you all. I admire your work ethic. I bow my head to your knowledge and expertise. There's no resentment on my part, I can assure you of that, and Sarah and the boys will back me up there. I just want to know where I am. That's all.'

They all fell silent looking straight at me. Not nastily. I don't think I had made a fool of myself. Sarah was smiling. It fell to Lukasz to reply. Lukasz was Sarah's number two. He was a Polish guy, late twenties, with crazy hair and a wicked smile, and he was funny. He had been here a bit longer than most of us. I really liked Lukasz.

'Wow, Jack. Lot of questions.' He opened with a big grin.

'Yes, we obviously get paid. Hmm, well it's more like an allowance, I think. There's no money as such. And we all get the same. Everyone. Even the big boys in the dome over there.' He pointed to the control dome, and continued:

'Well that's what I'm told anyway. We all get the same. As for how much? We all get enough. We get as much as we need. For example, you will always be able to get three meals a day. Always. Every day. But you will not be able to get four. Your watch will glow red and they won't serve you. And if you only have two meals one day you won't get four the next day unless you are suffering from malnutrition or some shit. The concept of saving doesn't really work here. And as for an account. You seen any banks since you've been here? That's a good thing surely? No fucking banker bastards. What you going to save up for anyway? A new house?'

Everyone laughed, me included. Lukasz had hit his stride now. He continued.

'As for the new shirt Jack. You have seen the clothes shop? Some nice stuff in there. The fucking hemp itches a bit on first wearing but it's OK after a wash. Same principle. If you need it, you're watch will glow green, and you take it to the assistant who registers you've bought it and that's it. Happy days. However, should you go back to the shop the next day and try to buy another shirt, your watch may glow red, because you don't need it. Same as the fourth meal in the restaurant. Same with all clothes, boys and girls.'

At this point David cut in. 'Yeah, it's killing Mum. Rationing on shoes and handbags.'

Sarah gave him a soft punch in the arm, and everyone laughed again. Back to Lukasz.

'This is funny right. See little Mateusz sitting here next to me?'

Mateusz bore the look of a man who had heard this tale that was coming a hundred times. Resignation as to what was to come poured out of him.

'So, Mateusz fancies this little Italian chick who sometimes works at the food counter. Foxy looking lady.' He made all the appropriate hand gestures to emphasise his point.

He continued, 'He'd been banging on about her for weeks, so it gets to the stage where we're saying, "Well go on then for fuck sake. Make your move before someone else grabs her." Give him his due, he'd started to develop a dialogue with her. I mean, I couldn't see anything coming from it, but you never know. Subsequently, he develops a plan. He'd noticed that she seemed to have a routine of sitting alone after her shift finished on a Saturday evening, around seven, drinking a coffee then presumably heading back to her apartment. Therefore, little Mateusz's genius plan was to get all dressed up, ask if he may join her for coffee, and then suggest they maybe go upstairs and watch some fucking shit girlie film or something.'

Mateusz was visibly wincing by now. But there was no stopping Lukasz.

'So, he's got his best shirt, and shoes, but he thinks he needs a pair of trousers to set it all off. And he asks me to go with him to the shop to give him a second opinion. I'm his friend. I am your friend aren't I, Mateusz?'

Mateusz gave him that look that said yes, he was his friend, but he was also a nightmare. Before he could confirm or deny anything Lukasz was up and running again.

'We're looking at all these fucking trousers. They've got all the sizes. They've even got a size that fits podgy bastards.'

Mateusz was short and chubby. Some people just were.

'He tries a couple of pairs on and we decide on this particular pair. But when he goes to the assistant his watch is glowing red. He tries tapping it but no effect. Still red. So, he thinks maybe the other pair were cheaper, and he tries to buy them. But still his watch is red. He is confused. Now I don't know why he thought he needed these trousers. Did he think he was Danny fucking Zuko? Good luck with that! Trousers or no trousers, he was Mr Potato Head. I am sorry. Poor Mr Potato Head.'

With that he gave Mateusz a big hug. Mateusz accepted it and said nothing. He still had that resigned look about him.

'He pleads with the assistant. Not loud or rude. Mateusz isn't like that. He cannot understand why he can't have these trousers. "Because you obviously don't need them" came the reply. "But I want to impress someone," he says.'

Lukasz started laughing at this point. It was all a bit cruel and he put his arm round Mateusz's shoulder once again. There did seem to be genuine affection between these two.

'The assistant feels sorry for him, but there's nothing she can do. She tells him the trousers he is wearing look fine to her. They make him look a very handsome man.'

This was too much for Mateusz. 'She didn't say that, you cock.'

Lukasz was laughing so much.

'No, you're right Mateusz. I made that up. Anyway, in the end he gave up and walked out of the shop, a sad little Mateusz. Now, get this, as we're walking down the stairs, just as he thinks things can't get any worse, he spots his sweetheart sitting at a table, holding hands and snuggling up to a boy. A fucking German boy! What a kick in the nuts.'

He paused at this point and put on a serious face. 'I'm sorry. She was clearly no good for you.'

With a shrug Mateusz agreed. 'No. It would appear she wasn't. Why do you have to keep telling that story?'

'Because it proves a point.'

'What point does it prove Lukasz?'

'You obviously didn't need those fucking trousers. Did you, my friend? The watches. They know.'

It was almost like a comedy routine and we were obviously not the first to have heard it. Mateusz did not seem overly bothered. Lukasz had his stage. They were both cool so everyone at the table laughed.

At this point Mateusz piped up. 'Next time ask Lukasz about Barbara and the shells.' He grinned as he said it.

Lukasz laughed out loud. 'Oh man. Did I fuck that up good and proper? Those fucking shells. Next time my podgy little friend. You will have your moment at my expense for sure. I promise. Now it's time to get your beauty sleep. Ha ha, fucking beauty sleep … Mateusz. That's a laugh. We've got another busy day tomorrow.'

With that we all got up to leave.

'Well thanks for answering my questions, Lukasz. It's all so much clearer now.' I smiled at him as I thanked him.

'No problem. Anything you need to know. Come to us. We're more than happy to help.' With that he shook my hand before he grabbed Mateusz and they headed off to their respective apartments, followed by all of us.

5

The beginning of the end manifested itself at the end of my third week down here. It was a Saturday, but it was still a workday, me included, so I arrived in the social dome at my usual time of around eight thirty to grab some breakfast. As I sat down at a table to the left of the stairs as you look from the entrance, I noticed the set-up for the new arrivals had gone. Its place was now occupied by more tables and seating. That was it then. Everyone who could be brought here was now here. Sadly, I wasn't totally surprised. The new arrivals during the last week had looked in a terrible state. Like in a 'may not live for long' state. The doctor had said that first morning I was here that he didn't hold out much hope for anyone by the end of that week. When I had visited him a week later as requested, he thought it would be a few days and they'd stop. But they had kept going for a further week and a half which was amazing. It was staggering that the whole operation above ground had held out.

You just have to try your hardest, don't you? Still the feeling remained that those recent arrivals would be in the hospital for some weeks yet.

I checked out fine. Next visit in six months' time. Oh, by the grace of God.

Sarah and I were discussing this that same evening, while we were sitting in the observation lounge watching the weird and wonderful goings on outside. She had seen some of the later arrivals in the hospital and was not confident as regards their chances. We agreed it was a noble effort to persevere with trying to save as many people as possible, even up to the point where it may have been too late for them. As I said this, I was watching a couple of Aja hoovering up what I could only assume was our rubbish, off the seabed. And please remember when I say 'our rubbish' I am referring to our exploits on land. This operation generated zero waste. Everything was recycled. Everything! Anyway, it occurred to me that no one had really mentioned the Aja much since we'd been down here. I mentioned it to Sarah.

'Think the jury's out, Jack,' she said.

At this point two guys sitting at a table next to us leaned across to where we were sitting.

'Excuse us,' said the first guy. 'We couldn't help overhearing your conversation.'

The pair of them were of a tanned complexion. Five feet five in height, early thirties. Possibly Spanish. Good looking guys.

'May we?'

'Of course,' Sarah said. They moved their chairs over to our table.

'I am Raul. This is my friend, Adriano.'

'Pleased to meet you chaps. This is Sarah and I'm Jack.'

'Ah, very beautiful,' sighed Adriano.

'Thank you,' I said. Bit of comedy to break the ice there.

We explained we were relative newcomers and we were working on a cure for what was happening above. Well, Sarah was working on the cure. I was bumbling about the lab like a fish out of water. That made them laugh.

'Raul and I have been down here now for ten years?' He looked at Raul. Raul nodded.

'Yes, ten years,' he continued. 'We fit the panels to build the domes. The robots do most of the work for us now, though there are some tasks they will never be able to do.' That last bit he said with pride. 'There are twenty or so of us working in shifts, seven days a week. You may have seen our subs passing by the window?'

'Yes. Yes, we have,' I said. 'Building these domes must be some task.'

'Yes, it's a skill for sure.' Adriano was proud of what they had accomplished, and I could see he welcomed my admiration. This time Raul cut in.

'It's a good job. It was a particularly good job. Six months on. Six months off. Good pay. We could go travelling in our "down" time or as the years passed, go back to our homes and wives in Portugal. Good life.'

Ah Portuguese. Glad I found that out before I asked them if they were Spanish. That wouldn't have gone down well.

'Did they allow you to bring your wives and children down here?' Bit of a risky question from Sarah there. Had to be asked though.

'Yes, our wives are here, and we are grateful for that. No children yet. Both Adriano and I and our wives were of the same viewpoint. Why bring little ones into a world that is doing its best to destroy itself? It's a cruel thing to do.'

'You could see this coming?' Sarah said.

'When people start messing with things they don't understand, no good comes from it,' Raul said.

'We disrespected the natural order.' Adriano this time. 'There are many things of which we have absolutely no comprehension. The Parade of the Mimics. Always sometime during the first week in May. Once you've witnessed that you will understand what I am saying.'

The Parade of the Mimics? Both Sarah and I looked quizzically at each other. No time, Raul had moved on.

'You don't much like them do you, Jack? Even as they clear the sea of our filth you view them with hostility.'

I looked at him and shrugged my shoulders with a 'guess so' manner.

'You think we are down here because of them. You are wrong. We are down here because of our greed and our ignorance. We abused them in the same way we abused everything. Take the fishing thing as the prime example. Greed, Jack. Pure and simple.'

It was Adriano's turn now. 'We both come from Tavira on the southern coast, not far from the Spanish border. There's loads of fishing there. And many restaurants and merchants that depend on the fishing. So, when all hell broke loose with those creatures getting caught up in the nets, you know what we did?'

Both Sarah and I shook our heads.

'We used smaller nets, so we were sure of just catching only what we needed to catch. Sure, it was a more expensive way of fishing, so we balanced the books by charging the tourists more.'

With that they both laughed at the simplicity of the solution.

It was Raul's turn again now. 'Have you ever wondered, Sarah and Jack, why they can breathe air?'

'A thousand times,' Sarah answered him. I think she wanted to insinuate to this pair that we were not morons or, for that matter, part of the problem.

'Of course you have. You are a scientist. You seek the truth. Have you ever considered the possibility that a long time ago these creatures may have lived on land breathing the air, but were forced into the sea when we poisoned the atmosphere so much it burnt their lungs ingesting it?'

'The thought had crossed my mind,' she said. 'There's no evidence of them though. No written reports of sightings. No fossil remains. Nothing.'

'I take your point.' Raul said. 'All I'd say is have we looked everywhere, and have we understood everything we have read?'

With it all starting to get a bit metaphysical both Sarah and I began the shuffle to signify we were off.

'I genuinely hope we haven't hi-jacked your evening,' Adriano said apologetically. 'It's nice to meet new folks down here.'

'It's been a pleasure talking with you.' Sarah reassured them. 'One question though.'

'Go ahead.' Raul that time.

'Will you consider having children now?'

Adriano jumped in. 'When it settles down. You bet, Sarah.' Raul nodded in agreement.

We bid them both goodnight and headed for the exit door. As we did, I took one last look out into the ocean, and would you believe it one of those creatures was staring at me through the outer skin. Definitely. That eye was matching my stare much as I had seen in previous encounters. Only difference was this time the expression, if there was an expression, was more one of acceptance. And the light show from its torso was faster and more furious than before.

'You've made a friend, Jack,' shouted Raul, and they both laughed heartily at their joke.

I followed Sarah out through the door. As we walked down the stairs to the emptying restaurant area, she turned to me with a grin.

'Well, that's us told then, isn't it?' And we both laughed as we headed to our respective apartments.

March 17th was a Wednesday. I had been here just over six weeks, Sarah and the boys seven. For all that time I had never seen them at breakfast due to their earlier start time in the lab. This morning they were sitting at a table waiting for me. Due to the fact they were in what had become our preferred spot, just to the left of the stairs, I spotted them immediately. In doing so I had done well. The place was full this particular morning. All three got up from their seats as I approached, and on my arrival, we engaged in a group hug. As we stood in an embrace my eyes caught sight of the message board. Today there was only one message. In large neon letters it read, 'All work is optional today. Services will be held during the day in all our preferred places of worship. Today, as in every day, we are all as one.'

If it was a shock, it was not a surprise. The last set of new arrivals over the previous three weeks had shuffled to the now defunct assembly point looking half dead, and word had it that after hospitalisation three of them had not survived. That said, the thought of ten billion people perishing on the surface was dreadful.

My mind drifted to the family I had left behind, including Mum's lot in Australia. I thought of beer buddies, friends and people around my town. Yes, I thought of the lady in the newsagent too. Must confess I had had an eye on new arrivals in the hope that maybe she would have been among them. Sadly, to no avail. And I thought about Tom. Wow, if the thought was painful to me what it was doing to my compadres didn't bear thinking about. As we slowly moved apart, I saw the same expression on all their faces. The sad smile. All watery eyes and lost for what to say, because what could you say? I knew Michael would struggle the most. He had always been the closer of the twins to Tom, following him in his chosen science and all that, and now he was clearly the most withdrawn of the three of them.

Sarah was the one to speak first. 'Will you be OK if we leave you and go and get on with something? Everyone's going to work today, or nearly everyone, I think. It's cathartic. Get some breakfast inside you and we'll see you when you're ready.'

I assured them I would be fine and that I would join them when I had finished eating. They remained at the table while I grabbed some food, and once back they left for work and I was joined by two French chaps. Understandably, conversation was limited, but on leaving the table we each embraced one another before we left to deal with the rest of the day. On my way to the exit door, I'm sure I spotted various ex-government ministers conversing with fellow diners. If they were genuine it would have hit them hard. This was not a time to be cynical.

I did wander into the worship dome briefly during the break for lunch, my first visit I am ashamed to admit. It consisted of numerous small buildings, to accommodate the various faiths. The separate buildings bore no architectural style as such, designed as they were as box shaped halls, all of them spread over two floors. It looked hastily put together and I imagined each would develop their own idiosyncrasies over the coming years. At that time, if I were being cruel, it more resembled a fast-food mall without the neon and accompanying tat. The only identifying markings were each religion's recognizable symbol above the entrances. I spotted the Islam Star and Crescent to my right as I entered, the Wheel of Dharma to my left. Behind that was the Khanda and behind that the Om symbol. The mark of the Christian Cross adorned the first building upstairs, next to a Synagogue. And so on. The thought crossed my mind that the specific placement of these places of worship would have been justification for a war up top in years gone by. The vibe I got down here was people were just grateful that this human need had been accommodated. I hoped that would not change over time.

Around the circumference of the dome were the flags of all nations at half-mast. I didn't count but I was told there were one hundred and ninety-six which sounded right. In between some of the flags were chairs for people who didn't fancy the close confines of their place of worship. It was in one of these chairs where I chose to sit for a few minutes. Twenty or so were also sitting around the dome, and we watched various souls coming and going as we sat, just a nod to acknowledge one another. I couldn't face a full-on service. How on earth do you find the appropriate words to mourn the deaths of ten billion poor souls? I shut my eyes and pictured the Priory Church back home. I thought of the people who had built it all those hundreds of years previously, and I thought of their reasons behind building it. The desire for it to remain standing for maybe a thousand years, its only tangible use being to preserve the presence of God in our minds, spirits and souls. If I were to say I felt the presence of God at that moment I would be lying, but it occurred to me after all that we had done in the years leading up to this, for some reason the chosen few of us were still here. Amidst the catastrophe that was this moment, it became apparent to me that the great plan did not have us down for extinction just yet. That thought gave me some solace.

6

Michael had been spot-on. It was now the last days of April and as predicted, the skin of all the domes, as well as our apartment windows, now radiated a light blue colour. Not that Sarah and I could see this, sitting as we were on one of the benches in the gardens. The foliage was thick and all over the outer skin of the dome. This was our Friday evening glass of cider. We had weekends now. We were still working on a cure, but some of her time was now spent working in conjunction with the farm and food cultivation. Devising ways of improving yields and suchlike. There was still urgency to her work, as there was to everyone's. It was just restrained now. People had time off.

Our watches allowed us to have two glasses of cider three times a week before they glowed red. Not ideal compared to the old ways, but then again, a lot of things weren't ideal compared to the old ways. I adopted the mindset that I was being looked after. I was being enabled to lead as good and as productive life as I could under the circumstances.

Sarah was elsewhere that evening. Anything I said was met with a reflective 'yeah maybe', or just a 'hmmm'. She was unmistakably distracted. Was it me? Had I messed up at work and she was trying to find the words to tell me I was sacked? After all these years I could still never really tell what was going through her head. Mostly it was part of the attraction, the 'mysterious lady' kind of thing. This evening it was unnerving. I knew there was no point in asking her what was up. That would have been met with a 'nothing' and irritation on her part. We sat in silence transfixed by the waterfall in front of us. Yes, this place had a waterfall now. How could anyone have any concerns in a place like this?

'Shall we go, Jack.' It was not a question, spoken as it was as she finished her drink. We walked toward our respective places of rest in silence. As we approached No 61 AA1 she asked me if she could come in for a few minutes. This was a first, and a bit ominous. Of course, I invited her in.

'Love what you've done with the place,' she said with a slight grin.

I'd decorated the coffee table with a plant. That was it. I offered, but she was not in the mood for tea or coffee.

'Jack, there is something I have been meaning to discuss with you.'

I was sacked?

'I feel terrible. I should have told you years ago. The time was never right. I lacked the courage. And the longer I left it the harder it was to broach the subject. But it's no excuse and I honestly don't know if you will ever forgive me, which would break my heart, but you would have every right not to.'

She was on the ropes for sure. That last statement had been followed by her welling up. I offered her a tissue to wipe her eyes. She refused, cursing her weakness. I didn't say a word. She'd been building up to this for some considerable time, evidently, so it would have been an irritant me wading in. In addition, I wanted to hear what she had to say. I wanted to watch her facial expressions. I wanted to hear how she justified her behaviour because I now knew where this was leading. Come on Ms Tough Nut, let's have it.

'David and Michael.'

'Yes, my godsons, Sarah.'

'They're not you're godsons, Jack. They are your sons. I'm so sorry.' With that she burst into floods of tears.

To be fair to her I think she had tried to hint at this a few times before. I remember one such occasion round my place, after she first left Tom. And I had always suspected something was up. I had always been a far better godparent than I ever could have imagined, so had I been putting in subliminal efforts I would otherwise never have made? And then of course David grew up into an outgoing occasionally boorish young man. He most certainly did not inherit those personality traits from Tom. He was highly intelligent though, they both were, but that would have been Sarah's gene pool. And the jet-black hair?

I was less surprised than maybe Sarah would have imagined. But it still came as a massive shock hearing her say it. I composed myself. Sarah had recovered somewhat. I had been staring at her the entire time her words had been circling around my thoughts. She did have the look of someone whose heart was breaking, who was staring at the void. And even after that revelation I still loved her, and I hated seeing her in pain. Yes, after all that she had come out with. I must confess I had enjoyed watching her squirm at the beginning, yet now compassion for her suffering had taken over. At the same time, I was angry though, and that wasn't easy to hide.

'Why Sarah?' Keep it simple. Let her do the talking.

'It's no excuse. I may have mentioned before, I was very broody around that time.'

Yeah, that time. The whole damn scenario felt as fresh as if it were yesterday.

'When we came back from the Downs. After you'd had your thing. All I wanted to do was have your babies.'

'But you were in love with Tom.'

'I was in love with you both. I didn't plan for any of it to happen. My head was all over the place. After you left, I spent that whole night mulling it all over in my head. By the morning, my plan was to leave town as soon as I could and move closer to Cambridge. I had work friends so I could begin to make a new life there. And if you had got me pregnant that last time, I was sure I could deal with the single mother scenario. Anything was better than the mess I had made.'

'Tom won the day though, didn't he?' I felt bad talking about Tom in this context, after what he'd been through. It didn't seem right, yet I couldn't see another way of getting to the bottom of this.

'It wasn't quite as simple as that. I'd made my mind up, so the following morning I went round to Tom's place to tell him I was leaving town for good, and the likelihood was our paths would not cross again from that moment onwards. I'd spent the previous night rehearsing this speech, so I started totally focused. Unfortunately, as I was coming to the end of it, I made the mistake of looking at him, directly into his eyes. I'd been avoiding doing that beforehand, like all good cowards. He looked so lost, so fragile. What I was saying was killing him. He was so pure and honest I couldn't continue. I couldn't destroy this beautiful, innocent man. I stopped talking and threw my arms around him, and that was it. From that point there was no going back. We kissed, and my fate was sealed.'

'I was feeling it too at that time, Sarah.' I had to get my two pennies' worth in, although to be fair after the Downs, I felt more spiritual relief in unburdening myself upon Sarah than any other emotions.

'It was different with Tom. Look, I always imagined that in time you'd give it that shrug of the shoulders, dust yourself down and find yourself someone new. I think I've said that before. I'm not saying I didn't feel awful in my treatment of you, Jack. I'm just saying I trusted your coping mechanisms. I guess I underestimated the strength of your feelings towards me. I was amazed you stuck around as I've certainly said before. I really was.'

It was my turn to speak. 'In truth, I really don't remember much about the immediate aftermath. I knew we were finished, that was it. Looking back, I could well have spent the following months in a heroin daze for all I can remember.'

'You didn't go on heroin, did you?' she said with shock and concern in her voice.

'Well if I had done, I would have drunk the whole bottle.' And with that dozy comment I did exactly what I didn't want to do. I started giggling, as did Sarah. She wasn't out of the woods yet though.

'So, with Tom it was more … what?' I was getting to a place I really didn't want to be, and I bitterly regretted coming out with that as soon as I'd said it. I quickly followed it up with a new thread to try and consign the previous question to history.

'OK, so how did you know I was probably the father and, more importantly, did Tom ever know or suspect?'

'Tom was what you would quaintly term a 'Jaffa'. I sussed that almost immediately on meeting him. I just see these things. I have no idea how. He didn't have the faintest idea he was infertile and no, I honestly don't think he ever suspected the boys were anyone's but his. I'm not proud of what I did. I clearly wanted it all. I could blame my hormones at the time but that's a cop-out. I did a bad, bad thing and not a day has passed when I haven't thought about what I did.'

'And when I re-emerged from my withdrawal from the soap opera?'

'To see me six months pregnant? I saw the shock on your face and the awkwardness on Tom's. I couldn't have felt more ashamed. But it was the path I was on then and there wasn't a thing I could do about it. A series of events set in motion. A lie I had to keep inside me. As I said, I hadn't expected to see you again. Around town maybe, though I'd tried to avoid your old haunts for fear of causing any unnecessary pain.'

'OK. I understand all that. But you made me the boy's godfather?'

'That was more Tom's doing.'

'Oh, it gets better.'

Her eyes were red and bloodshot, her skin pale. All her natural assertiveness had dissolved. She looked at me with that hopeless face that yearns for a forgiveness that can never be given. Like the ultimate crime of passion maybe. However much you explain away the circumstances you are still a murderer and that is how it will be forever. There's no escape.

'What about the boys?' I said.

'As far as they're concerned Tom was their father and they continue to grieve for him as such.'

That was Sarah's way of saying, 'I know I'm the biggest bitch that ever existed and I've ruined your life, but please don't tell the boys.' She could have even topped it off with a 'for Tom's sake', but she was better than that. In her defence she could have brought up the fact that I hadn't exactly displayed good potential for raising a family with my dream confession to her on the Downs. If the truth be told I didn't know what to think. I wanted to hug her, and I didn't want to hug her. The boys had grown up into successful intelligent interesting men. What was the problem? Oh, maybe it was the fact that I had been denied the opportunity to be their father, making them bit part players in my story, like Rosencrantz and Guildenstern, albeit without the betrayal on their part.

Too much. It was late and it was too much to absorb in one go. Looking back, I think I behaved well under the circumstances.

'Let me sleep on it,' I said.

'Do you hate me?' she said as she got up from my sofa.

I didn't but I couldn't say it, so I shut my eyes and shook my head with a sigh.

With that she gathered up her bag.

I remained silent.

'Goodnight, Jack' she said weakly as she closed my front door behind her, leaving me standing and staring at the space she had vacated.

Unsurprisingly, I didn't sleep much that night, all the events of all those years ago running around in my head. For twenty minutes or so she would be the ultimate villain, the scarlet woman. How could she have done what she did? Then the aspect would change. Tom had gone through his life experiencing the joy of being the father to two wonderful sons he would otherwise never have had. And he would have been a better father to them at that time than I would have been. Maybe, or maybe I would have transformed into a good parent. I'd been an exceptional godparent, hadn't I? Tom would have had his stupid bees to fuss over. Maybe without Sarah he wouldn't have ended up as the all-conquering hero taking on projects he should have stayed away from. And we'd still be living our lives on terra-firma moaning about not having cod and chips for dinner anymore. Too much.

The truth was the cancer would have killed Sarah without Tom's input. It always came back to that.

And we never really learnt to live alongside the Aja, so the likelihood was we would most likely have finished up down here with or without Tom's assistance. On top of that, in what was an unorthodox way, I had ended up where I was with a loving family, if a slightly disjointed one.

The arguments carried on going round and round in my head. My main problem was my current location. Had this all unfurled itself a year ago I could have at the least embarked on a ferocious two-week bender to vent all my frustrations, although I had a history of mixed results with them. But it would have been an option. Or I could have taken a more enlightened route and booked a flight to the States, with a view to losing myself in the Big Country, following in the footsteps of Dean Moriarty. Escaping from all responsibility and seeking adventure and spiritual enlightenment. Down here that was not an option. It was just too confined to set out on the journey of the massive sulk. Whatever happened I had to face Sarah tomorrow. And I had to keep it together. I would see the boys, who had now miraculously, before my very eyes, become my sons. How would I approach that? Eventually, I drifted off. I could deal with it in the morning.

7

One of the strengths of our new home was, by its very nature in those early months, that it didn't allow you the luxury of time to dwell on stuff for long. Without fail there would be something new to focus on every few weeks or so. The current time proved to be no exception. It would be May in a few days and that meant 'The Parade of the Mimics' whatever that was. There was a marked conspiracy of evasiveness amongst those who had witnessed it before.

'I can't explain. You have to see it for yourself', was the stock response from everyone I broached the subject with.

Sure, Sarah and I had been frosty for the days immediately following her little revelation. The boys put this down to a little tiff. Sarah was not just spikey in choice of hairstyle, and I had certainly had my moments as regards the stroppy department over the years. We all still sat together for meals with our colleagues, so civility had to be maintained. Particularly, bearing in mind where we were and how we were steered to conduct ourselves. Fortunately, conversation was made easy due to the expectations of the forthcoming event. Theories were put forward and discussed. These led on to more philosophical ramblings about our existence down here. We could still fish. Our subs set out on regular fishing trips. Lots of sardines, sole, hake and seabass so biggish nets, but now rather wonderfully no bycatch. It was interesting to listen to the guys who manned the subs talking about the Aja helping them by herding the fish and keeping the sharks and other disrupters at bay. Thus, there was co-operation. No one had seen that four-minute thirteen seconds performance since we'd been living in the domes and indeed lengthier residents had never seen it. Had it been intended as a warning and not necessary now as we were all in sync?

An interesting topic without a doubt, which also served to muffle the tenseness between Sarah and myself. We were heading off to our apartments at separate times but the medication of time passing, and immediate priorities, was taking effect.

On the evening of the first of May every inhabitant had found a vantage point to witness the event. The observation area on the first floor of the Social dome was rammed, us included. The messaging board downstairs now showed the scene outside, the same scene we were looking at. There was apparently also a viewing portal designed as part of the skin of the third accommodation dome. I'd never seen that. The Parade of the Mimics always happened in the same place, on the left-hand side of our world, which made the observation area ideally situated. And it always happened, when it happened, between seven and eight in the evening. That evening was a no-show, as was the next. For us newbies our initial enthusiasm was beginning to wane by the third night of May, though it was noticeable that this was not the case for the experienced dwellers. They noticed our somewhat resigned manner as we assembled just before seven.

'Stick with it guys. They always come.' And would you believe it, that night they did.

The view in front of us was unusually devoid of life. No fish of any sort. No sharks or rays. No crabs scuttling across the ocean bed. No Aja.

The whoops and hollers started soon after seven when the first of the orbs was spotted to the extreme right-hand side of our view. The Parade always passed from our right to left I was told. After a few minutes we could see over twenty of these orbs moving slowly towards our vantage point, all at various heights and distances from us. Keeping the whole show contained within our viewing range as they passed us. By seven fifteen our observation screen was full of these weird orbs, easily thirty of them by now. All different sizes, from a tennis ball to a medicine ball, floating slowly past. And they were all worlds. They were the views astronauts enjoyed when they took pictures of Earth when in orbit above it. Bright blue seas, the various shades of brown signifying deserts or wilderness, the green shades of vegetation and the whites of the Arctic areas. Clouds floating above it all. All of them, little worlds. Noticeably, while they displayed all these features that were familiar to us from the photos, they were not the same. The land masses were different to ours. There was no India or Africa for example. One of the largest orbs had an almost circular land mass surrounded by ocean. Others were more fractured, largely composed of islands. Curiously, the proportions of land to sea appeared similar in all these fantastic worlds. Just different in detail. As they slowly disappeared into the darkness of the ocean to our left, I afforded myself a sneaky sideways glance at Sarah and the boys standing next to me. They bore the same expression all the new arrivals had. The look when everything you knew and believed to be true had just been turned on its head. When the last small orb had succumbed to the darkness a small ripple of applause started up. This soon built to a riotous cacophony of bewildered clapping, so loud it drowned out any conversation; not that there was much. After two or three minutes the applause slowly subsided. But no one moved. The show wasn't over yet.

We stood where we had been standing for five minutes; a hum of indecipherable muffled chatter filled the room. Similar in a way to the hum at Lords before the start of the day's play. The occasional cough, no one moving from their chosen spot. Still no sign of any of the usual inhabitants of these ocean depths. The room was full of the odd tension of anticipation when, once again something began to stir from the far right of our viewing platform. Initially, it resembled a huge mass with no distinctive shape or structure. The conversation rose slightly in volume before it fell silent as individual shapes began to form within the approaching coagulation. By the time it had reached our vantage point it was all individual shapes moving slowly past us, all the same greeny brown colour. Most of them were the size of a family car, filling our vision. Ah, but what shapes! Aircraft,

215

helicopters, lots of tanks. There were some missiles as well as rocket launchers. Submarines. All of these I would describe as 'soft toy' versions of the real deal. The kind of thing a small child would play with in a bath. No discernible markings but maintaining enough of the intended shape to inform the viewer of what they were meant to see and understand. There must have been over a hundred of these 'apparitions' filling the lengths and depths of our vision for over ten minutes. I would imagine I was not alone in re-imagining military parades from places such as Moscow and Pyongyang over the years on the TV. This was for sure one surreal version of those. As with the orbs, these formations, once past our field of vision, dissolved into the gloom out to our far left. This time there was no applause, just an uncomfortable silence. The whole performance hadn't lasted thirty minutes in all.

That was it. We took a cue from the more experienced observers amongst us, and slowly the crowd moved off, still not much chatter. David, Michael, Sarah and I grabbed our usual table by the stairs and were joined by some of our regular colleagues, one of whom had been down here for a few years. This made the poor chap the focus of our hunger for answers. He was an extremely good natured middle aged American, Jeff, and he immediately sussed the coming scenario. He put his hands up in the mock gesture of surrender.

'Listen folks, all I've seen is what you've just seen. Same every year, never changes.'

'Well, what on earth is it?' said David slightly impatiently.

'It's the Parade of the Mimics. That's what we call it. You can call it whatever you want.'

Jeff was teasing a bit. He had a big smile on his face. I imagined he could still remember the first time he had witnessed the phenomenon, and remember the shock he had felt in the moments after. This didn't help David, though, and his open frustration prompted one of Sarah's looks.

'Yes, I know what you call it. What I want to know is what the fuck is it?' he rasped.

Jeff wasn't offended and he showed David some mercy.

"It', David, is hundreds of billions of microbes of various types. And to answer your next question if it's how they assemble themselves in that way, nobody has the faintest idea, but you must concede it is some achievement. The same every year.'

Michael's turn this time, 'Does anyone have an idea why they do it?'

'Oh yeah', replied Jeff. 'They do it because they want it to be seen by us. That's why it's always in the same place around the same time every year. They specifically want us to see it, once a year. Without fail.'

My turn. 'Does anyone have any idea as to what they are trying to tell us Jeff?'

'Best question of the evening. We'll make a scientist of you yet.' He smiled again, leaning across and squeezing my shoulder. 'The best minds to have inhabited this planet for the last twenty years have been working on the answer to that and they're no nearer to finding it now than they were when they first started.'

At this point Aaron leaned over from an adjacent table. He immediately apologised for eavesdropping on our conversation and then he spoke.

'The real sobering thought, is the further we try to delve into these mysteries, it becomes increasingly apparent that we have been ignorant for so long of so much of our world we once believed we ruled over.'

We all dispersed to our apartments very thoughtful that evening.

Two days after that bizarre vision I relented and partook in a couple of glasses of cider with Sarah in the gardens. I figured performances such as that made crying over spilt milk from thirty years ago a bit facile. We talked. There was a tension in the air that gave the evening an edge I rather got off on. Listen to me, my sixty first birthday just a few months away. We finished our drinks and walked out of the gardens heading for our homes. We stopped outside my place. Sarah hesitated, then asked if she could come in. Christ sake, what now? I opened the front door and we both went inside, sitting ourselves down on my sofa in front of my decorative plant on the coffee table. I asked her if she wanted a tea or coffee. She refused yet again and looked at me for a while. As I braced myself for the words she had surely come in to say, she pulled a bag of overnight toiletries from her hold-all.

'What do you think?' she said nervously.

'Doesn't the CCTV in the bedroom bother you at all?'

She smiled that killer smile. 'It hasn't been on since you moved in. They're overly cautious but they aren't snoopers. Or voyeurs! Trust me, we're alone.'

With that we kissed and effectively consigned what had passed to history; for that night anyway.

8

By the late autumn, to all intents and purposes we had become resigned, or acceptant if you wish, of our new lives. We still focused much of our attention on finding the elusive 'cure'. The business with the actual air was another challenge and did once prompt me to ask one of my regular dumb questions when I was with Sarah one evening. As follows:

'We're all breathing the air down here, aren't we?'

'Yes.'

'And we don't get sick, do we?'

'No.' She wasn't daft, far from it. She knew where this was going. 'We generate this air ourselves down here, so it is essentially artificial but functional.'

'Yeah OK, I understand that. Hence, my question is why don't we generate a massive amount of this air and blast it out up top so we can live up there again?'

A fair question I thought.

'Because it would quickly disperse and in no time disappear into the reaches of the outer atmosphere. Unfortunately, the air up there now would hardly be affected at the time of impact just through its sheer mass. If you remember, Tom designed a chain-reaction to take place. That's how he got his air to "stick" so to speak. Sadly, the trauma of the whole episode combined with his disintegrating health meant the key to "unsticking" it got lost somewhere in the recesses of his once magnificent mind.

'Michael and his team are working on that one and they are all incredibly talented, but they are not Tom, and never will be. I would be incredibly surprised if they come close to solving that little conundrum in the near future. I'm sorry, I think we have to accept that we are down here for a while.'

Now I personally didn't have a problem with that. I accepted that our controlled society was in place for my protection, for everyone's protection, in our quest to

219

prolong the existence of humanity. It didn't bother me that the freedoms that we once took for granted no longer existed for us. I'd lived through lockdowns before. For heaven's sake my early work life was a mission to save people from themselves and stay indoors. At least Aaron wanted us to mix with one another. I'd always considered our supposed freedoms to be something of a myth anyway. Diego Maradona may well have emerged from a Buenos Aires shantytown to become one of the most recognisable men on the planet, but he was one among billions. The rest left to live a life of squalor. Ask them about personal freedom.

My age also had a say in my acceptance. People like Sarah and myself had enjoyed a large proportion of our lives up top. We'd been given a fair crack at it. I could understand how it must have been tough for the younger set, who now made up nearly ninety percent of us. They would have been justified in feeling they had been robbed, all the hopes and dreams that would have been instilled into them by their parents suddenly disappearing into thin air, or rather Tom's air, to be precise. Hats off to them, they dealt with the upheaval remarkably well.

There was a huge distraction for them, though, that I'm sure helped. It was no secret that the apartments in the third accommodation dome were larger than those in the other two. They had two bedrooms for one thing and the other thing was they were largely uninhabited. And bearing in mind the male to female split down here was virtually fifty-fifty, all that had to happen was to light the blue touch paper and stand well back.

During the summer, the Social dome had transformed into a massive pick-up joint. They may have been the best minds we could have brought here but if they worked hard, they sure played hard. Requests for downtime periods as regards the bedroom CCTV screens escalated. The cinema did good business, all rom-coms naturally. The huge messaging board went into overload, all cryptic requests for rendezvous and romantic assignations. This was all part of the great plan. Specialist nurses and post-natal wards in the hospital were prepared. There sure was something in the air.

Soon Sarah and I struggled to get our regular pitch in the gardens. It was all young love holding hands and gazing at the streams and flowers in fond embraces. David and Yvette, his 'fit' French lady were regulars in there. David had a pragmatic way about him. We didn't flaunt it, yet it was clear to him that we were a mature in years 'item', to use an old-fashioned turn of phrase, and it didn't faze him a bit. Yvette was a love too, which made it a pleasure to spend some time with them. Michael, while all this was happening around him, was more comfortable hanging with his highbrow science set. He wasn't as hormonally driven as his brother which I thought, and I know Sarah thought, was a shame.

This summer of love had clearly worked for many. There were a lot of girls about now visibly fuller of figure. For some it had been an amusing distraction and for people such as Michael it was something that happened to other people. It was the middle of November the individual domes had reverted to a grey interior, and through all this Darcel had not reacted well. It was Michael who first brought him to our attention, just after the Parade of the Mimics. By all accounts he was a brilliant particle physicist. What is it with particle physicists? And although his name had French origins, ironically it had once meant 'dark', Darcel was English. He was just under six feet in height, skinny, black hair and a long thin undistinguished face. He resembled, to me anyway, one of those old police identikit drawings of a wanted felon. Some people, you can look into their eyes and you think you can see their soul; my lady in the newsagent a prime example of this. You couldn't see anything in Darcel's dark brown eyes. Not a thing. Unsurprisingly, he was not chatty, so it was a relief when he left us. Michael reckoned he was the best chance we had of unravelling the issue with the air up top. I had no idea of just how good he was at such things, but I had my doubts even after just one brief meeting with him. He may have had the ability, but not the temperament, to my mind.

And of course, after that initial meeting I couldn't keep my eyes off him, when the set up forced him to mingle with his fellow aquanauts or whatever we were. All summer I watched him when he appeared.

He preferred to sit alone, head buried in his food or a book or something. That was him, oblivious to the hormones and pheromones in the air all around him. Michael said he pretty much kept himself to himself in the lab and by the end of the summer had become unapproachable.

'No, no, no. You're wasting my time. Go away, I've got too much to do,' had by all accounts become a standard response by the time autumn was approaching.

I wasn't the only one keeping an eye on him. Members from the control dome would sit amongst us during mealtimes, and I was having breakfast with a former cabinet minister in the Swedish parliament one morning when Darcel kicked off.

'I'm not eating this slop you bastard! I hate you! I hate you all!' he screamed at the poor chap serving him.

With that he slammed his tray on the counter so hard the plate of food bounced up and smashed to the floor. He didn't care about the fuss he was making. He remained standing where he was and glared at everyone looking somewhat startled at him before marching off in the direction of his lab.

'That boy is a problem,' Viktor, my fellow diner said.

By the way Viktor was an excellent chap. I dined with him a few times. He was maybe ten years younger than me and full of stories. Also, on more than one occasion, he expressed a yearning for a good old-fashioned pub crawl.

'I thought you'd like him,' Sarah had said with that look of female resignation to men's many weaknesses. She could talk, as evidenced by the copious amounts of empty Rattler bottles left round my house after one of her visits.

At what point then does a problem become a liability? I would say that happened one morning, a month or so after his outburst at the food counter. He had dug himself into a bit of a hole through his actions that morning, the result of which was that he received a frosty reception from many, the food counter staff in particular. He didn't eat alone just through choice anymore. No one wanted him joining them. He was ostracised which, though on the surface may have had minimal effect, would have eaten away inside him. Also, sadly, some people aren't too subtle. I certainly heard whispered comments when he was about. 'Weirdo' and 'freak' being favourites. Now I didn't hear these words spoken by the occupants of the table by the exit door to the first accommodation dome that morning, but Darcel clearly heard something that he didn't like. So much so that he picked up a plant in its pot and from near to our favourite spot by the stairs, launched it at these poor folks' heads. Fortunately, they ducked and it's as well they did. The pot smashed upon hitting the wall behind them, such was the force and fury in Darcel's throw. The crash caused everyone to look round, first at the recovering souls at the table, then to Darcel. As regards Darcel, they had to be quick because only a few seconds after his outburst, two drones had sped out of the control dome and upon reaching where he stood each one hit him with a taser shot. As he fell to the ground, two chaps from the same dome grabbed him and took him back to where they had come from. That was that. I was waiting for the 'there's nothing to see here folks, now move on' speech from someone but there was nothing. People were shocked, and the victims at the table were fussed over, but soon people got back on with what they were doing. I think for a lot of people it was a relief that the whole thing with Darcel had finally come to a head.

About the time I had been asking Sarah questions about the air, Darcel hadn't been seen for a week. Yes, harmony had been restored and I think most people were simply relieved to be able get on with things without the threat of that gloomy, erratic man hovering around. It bugged me though, so much so that the following morning after our air discussion I finished my breakfast and headed across the floor to the door of the control dome. It opened automatically as I approached allowing me to march on inside.

There were many floors to this dome. Lots of machines. Lots of panels displaying lots of lights with individuals monitoring and manipulating them. Control panels covered the outer shell of the dome as high as you could see. There were other individuals marching to and fro, among the consoles dotted around the building, stopping for a while, adjusting this and that. A low hum of electricity in the air. The whole insides resembled a huge glitterball. In front of the steps up to the next level was a grand old table where Aaron and Viktor were sat. They looked pleased to see me.

'Have a seat, Jack. We wondered when you'd come to see us.' Aaron gestured for me to sit at the seat facing them.

'You were expecting me?'

'You're our moral compass. Of course we were.' Viktor this time.

'OK. Well you'll know what I'm here about. I want to know what's ...' I didn't have a chance to finish my sentence.

'You want to know what's happened to Darcel,' Aaron said.

'Yes. Yes, I do,' I said.

'You're concerned we may have done something awful to him aren't you,' Aaron said.

'The thought had crossed my mind.' I felt bad saying this. These people had done nothing to harm me and here I was acting like the head of some liberation army come to depose the evil tyrants.

'Look, Darcel was a bloody nightmare,' I said trying to temper my approach. 'I appreciate you had to act. All of this is too important not to have done so. And I'm not here to pass judgement. I just would like to know where he is that's all.'

At that point I spotted a former home office minister chatting to a couple of Mediterranean looking gents over to my left. They were joined by a young lady who could well have been one of our Royal family's outer circle. As for the inner circle? Stayed with the sinking ship maybe.

'In answer to your question we took Darcel where he wanted to go,' Aaron said.

What did that mean? Did he 'want' to be flushed out into the ocean. Had he 'wanted' to be filled full of drugs to make him compliant? Or had he 'wanted' to be brainwashed?

Viktor continued, 'We're not some 1960s dystopian vision. Aaron is correct in what he says. We asked him where he wanted to go. He answered, and we took him there.'

Uncanny. Could they hear what I was thinking?

Aaron took over again. 'Darcel had been struggling down here for months. We knew he suffered badly from claustrophobia when he was selected but the hope was, he would recover. Yes, we took a chance, but you see he had a brilliant mind, and the view was that if anyone could solve our challenges it was him. Sadly, as you know, poor old Tom was no longer in a fit state.'

The reference to Tom made me bristle but Aaron was correct in what he said. I got the impression he realised how I would react to his words. These people knew so much about me. He continued.

'Darcel was fine at first, but March 17th had a very detrimental effect on him. Now he was locked in. This was his home possibly for the rest of his life. At first it spurred him on into his work. Sadly, when the results failed to materialise the downward spiral began.'

Viktor cut in. 'You only saw the tip of the iceberg, Jack. His apartment was a disgrace. We were constantly clearing away faeces from the windows. The mirrors were all smashed. We had him in for counselling. That just made him more aggressive. By the time he made his final move next door we were having to have him monitored around the clock. Oh, and he spread faeces on his CCTV screens too.

What do you do with people like that? Your apartment's CCTV is just cosmetic, as I'm sure you've figured out by now. You aren't a threat. Well done. Darcel had his own bespoke team watching him.'

'Jack, this place runs along the lines of John Stuart Mill's harm principle. Probably taken as far as it is possible to take it.' Aaron this time.

'Everyone can do what they want as long as it doesn't have a negative impact on others. For example, the watches prevent gluttony which would impact on our health support people as well as put pressure on the supply of food. Although it may seem authoritarian, we try to apply it in a benevolent way. Darcel was beginning to cross that line, but we had to be careful not to cross a line ourselves if you see what I mean? He finally crossed it when he attacked those diners a week ago. We can't allow violence against our people and we dare not risk vandalism of our environment. We're on a knife edge here. It takes just one act of anarchy and our world is at risk.'

'OK. OK. I appreciate all that, Aaron. You said you took him where he wanted to go?'

'After he recovered from the effects of the tasers we questioned him in here. Explained the seriousness of his actions. And then we asked him what he wanted from us. Was there anything we could do to help him?'

'And you know what he asked for?' Viktor said looking directly into my eyes.

'Go on,' I said shaking my head.

'He asked if he could go home,' Viktor said.

I breathed out heavily upon hearing his words. 'But that's certain death surely?'

Viktor shrugged his shoulders. 'The outlook is certainly bleak up there. No one is denying it. He was most insistent though. And yes, you could argue he wasn't of sound mind when he said it, but in all honesty, where was he going to go down here? What, we just keep sedating him until his mind gives up? Is that humane? At least up there he had chosen his path, whatever the outcome.'

Once again Aaron spoke.

'We're not proud of all this. All we're trying to do is explain to you how our choices were limited, and with our duty of care to all our residents we could not afford to take any more risks. Bringing him down here in the first place being the first risk we took, as I explained earlier. He would now be in the same situation as he would have been had we not brought him, albeit a while after the event.'

These words clearly hadn't come easily to Aaron, and horrified as I was, I also tried to show some empathy. What would I have done in his situation? Listening to what they had said I'd have probably had Darcel in a sub minutes after he had expressed his wish.

'Therefore, you granted him his wish?' I said.

Viktor looked up at the roof then back down across at me. 'We gave him the night to sleep on it, in this dome out of harm's way, and we told him that if he were still of the same mind the following morning we would gather his belongings and one of the sub commanders would indeed take him back home. Well, he woke after what appeared a good sleep and told us his feelings had not changed.'

'Jean-Claude is a good man, and a good submarine commander. We explained the whole scenario to him, and he agreed to take Darcel.' Aaron's expression was sadness as he explained. 'It can't have been easy for Jean. He did say there hadn't been much conversation when he returned. Darcel had wanted to return to London so as was his wish Jean took him back to the aquarium, your point of departure all those months ago.'

Another outpouring of breath from me before asking, 'So I have to ask. What's it like up there now?'

Viktor replied this time.

'We asked Jean-Claude to send out some drones after he had dropped Darcel off. Like you we were curious to find out what our world was like after all that had gone before.

Accordingly, he positioned the sub in the middle of the Thames facing Westminster Bridge, and, being only half capsized, he opened the hatch in the sub's roof to release the drones. Immediately a crow attacked him, then another. If he hadn't been wearing his mask, he would have lost an eye. Understandably he released the drones and quickly closed the hatch behind him.'

'They're not scared of us anymore.' Aaron continued the recounting. 'It would appear they've acquired a taste for human flesh and they're more than happy to grab any fresh samples. It's brutal but unfortunately, it's the truth. And when the drones returned the view wasn't any rosier. The streets of London are now full of feral hounds fighting over the remaining scraps. The pavements are covered with bones and broken glass. It's a tough one to take in.'

'He wouldn't have lasted five minutes, would he?' I said. It was a rhetorical question.

Viktor let out a big sigh. 'We understand there were plans for subterranean settlements dotted all over the world. We have no means of contacting them now, so we don't even know if they still exist, or if anyone survived. I wasn't aware of any near to London, but you never know. People never lose the ability to surprise you, do they?'

I sat there for a while trying to take in all they had said. I guess the trick down here was just to get on with it. If you stopped and tried to imagine where we had come from and what it had turned into you could soon be following a similar descent to the one Darcel had taken.

'We have to be so alert.' Aaron this time. 'Brace yourself Jack. I have to tell you at this point that we have lost all contact with the other underwater worlds such as ours over the last couple of months. Our subs don't have the range to reach them. We keep trying to make contact, but we may soon have to face the possibility that it is just us keeping this going.'

No one spoke for some time after that bombshell.

I let out a deep breath. 'The subterranean settlements?'

Viktor looked up in the air and let out a big sigh. 'Maybe. As I said before we don't know anything about them. Nothing. There wasn't time.'

He clearly wasn't holding out much hope in that direction, even in the light of his previous comments pertaining to Darcel's chances up top. So, maybe it was all down to us now. Dear oh dear! Part of me wished I'd never come barging in to see them in the first place. I had to admire their resolve though. They were literally carrying the weight of the world on their shoulders every day.

'I think it's for the best we keep all of that in here, don't you?' I said after a period of consideration.

'Yes, Jack,' Viktor said. 'That would most certainly be the best outcome.'

Part 5

1

My final five years were great! I say that with an appropriate sense of guilt, fully aware of the horrors and suffering that had gone before. Many innocent people had been less fortunate than me. Sarah would berate me at times for feeling this way.

'Jack, you've been through the wringer. You've earned everyone's respect down here. Don't dwell. There's nothing to be gained by it. Embrace your situation. I love you. The boys love you. For heaven's sake you have a grandson now. You've done it, Jack, now stop moping and give me a hug.'

Yes, I was a grandfather, though officially I was just an uncle. Not ideal; you just compromise for the greater good and accept the trade-off. David and Yvette had fully embraced the initial breeding season, along with over a hundred similar minded couples. As a result, they produced a wonderful healthy baby boy the following July. They named him Tom, which was a nice touch I thought. Michael became his godfather. This allowed them to move into the third accommodation dome with apartments specifically kitted out for young families. They had luxuries such as their own cooking facilities. Their dome had its own parade of shops specifically designed for a young family's needs. They had a school there too. Whatever feelings anyone had about the way the place was run, you had to take your hat off to the designers, on occasions.

Over the years, the occupancy of the accommodation domes grew and grew until, by the time I reached my seventieth birthday, they were full. As a result, a 'one in one out' policy had to be adopted. In a nutshell someone had to reach the end of their life before any new birth could be sanctioned. It was a draconian measure introduced out of necessity.

Supermarkets had adopted a similar policy many years before during times of global crisis.

Despite my initial reluctance, Sarah made a big deal out of my seventieth. There were the usual banners displayed all around the social area on the day. The kitchens produced a ridiculously over the top birthday cake. By seven in the evening the place was heaving. The concession that sold the whole thing to me was that a PA was set up, and I was allowed to play my, or more accurately Gran's, music, so people could have a dance if they wanted to. I was mindful of keeping the mood light and fun, and I have to say the sight of everyone dancing to 'Stayin' Alive' by the end of the evening remained with me until the end of my days.

One unexpected result of the evening was it acted as a form of audition. The following morning, I was having breakfast with one of the guys based in the control dome, Miguel, a former Spanish interior minister. He was very animated, complimenting me on my performance the previous evening.

'You sure got people moving, Jack. It was fabulous. Everyone loved it. You seem to have a vast collection of music.'

I explained to him how it was Gran's legacy with a bit of my mother's stuff thrown in, and how it was not just music. I had movies and books and art and press cuttings from the period and so on. He listened, nodding his head before he made his pitch.

'Have you ever considered passing any of that on to others?'

I had to admit I hadn't.

'As you know, we have the school in the third dome which provides our children, we hope, with the foundations of a full education. We teach them history. The trick is to make them understand the life we all lived before, without making them restless and resentful. They have only known this world we are now in, and there is a possibility this is the only world they will ever know.'

He coughed and gathered himself, mentally preparing how he was going to phrase the denouement.

'We want to fill them with wonder. We want them to appreciate the beauty that we have, in the past, created, and to inspire them to follow in our footsteps. We believe you can help us achieve this. What do you think?'

I was flabbergasted.

'I've never taught in my life, Miguel. I wouldn't know where to start.'

'Well, we are thinking of an age group of six to seven years old. Initially your classes would comprise of no more than ten boys and girls. We'd give you the observation room upstairs for hour long sessions, maybe longer if you feel comfortable after a while. We'd give you a screen to show films, a little PA to play your music. You may want to just talk to them, within reason about anything. Hell, I'd even sit in with you for the first couple of sessions to give you moral encouragement if you need me to. What do you say?'

As I looked at him, I had to confess to feeling rather good about this, although a touch nervous. It was most certainly an honour to be asked. Yes, I was doing good, important work in the lab but here I could really contribute if I got it right. I just had the feeling that I was being presented with an opportunity that I would regret in later years if I passed it up.

'Can I think about it?' I said, attempting to be upbeat in my request.

'Of course,' Miguel said, smiling. 'I'm here every morning along with most other folk. Let me know your thoughts, maybe once you've slept on it.'

With that he got up, wished me a good day, and headed back to the control dome.

'Do it, Jack. You'll hate yourself in years to come if you don't. You'll be a natural. They must think a lot of you for them to ask. I'm proud of you.'

Well Sarah sure wasn't sitting on the fence as regards my next course of action. Michael was equally enthusiastic during our evening meal.

'I'll look in on David and Yvette later. Tom may be just too old for your initial classes. I know they will be supportive. We all will be.'

Seems Sarah had made her mind up. I still wanted to sleep on it but hey, realistically what did I have to lose, and as they say, God loves a trier.

Miguel was sitting with some colleagues the following morning. I caught his eye and he beckoned me over to his table.

'OK. I'll give it my best shot. No guarantees I'll be any good though,' I said, a bit defensively.

'That's great news.' Miguel got up and shook my hand vigorously. 'I'll let the other guys know and start getting you set up. You'll knock 'em dead, I just know it.'

The first session was scheduled for the following afternoon between three and four. My class was six boys, four girls, various nationalities. The first half hour was mainly introductions, followed by me explaining what we were going to try to achieve during the hour long get togethers. A tough one, being as I was still unsure myself. For the second half of our session I played some songs from the movie 'Mary Poppins,' which I thought may act as an icebreaker, followed by a sing-along. Give them their due, they listened and some asked if I could show them the film some time, which was positive I guess. The sing-along nailed it. Armed with my guitar and a basic dozen or so chords I began my rendition of '*Chim Chim Cher-ee*', encouraging them to join in. Unfortunately, they found it almost impossible to do, even if they had wanted to, due to them all falling about in painful laughter at my pitiful attempts to evoke the magical spirit of Dick Van Dyke.

Well, they left smiling. That at least was a good thing. Miguel seemed impressed too, shaking my hand enthusiastically as the kids trooped out. My reviews the following day from the mums and dads were positive.

Over the following months the sessions developed as we all got to know each other a bit better. My classes gradually doubled in size, and the length of our time together expanded to two hours, which meant I could show them movies. 'Yellow Submarine' was a hit with all of them. They loved the music, which allowed me to introduce them to more of the sounds and the art from that period. And Blue Meanies. If they were in the mood, we'd wind up the session with everyone joining in as loud as they could to the rousing finale to 'Hey Jude'.

Sometimes one or more would stay behind for a chat after the others had left. We would sit talking for half an hour or so while gazing out at the view the other side of the window. Ruben, a Dutch boy, always stayed. I knew his mum and dad quite well. They were a nice family, so I sort of knew Ruben before the classrooms.

Ruben loved the song 'Puff the Magic Dragon', and he was always pestering me to play it for him, which was not a problem. It had always been one of my favourites when I was his age, even, as it was, a bitter-sweet tale of growing up and moving away from childish things. In the last verse though, Puff was back in 'Honali', so everything was OK again.

The afternoon that sticks with me was just Ruben and me. I'd played his favourite song and we were sitting watching the inhabitants of the depths going about their business. Ruben always liked to ask questions. I encouraged him to, promising always to give him the best answer I could or come back to him if he had flummoxed me. He was in a question asking mood that afternoon.

'Jack?'

'Yes, Ruben.'

'Someone told me that up there some people lived alone in houses as big as our whole home here.'

'Yes, that's true Ruben. Some even bigger than this.'

This clearly made absolutely no sense to Ruben. He had the same look I used to have when people tried to explain quantum physics to me. I understood the meaning of the individual words but the combinations may as well have been in Nadsat.

'And some people had to squish up to make room for the people who lived in the big places?'

'Sort of. Some people just had bigger homes than others.' This was going to get difficult to explain, certainly impossible to justify.

'Some people who sang songs had big homes, didn't they?'

This particularly resonated with Ruben. I had noticed, particularly after I had been playing music, he would wander about trying to grab something out of thin air like you would a fly. I asked him one day what it was he was trying to grab hold of. It was songs. He thought you could capture a song out of thin air.

In his defence, metaphorically, that's usually how it was done.

'So why did people who sang songs have big homes, Jack, and everyone else had to squish up?'

I looked at him, shaking my head in acknowledgement of his question.

'I know it doesn't seem right. That's just how it was. If it helps, I'm quite sure Peter, Paul and Mary wouldn't have lived in a ridiculously big house.'

Remaining mystified trying to understand our past he continued to probe.

'And some people who didn't even sing songs had big homes. And the people who had to squish up got to watch them in their big homes on the television.'

I gave out a noticeably big sigh. 'Yes, that is also true, though I must tell you I neither lived in one of those big houses nor spent my time watching those people in their big houses. The main reason being they were usually idiots.'

Wealthy idiots mind.

Ruben laughed when I said that, even though it all still made absolutely no sense to him. We sat in silence, which was a bit of a relief, and watched what was happening outside. A group of Aja had appeared and were gliding around together in front of us bunched up quite tightly. Their tentacles on occasion became gently entwined with one another as they passed by. Blues and reds and yellows shone from their skins. Colours we still had not the remotest clue as to their meanings. I looked across at Ruben noticing his eyes had lit up at the sight of them. He wore the smile of a child who has been taken to a favourite place, like the seaside or McDonald's.

We sat in silence a little longer before Ruben sparked up once again.

'Jack?'

'Yes, Ruben.'

'Some people weren't very nice before, were they?'

'No. Sadly, there were some bad seeds.'

'There were people who used to take young boys like me and do bad things to them, weren't there?'

This was territory I had hoped not to stray into. This boy deserved an answer, though. Fortunately, there had been no repeat instances of the Darcel business. Everyone pretty much behaved in a civilised manner now. Getting on with life was the way forward and, in the circumstances, the correct way. There weren't any threats in the way Ruben was alluding to anymore.

'I'm afraid to say there were, Ruben. But all those horrible people aren't around now, so don't worry about them.'

'Oh, I don't.' Ruben said this with some confidence, smiling as he did so.

'The Aja will protect us from the monsters now, won't they?'

As he said those words, I'm sure at least two of them fixed their gaze on us from the watery depths outside. With that Ruben waved at them saying, 'Hello. Hello Aja. I'm Ruben and this is my friend Jack. You'll look after us now, won't you? We love you.'

And that is how we lost the top spot in our wonderful world!

Not through a battle or a great war. In the end we surrendered our place at the summit of the food chain, through an unconscious spin off from the positive eugenics at work down here. In just a few years the beliefs I, and my generation held to be true, would be largely ... well as *dead as a Dodo*. They would have been purged.

We would eventually re-emerge from the sea and once more make our home on the land. Of that I had no doubt. And when little green men visited our planet and asked to be taken to our leaders, we would point at the sea, or maybe at a garrison close by, and say matter-of-factly, 'That's where you'll find 'em, guys. Big buggers. Lots of flashing lights. You can't miss 'em.'

Sarah never fully forgave Marco and Elena which was unkind of her. The whole thing was my decision and mine alone. I was big enough and ugly enough to make my own decisions, certainly by that stage in my life. Granted, the closer to them we got, the more their desire to have children got a mention. And yes, Elena was in her mid-thirties which was a concern, but this was just conversation, general chit chat. I don't believe there was ever an agenda in our meetings with them. They were a nice couple. Marco worked in the farm dome, now domes, and Elena in the kitchens and serving area. By the time they hooked up, birth controls were in place, not their fault. It was never intended to be a race. They were a friendly loving Italian couple who just wanted to be together and eventually have a family. That was them in a nutshell.

I, on the other hand, was everybody's best friend, favourite uncle, ideal companion for a glass of cider, entirely due to my little enlightenment sessions upstairs. By my seventy fifth birthday I was holding four of these, every week, all two hours in length. My initial group had stayed with me. Ruben was now ten years old, so now I entertained a mix of starter sessions and then gatherings up to Ruben's age group. I had the privilege of being amongst the boys and girls as they grew and progressed, and the good fortune to possess Gran's vast library to draw on. This made me a draw for the mums and dads. I think some of them saw me as a lifestyle guru, which I most certainly wasn't. In the main, they just wanted to talk to me about their sons and daughters. When they had exhausted that topic, they wanted to know about me. I was economical with my history, preferring to focus on Gran's archives and the joy they had given me both as a source of study and now as the backbone of my teaching.

David and Yvette's Tom was now in his 'teens. Of course, he was a wonderful boy, as I would say as a covert grandparent. It was always a pleasure to spend time with them and Michael, and of course the ever-present Sarah. Even with our little family unit having its own unusual quirks, it felt to me as if I had finally achieved contentment, which was a truly magical feeling.

My only concern was outstaying my welcome. My general health was still good, thanks in part to my guardian wrapped around my left wrist. I had taken the doctor's advice from all those years ago and had made my peace with it. It had undoubtedly helped through the control of what I ate and drank and when I took exercise. My knees had seen better days. There were more 'comfort' breaks as the years wore on. My eyes strained slightly with the laptop screens. Otherwise, I was OK really. Yet I sensed the beginning of the decline was not far away, a few years maybe. Maybe less. In my vanity I wished to be remembered at the top of my game. On top of that was the fact that old age was an indulgence down here. Sure, I was satisfying a need with my groups of varying ages, but the whole driving force, the ethos here, was to maintain, continue and develop humanity. However well respected and regarded I may have been, I was part of the old guard, and it was, I felt in my case, now time for fresh blood. It was selfish and selfless on my part, and it was the right thing to do.

'You're a ground-breaker Jack, I'll say that for you. See, I told you that morning over breakfast you'd have a significant part to play down here.'

I don't think Aaron particularly wanted to see me check out, but he could see my mind was made up. His co-interviewer whom I had never met before was a large black Southern States American by the name of Reg, with accompanying dreadlocks and southern drawl. He just seemed full of admiration for what I intended to do after I had made my pitch to them both.

'Ya'll bow out the Champion of the World, Jack. Not many can say they done that.' He said champion and world as if with capitals as people did when they needed to emphasise words.

We discussed the whys and wherefores for over an hour. I insisted Elena and Marco be given the green light as soon as I had signed on the dotted line. Also, I wished to stick around long enough to witness the birth. In the meantime, it would be business as usual as far as I was concerned.

I shook hands with them both before I left. Aaron commended me on my altruism declaring I would be a sad loss for the community, but a true spirit to be admired. He didn't need to say that, but it made me feel good about myself and confirmed I was doing the right thing here. Now all I had to do was explain it to Sarah.

'You've done what? No, no, no, no. We're going straight back in there and you're going to tell them you've changed your mind. What on earth were you thinking? Is this some kind of sick way of getting your own back? David and Michael? Yvette? Little Tom? No thought of how they feel, it sounds like. Did bloody Marco and Elena put you up to this? And those pigs in the dome agreed to this? Well don't think I'm following you, not for one minute. I respect this life and I love my family, which clearly you don't. Have you lost your mind? Everything has finally fallen into place. We have a wonderful life down here and you've gone and ruined it. I'll never forgive you, Jack!'

Could have been worse I suppose. In the end, and after many tears and me being persona non grata for a time, there was no storming in to tell Arron and Reg it was all a big mistake on Sarah's part. It would have been to no avail anyhow. Once Marco and Elena had been given the go ahead the wheels were in motion. And they most certainly took the lead. Elena was pregnant in a matter of weeks. As with all the big decisions in life, once made and initial action has been taken, there's no going back. Sarah would have appreciated this more than anyone, surely.

There was most certainly an edginess around my last few months. Elena became increasingly embarrassed about her steadily increasing lump whenever Sarah was around. I think the boys silently admired my motives though they were genuinely sad. Would they have been more emotional if they had known the whole truth about them and me? Who knows? Sarah and I maintained our close relationship but there was palpable tension around us, manifesting itself on occasions like a wasp in a beer garden. She probably thought I had betrayed her in some existential way. Of course, there were times when I regretted what I had done. Sarah and I could have walked into the gardens any time and be as near to paradise as anyone could be. The thing is, and I had to keep reminding myself of this, nothing lasts forever. Ever. This way I was leaving on my terms, not through a haze of medication and well wishing.

And so, Marco and Elena had a baby boy which they called Antonio. I thanked them for that. I had mentioned I had known an Italian lad named Tony many years ago, omitting the details of our meeting. It was a nice return of a favour that they should name him so. Now it was my turn to fulfil my end of the bargain.

I deliberately engineered my final day as low key as possible. All Gran's stuff I passed on to Michael as he had expressed an interest in maintaining the legacy; unbeknown to him, his Great Grandmother's legacy. I mingled for the last time, subconsciously saying goodbye to everyone. At three in the afternoon I went to see Aaron and Reg for the final prep regarding the following morning.

'Are you ready for this, Jack?' Aaron said. Once again Reg was sitting alongside him.

There followed a massive temptation to say no, I had changed my mind. That would have been a right laugh, wouldn't it?

'Sure,' I said. 'Ten o'clock tomorrow morning at the rear of the hospital.'

'That's it. I'll be genuinely sad to see you go but remember, you've done a good thing here.'

Aaron was giving away some emotion as he said the words. I wondered if he had ever envisaged a conversation such as the one we were having, when he initially threw his quickly gained wealth into a new world at the bottom of the ocean all those years ago. Probably not, I thought.

'Present will be Sarah, David, Michael, Yvette, Tom, Marco, Elena and little Antonio. Is that correct?'

'Yes, Aaron. And if you could make yourself available, I would welcome you being there also.'

'I would be honoured.' His eyes reddened after he had answered.

'Before I go could I ask one question?'

'Of course.' Aaron leaned forward eager to know what was on my mind.

'It's about the Aja.'

'OK. Fire away.'

'Right. So what was the four minutes thirteen seconds all about?'

They looked at each other and smiled. Reg spoke first.

'Truth is, Jack, we don't really know for sure. They've never repeated it since we've been down here.'

'No, they haven't, have they?' I said.

'The general feeling,' Aaron took over, 'having spent a lot of time going over this with a lot of people, is …'

He trailed off giving his next words some thought before he said them.

'Our opinion is they did it because they could.'

I was no expert, but I always suspected they were showing off in their own way.

'We don't believe they were being malicious. They constructed a rotating sphere if you remember, seven or eight of them. If you stick with the image of a sphere, then remember back to occasions when maybe you threw a ball

243

for a dog to collect. You were having a game. And maybe sometimes you stood with the ball teasing your dog, pretending to throw it. Being mildly cruel I suppose but as I said, not malicious. Just letting your dog know who was in charge.'

After Aaron spoke Reg gave a big smile and looked straight at me.

'They was fuckin' with us.' As he said it, he nodded. He knew I wasn't a fan.

Now it was Aaron's turn to speak again.

'You're the first of the new frontiersmen to leave us in this way. None of us are getting any younger and you will no doubt have noticed this is one area we haven't really prepared for very well.'

'Well no, I hadn't spotted any carers as such around the place. It was a factor when I made my initial decision.'

I thought back to Gran's final days. Wonderful people looking after her but in some respects the set-up left a lot to be desired. I could forgive these guys admitting to it being a stumbling block.

Aaron replied. 'I understand. Which leads us to the subsequent generations. This has worked down here due to everyone being on-message. My fear is that the current ethos of this underwater world will be lost over the years, leading to the new inhabitants questioning its purpose. The desire to return to the surface will be overwhelming.'

At this point Reg cut in, 'Which in some ways is a good thing. It's what we are ultimately working towards, surely?'

'Yes,' Aaron continued, 'but attempts made to return to the surface may generate a momentum that could be devastating if it isn't thought through. I'm not saying it's perfect down here, Jack. Not by a long stretch. People shouldn't live under these draconian rules.'

'Folks need the freedom to fuck up.' said Reg pointedly. 'But these rules are keeping humanity going while we are here.'

'Apparently the packs of wild dogs have mostly died off up top. Bugs and insects seem to be the ruling elite now. All thick vegetation and bright colours.' I felt Aaron was setting me up here.

'The air suits the bees then,' I said.

'It would seem so.' The irony was not lost on either of us.

It was Reg's turn to speak once again.

'Stop me if I'm speaking out of turn, Aaron, but you're protective of this place aren't you, which is understandable.'

'Yes, I am.' He stopped and smiled. 'I am aware that it's not a long-term fix though. And no doubt I won't be around when the inevitable evacuation happens. I just worry that's all.'

Aaron was not a bad man, but Reg was correct in what he said. This was Aaron's baby, and he was loath to let it go. I wondered if the apparent absence of a plan for death really was an oversight, or maybe something more altogether; not sinister as such, but nevertheless a refusal to accept that all that he had created would someday have to end. Not by a democratic process, but by the end of his own natural life?

Now that's one existential crisis!

It was nothing humanity hadn't witnessed before. Aaron was merely displaying aspects of the human psyche which confirmed that all set-ups such as this, as had been the case throughout the ages, can only ever be temporary. And the way humanity viewed the world and our place in it was changing, wasn't it?

The three of us sat in silence for a few moments. Then Aaron spoke.

'We're not going to hold a service as such. Having said that we will ensure that our family down here are aware of why you've done what you have done. We'll do it subtly. We may be a tad authoritarian but we're not about to go all *"Logan's Run"* on everyone.'

This was his way of telling me there was no plan for my actions to become a precedent. I thanked him for that.

On my way-out Reg grabbed my arm.

'Have a few drinks this evening, Jack. Don't worry about your watch.'

'Unbelievable!'

Sarah and the rest of our little family joined me at one of the many idyllic tables in the gardens.

'How many, Jack?' she tersely enquired, as I got up to get my fourth glass of cider.

I proudly, and in a slightly inebriated manner, displayed my watch showing bright green.

I sighed once I had sat down again. 'Wow. One night I can get as drunk as I want.'

'Looks to me as if you're there already,' she said.

After a while, the others bid us goodnight, all of them giving me big hugs. This left just Sarah and me, sitting watching the waterfall and the inhabitants of the rock pools, as we had done on so many nights.

'Thanks for getting me down here, Sarah. These have been the happiest years of my life.'

I still felt a bit rotten saying that but, hey, it wasn't like I was milking it, was I?

'It's been good. Apart from this last nine or ten months that is. I understand now why you did it. You're a good man and it's a noble way to depart, but it's broken my heart.'

With that she began to quietly sob. I suspected that along with being sad at my leaving tomorrow morning she was contemplating that her time was approaching too.

We didn't speak much after that and I didn't have another drink. We sat in each other's arms watching our fellow nature lovers gradually call it a night. It was July. It seemed at that moment as if everything was in bloom.

As we walked back home Sarah told me she wouldn't be staying with me this last night. It would be just too painful for her. We embraced outside No 61 AA1 and she headed off, a little tearful once more.

It was just Sarah and me at breakfast the next morning. The others planning to join us at the witching hour, not long from now. I tried to lighten the mood by declaring my sausages were a bit overdone, to no effect. By this stage I just wanted to get the whole thing over and done with. I sensed Sarah was trying to hold on to the passing minutes. I just wanted them to pass.

'May I join you?' Eva said, not waiting for a reply as she sat at our table.

'I wanted to have a little word with you, Jack, if I may.'

'Sure Eva. Fire away.' Sarah was scowling at me as I said it, but I wasn't planning to end my time here on a sour note, with anyone. Even pushy Eva.

'That film you showed the other day, to Ralf's group.'

Eva was a German lady and Ralf was her ten-year-old son. I knew immediately which film she was referring to. I had let the eldest of my groups watch *Spartacus* the day before yesterday. They had all loved it, and it had been hysterical during the evening meal sitting watching some of them suddenly standing up and shouting out one after the other 'I'm Spartacus,' 'No, I'm Spartacus,' and so on.

'It's a classic movie.'

'That director was a pervert.' She clearly didn't agree.

'Stanley Kubrick was one of the most important film directors of his generation. The diversity and scale of his movies is breath-taking, surely.'

'Well, I don't think so. I think he was wrong. I wish you hadn't shown it to Ralf and his friends.'

'I'm sorry you think that way, I really am. My intentions were sincere I can assure you.'

At this point Sarah kicked me hard in the shins.

'Eva, you must excuse us. This is an important morning for Sarah and me, and we have a lot to talk about.' With that I looked across at Sarah and then back to her.

'Oh, oh I'm so sorry. So rude of me. I will leave you to talk. Please forgive me.' And with that she was gone.

247

'Bloody woman. Why did you give her the time of day?' Sarah was both angry and upset.

'It's just another day for her, isn't it? It's how it should be.'

We didn't speak much after that. We held hands across the table, catching each other's gaze, then looking around, then catching each other's gaze once more.

When the time came, we got up and made our way to the hospital, teaming up with Marco, Elena and Antonio en route. David, Yvette, Tom junior, Michael and Aaron were there when we arrived at the back of the hospital where the event was due to take place. It was explained that this was probably the best moment to say our goodbyes. Elena begged me to hold Antonio just briefly, the symbolism of that moment not lost on anyone. I hugged everyone in order, beginning with the Italians and finishing with Sarah.

'Have a safe journey my love. I'll see you when it's time.' And with that we kissed, and she moved slightly away mopping her eyes as she did.

I was told to go behind a linen screen and undress. I handed them my iPad and removed my watch, shedding a tear as I did so. Two male nurses then bound me in long white strips of cloth leaving just my face in view. Once they were happy that I was properly prepared, they led me back to my people, now congregated around the large tube that was to be my point of exit from this world. I smiled at everyone as I got into the tube. Once I was comfortable, a strap was placed round my wrist where my watch had been, with a lead that fed into a laptop that one of the two doctors present was holding. It was explained to me that this would stop them from 'flushing' me into the ocean while still alive. That was a relief. The other doctor then asked if I was ready for the injection. I let him know I was.

At first, I felt nothing, then after a few minutes everything started to feel a bit hazy. I remained conscious and I could still see everyone looking into the tube at my face, while their faces began to gradually lose their definition. It wasn't painful, in fact it felt quite soothing, like I was in the ultimate pampering salon. All my cares and concerns were leaving me, and my focus gradually turned to what was ahead. Pretty soon all sense of hearing had gone, and all the faces were a blur. It didn't matter. I knew I probably had less than a minute before all my readings would be flat, which would cue the face covering being attached and whoosh, I was out of there.

I was in darkness now, but it wasn't at all scary. It was warm and I felt as if I were floating, with a blanket covering me, preparing me for my journey. I thought back over all that had gone before. It was fair to say humanity had for a time been on the brink, but it had turned a corner now. For the first time in a long time, I felt optimistic.

I wondered if I would meet all these people in some metaphysical form again. I wondered if we would all be united. Sarah, the boys, Yvette and young Tom. Maybe my friend Tom would be there. And hey, no one knew about the lady from the newsagent, did they? They may have thought they knew everything, but they didn't know about her. I wondered if I'd see her again, and maybe spend more than a passing moment with her.

Amazing, isn't it? Even when we are nearing our last breath it seems we're still looking ahead.

And then everything gently fell apart.

Oh yes!

See you in the next life ... Jack...

Acknowledgements

Rather than get into a 'and everyone who knows me' scenario, I am keeping this to the kind folk who helped me create this thing.

To Crawf and Baz who read the 1st draft and gave me the thumbs up to persist with it. To Diana Jackson for giving me an insight into the literary world, and then kindly agreeing to publish the finished manuscript through Eventispress. Also to Lauren C Waterworth for the fantastic cover images.

To lovely cousin Lucy x for introducing me to the following literary folk. To Caroline Maston and Will Templeton for your time and feedback. To Katherine Middleton for teaching me to write and spending hours of your own time giving me your thoughts. And to Alex James for applying the final polish.

Thank you so much.

Dedication

For Mum and Dad. See you in the next life...